SOUTHWEST NIGHTS

SOUTHWEST NIGHTS

SEMIAUTOMATIC SORCERESS™ BOOK 1

KAL AARON

MICHAEL ANDERLE

DISRUPTIVE IMAGINATION

Copyright © 2021 LMBPN Publishing
Cover Art by Jake @ J Caleb Design
http://jcalebdesign.com / jcalebdesign@gmail.com
Cover copyright © LMBPN Publishing
A Michael Anderle Production

LMBPN Publishing
PMB 196, 2540 South Maryland Pkwy
Las Vegas, NV 89109

First US edition, March 2021
eBook ISBN: 978-1-64971-618-7
Print ISBN: 978-1-64971-619-4

THE SOUTHWEST NIGHTS TEAM

Thanks to our Beta Team:
Allen Collins, John Ashmore, Jim Caplan, Mary Morris,
Larry Omans, Kelly O'Donnell, Rachel Beckford

JIT Readers

Dave Hicks
Diane L. Smith
Jeff Goode
Deb Mader
Wendy L Bonell
Dorothy Lloyd
Zacc Pelter
Angel LaVey
Jackey Hankard-Brodie
James Caplan
Peter Manis
Paul Westman

Editor
Skyhunter Editing Team

DEDICATION

This book is dedicated to my wonderful wife, who has always believed in me. It's also dedicated to my bird Momo who helped me get up early to write by squawking many days before my alarm.

— Kal

*To Family, Friends and
Those Who Love
to Read.
May We All Enjoy Grace
to Live the Life We Are
Called.*

— Michael

A little vibrating mirror ruined Lyssa's day. Trouble was coming, and it was barely past noon.

She sighed and set down her pint of strawberry ice cream before pulling out the small pink compact that was her leash as a Sorceress. Some people were so rude when a woman was having a snack.

"I'd thought he'd let me settle in," she muttered and stood. "He's been working me like a dog these last six months, even before the move."

Her living room remained mostly bare, with a modest TV hanging on the wall, a couch, and an IKEA end table. Her feeble decoration was limited to a sad-looking ficus. She'd just moved to this apartment in Scottsdale, Arizona, a suburb of Phoenix.

Outside, rocks and cacti formed her front yard. At least she didn't need to water the plants.

Lyssa wasn't like her foster mother, Tricia, who also was a Sorceress. Tricia focused on plant-based sorcery.

"Elder Samuel?" replied a low but calm and reassuring

male voice, interrupting her thoughts. "That's whom you're referring to?"

The sound came from no direction, though she could hear it clearly. No one but she would be able to hear it, but covering her ears wouldn't block it. The source of the voice, the spirit Jofi, was sealed in a physical vessel locked in a safe concealed by sorcery, but she could still make his voice out with ease.

"Yes, Samuel." Lyssa frowned. "He told me he was going to let me settle in. He promised me after that whole hostage rescue thing on Labor Day. I think he's pissed at me."

Samuel was an Elder Sorcerer and served as an annoying combination of Lyssa's boss and the regional governor. He wasn't the kind of man who stopped by to discuss the latest viral video. Any contact from him meant work.

"You don't feel two weeks was enough for settling in?" Jofi asked. "And did you expect to have Labor Day off? I've often observed you don't follow conventional human patterns."

Lyssa rolled her eyes. "It's the principle of the thing. He's the one who promised."

"You seem settled every time you clean me. I don't understand why you're so frustrated with Elder Samuel. Or why you think he's upset with you."

"He's probably still mad about that herbs and spices joke." Lyssa snickered. "He doesn't want me to relax. It's a petty punishment for a hilarious joke."

"Perhaps teasing him about his resemblance to a fictional character isn't worth it if it will result in punishment, but I don't always understand your sense of humor. Please take no offense."

"I don't need lessons in what's funny from you, Jofi." Lyssa snorted. "You're a spirit bound to two guns, not a spirit of comedy. Of course, you don't understand. Trust me, he's an old man with white hair who walks around in an all-white suit. Jokes about secret herbs and spices are spot-on. It's like he's begging for it."

"His appearance is a product of his regalia," Jofi replied. "I imagine all Elders would strive toward their maximum ability when conducting official duties."

Lyssa didn't want to admit Jofi had a point. A Sorcerer could use their abilities without their special enchanted costumes, their regalia, but only at the cost of significant power. Disguises also cost power.

"Sure, sure." Lyssa waved a hand dismissively. The finer points of mocking her boss with fried chicken mascot jokes were wasted on Jofi. She always let his deceptively human voice trick her into forgetting his true nature. "Let's get the pain over with."

Lyssa flipped open the compact, ran her finger across the mirror, and murmured the activation incantation in Lemurian. The surface grew cloudy and glowing yellow words appeared, written in the familiar dense, swirling script. Even at thirty years old, her dreams remained haunted by the many childhood hours she'd been forced to spend learning the ancient language.

She was never sure if Samuel used the enchanted compact mirror as an additional security measure or if it reflected his hidebound traditionalism. When she suggested he make it resemble a phone, he'd looked at her like she'd cracked open a portal to the darkest pit of an evil dimension lacking any sanity or goodness.

Samuel *could* accept a compact mirror, even a pink plastic one. He might not admit it, but facing the realities of modern living should be on the top of the list for every Sorcerer or Sorceress. How could they call themselves the Illuminated if they were afraid of technology?

His security measures wouldn't remain effective. Ever since the existence of sorcery had become public knowledge five years ago on M-Day, what had once been secrets shared only among the smallest of circles were slowly becoming public knowledge all over the world. That included the otherwise long-forgotten language of the lost continent of Lemuria.

An east Phoenix address appeared in the glass, complete with a ZIP code. Lyssa didn't have to leave the area. It took a moment for her to translate the rest of the message.

You are engaged as an officially sanctioned Torch of the Illuminated Society. United States Extraordinary Affairs Agency coordination is in progress. Limit activity per Shadow authorities' desires. This order is for immediate implementation. Only Shadow enemies are anticipated. The contract is Society-bound.

The Sorcerers and Sorceresses of the Illuminated Society loved their titles and labels. They were another way to separate themselves from the vast bulk of humanity.

A person wielding sorcery was an Illuminated. A normal human was called a Shadow.

Lyssa was special in a way. As a Torch, she was akin to Shadow Special Forces operators. She was trained in combat sorcery and given the latitude necessary for the violent suppression of threats as identified by the Society.

Some Illuminated referred to her as an elite, but others claimed her becoming a Torch was inevitable and one step away from nepotism. She came from a long line of Torches, including her parents and her older brother.

Lyssa stared at the message. The official order jogged a memory. She'd forgotten. How could she have done that?

She'd been distracted by the move. Her parents had died in the line of duty when she was a young girl. She'd come to terms with that, but then her brother vanished when she was a teenager. The fifteenth anniversary of his alleged death was approaching.

The Society insisted he was dead. She refused to believe it.

Lyssa could never let herself forget. She was the only one left who cared. For now, she needed to concentrate on her job. The best way to honor him until she found him was to become the ultimate Torch.

"A local address and pointing me at the cops to handle some normal people?" Lyssa forced mirth into her tone. Maybe she could fool Jofi. "He couldn't have called me to tell me? He's already accepting modern times. It's not like they had ZIP codes back in the old, glorious days of hidden sorcery."

"Elder Samuel has his reasons, I'm sure," Jofi said. "He has many decades of experience."

5

"You're right." Lyssa stood. "His reason is he's a fossil. Television didn't exist when he was born. World War I had just ended. That might not mean a lot to you since you're ageless, but it does to me."

"Why? I'm curious. I don't ask to be obstinate."

"Because it's hard to trust fossils to lead us into the new age, Jofi."

Criminals used phones without getting caught. A Sorcerer should be able to contact a Sorceress without an elaborate arcane item and an ancient language.

The Illuminated Society had allowed technology to advance too quickly while failing to develop the necessary countermeasures. It was inevitable they would have to emerge from their hidden dens spread around the world. They'd decided it was better to do it on their terms rather than wait for eventual discovery.

Their powers didn't justify being stuck in the past. Too many things had changed over the millennia, but the Elders and the Tribunal who ruled her kind acted as if all the Illuminated still lived on their lost continent.

Sometimes Lyssa wondered if her people accepted that Lemuria had been lost for ten thousand years. The center of the Society's power, the hidden island of Last Remnant, had been settled after the fall of Lemuria.

"It's fine, Jofi." Lyssa took a deep breath. "I'm annoyed, but I'll live, and we both could use some exercise. And you're right, he wouldn't call out a Torch to mess with me. I hope the job's useful."

"Does it matter?" Jofi asked.

"Sure. I might bitch, but I get the warm fuzzies when I save people from gun-toting lunatics."

Lyssa walked into her bedroom and over to a wall in her closet. She ran her hand over the wall while imagining a series of thick black ropes untwisting. A rectangle faded into existence, appearing shadow-like at first. It soon solidified into a safe door.

Her last line of defense was rather mundane, a keypad lock. She tapped in the combination, humming the tune she'd used as a mnemonic when she memorized the code.

"It's time to play, Jofi. You ready?"

"I'm always ready."

Inside the deep, wide safe, two black pistols lay crossed near the side, along with small boxes filled with enchanted rounds and magazines marked with strips of colored tape. A wrapped bundle of black clothes and holsters was piled on the opposite side. A skull-like mask sat on top. The clothes formed her regalia, that of the Night Goddess.

Lyssa yanked off her jeans and shirt and tossed them on the floor before pulling out the dark regalia inside the safe: a long dark coat over black pants, shirt, boots, and gloves. She tugged out a metallic mesh vest and slipped it on before her coat. It wasn't part of her regalia proper, but she had picked it up from a friend in Vegas.

The regalia offered decent protection, but the more passive armor she wore, the better chance she had of surviving without being dependent on constant sorcery. The dual holster went on before the rest of the clothes.

With concentration, she could change the regalia's appearance to resemble a normal outfit, though she'd lose some of the physical protection and sorcerous enchantments accompanying its true form. It also helped not to scream "Sorceress" to her own kind. They weren't all her friends.

There was nothing wrong with the Sorceress and the woman separating themselves when not on the job. Not everyone needed that, but sometimes a person needed to remind herself she wasn't the Grim Reaper when she spent so much time in a skull mask.

Elaborate raised sigils covered the regalia's pieces. They were hard to see without close inspection.

Although the look of the outfit invoked shaped dark leather, that was the product of how the outfit had customized itself when Lyssa had first bound it. The secrets and true nature of the material had vanished with the fall of Lemuria.

Lyssa grabbed the mask and slipped it on. It covered her face entirely, replacing the pretty dark-haired woman with a nightmarish mix of evil biker Goth chick, the Grim Reaper, and Santa Muerte. A thin layer of wispy, twitching shadows outlined her body, darkening and obscuring her features even more. Lyssa Corti was gone. Hecate the Night Goddess had replaced her.

She filled her pockets with magazines before holstering the pistols. Sorcery had its place, but guns cast a death spell all their own. Though, she *was* cheating with the help of enchanted bullets.

"You doing okay, Jofi?" she asked.

"I'm fine."

His voice was louder because his physical form, the two pistols, now lay right next to her body. Having a spirit bound into her guns was another cheat.

"I'll take your word for it," Lyssa replied.

A bright yellow Ducati Panigale V4 racing bike was parked inside her garage, ready for her. It wasn't a motorcycle that allowed a woman to keep a low profile, especially one dressed in such an attention-getting way outside of Mardi Gras, Halloween, or a comic book convention. As much as she loved her bike, working the job meant keeping Hecate and Lyssa separate.

She mounted her bike and gripped the handlebars, imagining obscuring clouds flowing over it. They appeared and consumed the bike, replacing it with a gray and black chopper, her Dark Mantle disguise. No one on the planet could mistake Hecate's ride for Lyssa Corti's Ducati.

She grinned. "Too bad I didn't end up as the Sun Goddess. That'd make this easier."

"At times, I wonder if you ended up with the right regalia," Jofi replied.

"Gee, thanks. I was joking."

"I know."

"Sometimes I can't figure out if you really don't understand human jokes or if you're messing with me." Lyssa shook her head.

She cast another spell, this one requiring more concentration. She layered thin strands of shadow, mentally sewing and weaving, along with a whispered chant. Her bike and body faded from view, becoming insubstantial until only a tiny, thin patch of darkness remained. The dark form flowed through the cracks in the garage, staying close to the ground as it moved toward the street.

Lyssa hit the road. She couldn't move as fast as she would have liked since using the thinning spell took more power than most of her techniques, even with the help of her regalia and Jofi. She was grateful she lived in a neighborhood with a lot of trees to provide cover, which was rare in Scottsdale. She needed a hidden tunnel like the one at her old house.

Once clear of her block, Lyssa ended the thinning spell and returned to her normal size. She kept her wraith form, which made her a full-sized shadow flowing along the side of the road. The bright afternoon sun made her more conspicuous. People would notice her, but they wouldn't know who she was.

A child playing on the street cocked his head and looked her way. He seemed more curious than afraid.

Lyssa didn't care about the occasional sighting. She'd traveled all around the county using the wraith form to ensure everyone knew Hecate called Maricopa County home. She'd even spent half-days in Tucson and Flagstaff the previous week to expand her reported range of terror.

Without her full safety spells and rituals being in use, traveling hidden too far along city streets was a good recipe for dying in a wreck. She released her cloak near a corner, popping into existence as she approached the intersection and stopping at the red light.

She didn't expect any cops to track Hecate down to give her a ticket but giving the locals fewer reasons to dislike her might help her in the future. No cop would ever fully trust a Sorceress with a hidden identity, but her time in San Diego had shown that she could pull them almost all the way with effort.

An old woman walking along a nearby sidewalk stopped and looked her way, then shrieked and clutched her hands to her chest. "I'm not ready to die! I've been doing everything my doctor said to lower my blood pressure. I've even been doing the *Dance Master DJ Supermix* game my grandson gave me for exercise."

It'd been a while since someone had mistaken Lyssa for Death. This many years after the revelation of sorcery on M-Day, she was always surprised that people didn't assume anything strange they saw was the result of sorcery. There might not be many of her kind around, but they were talked about and featured on the net and TV.

"I'm not here for you."

Lyssa's voice was pitched low and distorted by her mask. Her feminine silhouette was unmistakable in her outfit, but the mask and tone changes added enough questions about her identity to allow her to live in a normal house without reporters or assassins showing up and ruining her strawberry-ice-cream-and-reality-TV time.

"Oh, thank you." The old woman moaned gratefully. "I promise to keep doing what my doctor says."

"You do that. And call your grandkids more. Thank your grandson for the game."

"I will." The woman nodded, relief spreading on her face.

Lyssa sped toward the address. Samuel's message had said she needed to head out immediately, but it hadn't mentioned an expedited arrival. Getting there wouldn't take long without a spell. With luck, she wouldn't need to kill anyone.

CHAPTER TWO

Lyssa pulled up to an army of police surrounding a sprawling two-story house with a huge lawn. Trimmed palm trees surrounded the house. They also ran beside a pool she could see even from the front.

The whole place screamed "expensive." Maybe the old woman's doctor lived there, or the man who'd created *Dance Master DJ Supermix.*

"We're moving on up in the world, Jofi." Lyssa grinned. "Every time we do a job lately, it feels like it's at a more expensive place than the last."

"Is it better to battle enemies at more expensive places?"

"Beats the dives and gangland scum we mainly fought in San Diego, though people get angrier when you break things at expensive places."

Cops looked Lyssa's way as she pulled off to the side. No one made any attempt to stop her as she slowed her bike and wove between their cars. She pitied the poor men having to sit there under the cloudless sky, with the relentless Arizona sun punishing them for their forefathers' sin of being arrogant enough to build a city in the middle of the desert. Her regalia protected her from the worst of it, but the cops were all sitting out there sweating from both the stress and the heat.

Lyssa sought a particular target. She spotted a handsome, clean-cut, dark-skinned man in a dark suit standing to the side behind some police vans, Agent Damien Riley of the government's Extraordinary Affairs Agency.

The revelation of sorcery to the public at large had accomplished its least impressive and most easily predicted feat: increasing the size of the government bureaucracy. The American government had had no problem accepting the supernatural. It was just another thing for them to regulate. The poor IRS was still grappling with how to tax certain aspects of sorcery, but the EAA agents manned the frontlines, advising and monitoring the contracted Sorcerers and Sorceresses of the Illuminated Society.

A police lieutenant stood next to Damien, barking orders into a walkie-talkie. He shot an annoyed glance Lyssa's way.

Damien waved her down as she approached. "You took your sweet time getting here, Hecate."

"Too many red lights," she joked. "And frightened old ladies."

"Do you stop at red lights?" Damien asked.

"Sometimes. It's not like I can lie and say it was the other Hecate on her shadow bike."

Lieutenant Lopez's scowl deepened. Lyssa resisted a constipation joke.

Damien knew her identity, but the treaties that kept the Illuminated Society under control in most countries also ensured the right to privacy to any Sorcerer or Sorceress who didn't want their identity publicly revealed.

Though, when she thought about it, leaked identities weren't much of a problem, even in other countries where she might expect it. She had to give the Society's Elders credit for that. They must have held more leverage than she realized.

"Shouldn't we get to the task at hand?" Jofi asked.

"Sure," she whispered. She nodded toward the house. "What's the situation?"

Damien put his fist to his mouth and coughed. "I think Lieutenant Lopez should handle that. I'm just here to oversee."

"To make sure I don't accidentally summon a demon and release him on a golf course?" Lyssa snickered darkly. "You don't want to see a bunch of golfers running faster than Olympic sprinters?"

Damien frowned at her and folded his arms. She couldn't help it if the EAA didn't have much to do other than clean up after the Illuminated. He needed to get over it.

Lieutenant Lopez turned her way, wrinkling his nose like he smelled something awful. "I don't want you here, Sorceress." His jaw tightened as he took in her appearance. "Let's make that clear upfront."

"And let me make it clear I don't care much," Lyssa replied. "I was ordered to come here by my Elder. That means someone contacted the Society and begged them to send a Torch." She hopped off her bike. "A contract is active, and I'm required to execute it to the best of my ability." She gestured grandly with both arms. "So I'm here. Trust me, I'd rather be at home."

Lopez grunted as he looked her up and down. "You've got stuff around you. What the hell is that?"

"Shadows and darkness."

The cop grimaced. "Shadows and darkness?"

"We're straying from why I'm here. I assume it's not to scare some partying teens straight. That might be fun, though."

Lopez muttered something under his breath before clearing his throat and speaking louder. "The mayor's riding the department's ass about this. That's why you're here, but I don't want you to think we're too comfortable with your kind. Remember that when you're in there doing your hocus pocus."

"My hocus pocus involves a lot of beatings and shootings, Lieutenant. I just do it better than you can." Lyssa shook her head. "I'm glad I didn't waste energy hurrying over here at top speed if you're going to take this long to explain things. I can go back home, and you can send it by carrier pigeon. I'll write back a letter with my response and transport it via dogsled."

She didn't have time for this. Damien needed to do his job and expedite things.

"You think you're all that, don't you, Hecate?" Lopez asked, sneering.

"I think I'm a Torch of the Illuminated Society," Lyssa replied. "I think I'm Hecate the Night Goddess, controller of darkness sorcery. And I think you should stop wasting my damned time."

Lopez's nostrils flared. He glanced at Damien, who

shrugged. Nearby cops watched with rapt attention, their attention turned away from the house. It wasn't every day a skeletal masked Sorceress with dual holsters got in the face of a police lieutenant.

"Okay." Lopez rubbed the side of his nose. "We've got Jorge Alvarez and a lot of his main boys in that house. We weren't expecting him in town, but we got a tip he slunk back in. He's got massive balls to come back here."

"Why weren't you expecting him?" Lyssa asked.

"Because he pushed too far a couple of days ago." Lopez inclined his head toward the house. "And the feds have three dead FBI agents that can be pinned to him. The feds will be here soon, but the chief wants this resolved before that, so my captain wants it resolved before that too, which means we're going to do just that." He pointed at her. "And that's where you come in."

"Let's take a step back. Jorge Alvarez?" Lyssa shrugged. "Am I supposed to know who that is?"

She did her best to put a face with the name. A local politician, maybe? Familiarizing herself with the area was coming along slowly, but it didn't matter that much. Samuel was the main one giving her orders, and his area of responsibility was a lot larger than the Phoenix Metro Area. Most of her jobs since becoming a Torch hadn't been in or even close to her home city.

Lopez scoffed. "The big bad Society Torch doesn't know the name of a major cartel player? I thought you were supposed to be magical Special Forces? I guess TV adds ten pounds of badass to everyone."

Lyssa stomped over to the cop, slamming her boots

down on the pavement for extra emphasis. He backed away, his hand drifting toward his gun.

"Hey, everyone, just chill." Damien waved his hands. "We're all on the same side here. No reason to get rough."

"Are we?" Lopez asked, his fingers twitching near his gun.

"Don't antagonize him," Jofi said. "That will lead to an unpleasant and unnecessary confrontation."

"He's antagonizing me," Lyssa whispered. "I need to let this guy know who's boss."

"Your relationship with Elder Samuel is already strained. An altercation with the local Shadow authorities won't strengthen it."

"But it might make me feel better."

Lopez watched her, his jaw tight. If he could hear her, he probably thought she was a nut talking to herself. Like everyone else, including most Sorcerers without spirit sorcery and normal humans, he showed no indication of hearing Jofi. This was one of the few times she wished the spirit were telepathic.

"I'm not a cop, Lieutenant Lopez." Lyssa raised her voice. "I'm not Special Forces in the military of any country. I'm a Torch of the Illuminated Society. I destroy what I'm hired to destroy on orders from my Elders. I don't care if you're having some problem about that, so cut the BS and get to the point. Otherwise, stop wasting my time. Or maybe the feds will show up and decide they'll handle Alvarez their way. And trust me, if you drew on me, you wouldn't like how I rearranged your face."

Lopez licked his lips and inched his hand away from his gun. His eyes darted back and forth as if he were checking for reinforcements. Others watched, but they kept their distance, some looking at the ground as if they'd be safe if they didn't make eye contact with Lyssa.

"Do we understand each other, Lieutenant?" Lyssa asked.

"Yeah. Alvarez is garbage." Lopez grunted. "If you can help clean him up, we've got no beef. Drug smuggling, murder, trafficking, and I bet the bastard doesn't pay his light-rail fares, either." He took a couple of deep breaths and wiped his brow, then pulled out his phone and tapped before holding up a picture of a fierce-looking man with slicked-back hair and an evil gleam in his eyes. "This son-of-a-bitch is cocky enough to murder FBI agents and stroll back home like he had been on vacation."

Something felt off about the whole situation. The cop was right; ruthless killers were as common as glass, but the kind of criminal who rose to a position of authority in a cartel combined intelligence with ruthlessness.

Alvarez had to know the police would come for him. It was almost as if he wanted a shootout. Maybe he'd come back from his latest trip with some new toys, like a grenade launcher or a machine gun for his best *Scarface* impression.

"I get it. He's not a great guy." Lyssa snapped her head toward the house. "But I'm curious. After your little loving tribute to me, why does this require a Torch instead of a SWAT team?"

Lopez's constipated look returned. "The mayor wants, in his own words, a better liaison with all you witches and warlocks." He made air quotes around the word "liaison." "He says we need to know what you're capable of, now that we've got one local. We know this is a bad dude, so might as well throw you in there and let you turn him into a toad before we pitch him into a six by eight cage."

"I'm not a witch. I'm a Sorceress, Lieutenant."

"Isn't Hecate technically the goddess of witchcraft?" Damien asked.

Lyssa growled at him. He backed away with his hands in front of him and an apologetic look.

"And the night, magic, ghosts, and other things, too," he added hastily.

Lopez snorted. "Sure, sure. I don't care. Witch, Sorceress. Whatever." He gestured at the house. "Go in there and get 'em, Hermione. Bust them up."

"Very funny. For a guy who was going to wet himself before, you're awfully cocky now." She stepped toward him. "And like Agent Riley said, I'm Hecate."

Despite her correction, she harbored zero doubts that Lopez didn't know exactly what he was doing by calling her by a fictional witch's name. Maintaining a good relationship with her Elder didn't mean putting up with whatever crap someone wanted to shovel onto her. Lopez was already on her list of people getting a nasty fruitcake for Christmas.

Lopez glared at her, but he didn't do a great job of concealing his shaking. "I bet you wear that freaky mask because you're an old hag under there."

"Not exactly. Would you like to know?" Lyssa snickered. "Maybe I'm a zombie under here. Maybe I'm nothing but a skull, or I've got snakes for eyebrows."

"I'm not an idiot." Lopez tried to keep the quiver out of his voice.

"Could have fooled me." She shrugged.

"Now, you listen," Lopez growled. "I don't—"

"Hecate," Damien snapped. "Just let it go. And you, too, Lieutenant. She's right. The city of Phoenix requested a Torch, and the Society has sent one. Let her do her damned job."

Lopez ignored Damien and stared at Lyssa. "All your magic's in those special clothes, right? But not every one of you uses a mask. That's got to mean more than you say. We can't trust your kind to tell the truth."

Lyssa saw no reason to clarify that regalia enhanced rather than supplied the innate sorcery essence of an Illuminated. Essence manifested at puberty and reflected the fundamental nature of their powers, like her darkness sorcery.

The average person didn't understand that sorcerous abilities all related to that essence. While a trained and clever Sorcerer could do far more with their ability than a person from Shadow society might expect, there were still limits.

A smart Sorcerer worked within their conceptual limits rather than waste effort trying to copy techniques from different essences. No matter what, Lyssa was never going to be tossing fireballs around.

Regalia offered other special powers, usually protection and healing in general, as well as specific abilities, such as Lyssa's Night Goddess, which enabled her to see in the dark. Each costume was unique and bound to a Sorcerer or Sorceress in a Rite of Passage Initiation ceremony three years after they came into their powers post-puberty. Compatible essences and regalia types informed the theoretical choices. Some regalia wouldn't bind to a given Illuminated.

It wasn't as if the Society had been going out of their way to conceal all the details of sorcery, but they also didn't see a reason to kill every rumor and misunderstanding among Shadow society during the transition between secrecy and openness. Information asymmetry could be a useful weapon.

"Go read a book if you want to know about regalia." Lyssa pointed at the house. "My orders include paying attention to what you have to say. What level of force should I limit myself to?"

Lopez sucked in a breath before nodding at the house. "It's not supposed to be a massacre. You might not have to follow the same rules we do, but even if this guy is a total piece of trash, we want him for trial and to roll on the rest of the cartel. Same thing for his lackeys. If we end up with a house full of corpses, that's only going to set the cartel back a little while. But if we get enough of these guys to spill their guts, the feds can do some serious damage."

"You should have picked someone else if this is about keeping everyone alive when they're trying to kill me." Lyssa shrugged. "Finesse isn't my forte."

Damien sighed. "It's not like there's a Rent-a-Sorc app, Hecate. No one's saying you should let yourself get hurt. Just keep it reasonable and give them someone they can interrogate." He motioned around. "We need to get going on this before it's too late. Notice what you don't see?"

Lyssa looked around. "No media?"

Damien pointed at a helicopter overhead. "I could only do so much about the choppers and drones. I've been busting my butt to keep them away from here with EAA tricks, but that's not going to last long. We'd like this over before every teen with a phone shows up to get selfies with the #SemiAutomaticSorceress."

"Semi-automatic Sorceress?" Lyssa asked. "Did you come up with that yourself? I kind of like it."

Damien frowned. "Can you clear out the building?"

"Sure." Lyssa looked at the house. "Distract the idiots in the house in a big way in five minutes. I'll open the front door when the cops should join me."

"Understood."

Lyssa headed toward trees on the border of the yard. She'd need the time to strengthen her defenses. Whoever was watching the outside for the cops would have spotted her. She didn't go out of her way to hide her arrival, but that didn't mean she couldn't get inside without them knowing about it.

Five minutes would be good. It was enough time for the criminals to spread the word inside that a Sorceress was coming. She'd get paid and receive credit with the Society for clearing out the house either way.

"Engagements with only hostiles are always easier," Jofi said.

"You'd think." Lyssa patted her holsters. "But I don't know if you'll get to play today. It's not supposed to be a ruthless clearance job."

She could control herself. It wasn't like she couldn't, like certain other Torches she knew.

"At least I'm not Aisha," she muttered, shuddering at the thought of a prodigy Torch she hadn't seen for months and hopefully wouldn't see for many more. "Time to be a professional."

Every police siren went off at once, along with a loudspeaker blasting a loud rock song Lyssa didn't recognize. Lieutenant Lopez was good for something other than insulting her.

She spun from behind a tree, already cloaked in her wraith form. The tenebrous outline would stand out under the bright Arizona sun, but she'd chosen to approach in the shadows cast from the house.

Lyssa scampered up the side of the house. Layers of blackness covered her hands and feet to connect her to the darkened side of the house. She reached a top window and pressed her back to the wall, then pulled her hands away and yanked out two telescoping batons.

"Be careful," Jofi said.

"I don't know if that goes with this job."

With a flick of her wrist, Lyssa locked her batons at their full length. Arcane-looking symbols ran up and down their shafts, but that was for show. Her sorcery and skill would supply the power.

She half-closed her eyes, picturing twined streams of pulsing dark lines and running her hands over the batons until dark auras surrounded both. The spell would increase both their damage and knockout power. Shooting people was easier, but bashing their heads in relieved stress and kept down the number of accidental deaths.

A dark curtain covered the window, with a thin slit at

the bottom. She craned her neck to look. She couldn't see much other than a long hallway with no one in it.

Had they pulled everyone to the front? Even if she weren't there, some SWAT guy could have dropped off a helicopter and smashed in through the window.

"Time to make a big entrance," she whispered.

"Are you sure?" Jofi asked. "This might be a situation that would benefit from subtlety."

"They didn't hire me for subtlety. They hired me to take down Alvarez."

Lyssa smashed the window with two quick strikes from her batons before diving into the hall and springing to her feet, batons at the ready. Numerous doors stood on either side of the hallway before it dead-ended at an elaborate spiral staircase. No one emerged from the doors, ready to shoot the intruder.

Pressure built in her chest, a sign of sorcery. Her heart rate kicked up.

"What the—"

A small crystal sphere popped out of the wall halfway down the hall, and a curtain of flame blasted from it.

CHAPTER THREE

Lyssa reacted on instinct and bent backward until she dropped to the floor. The jet of flame ripped through the hallway, scorching the doors and walls on both sides. It scoured the wood and the drywall, slicing through them without setting them afire before missing her by inches. It was like someone had carved through the hallway with a burning sword.

The heat was intense even through Lyssa's regalia and spells, but the flames didn't burn her. Without anything to stop the spell, the blast hit the end of the hall and blew out what was left of the window in a house-shaking final strike. Pieces of wood and glass covered Lyssa.

She lay on her back and brushed the debris off her mask, unsure of what the hell had happened. Without her regalia enhancing her reflexes, the blast would have blown her out of the building. Surviving the first hit in a battle wasn't good enough when she didn't know the enemy's capabilities.

Why was a Sorcerer with these random cartel idiots? Had she made a mistake by not trying to arrive in secret?

A dark memory of somber-faced Elders speaking to a teenage Lyssa surfaced.

Some information wasn't made available to the assigned Torch. We believe that had your brother known what he was facing, the outcome would have been different. That was unfortunate.

Lyssa gritted her teeth and concentrated on the here and now. She didn't have time to get distracted by things from fifteen years ago, no matter how important. The best way to find her brother was to become stronger, and that included not letting gangsters and rogue Sorcerers embarrass her.

Hushed murmurs came from downstairs. Lyssa couldn't make them out, but there were a lot of men there. Their lack of screaming and fleeing in terror after the spell meant they had expected it.

Lyssa hopped up, clutching her batons tightly. Clever traps didn't do any good if they didn't hit the target.

"Are you unharmed?" Jofi asked, as calm as ever.

"My pride's hurt for getting surprised," Lyssa murmured. "Does that count?"

"No."

Shadows played across the holes sliced through the doors by the spell. She wasn't alone on the second floor.

"Someone screwed up," Lyssa whispered. "I don't know if it's Samuel's, the cops', or the EAA's fault, but someone should have known about the sorcery." She lifted her batons. "No more Miss Nice Girl."

There'd been more than enough time for whoever was

on the second floor to emerge from the rooms, but they were hesitating for some reason. Were there more traps? Why didn't the Sorcerer follow up on the attack?

The hushed words from below gave away to shouts, along with pounding footsteps. The sounds grew distant as they moved toward the other end of the house and the staircase.

"Keep on the door!" someone shouted from below. "We just nailed some SWAT bastard on the second floor. The rest of you assholes up there need to clean up! We'll get ready down here."

There was a mention of SWAT but no mention of a Sorceress. That was a bad sign for their internal communications. They also should have come after her immediately after the explosion, not that it would have helped. She was surprised they hadn't been expecting her rather than the cops.

A door creaked open down the hall, surprised eyes peeking at Lyssa. The owner of the eyes, a hard-looking man covered with scars, emerged more fully.

"It's not the cops!" he bellowed. "It's the Sorceress!"

Lyssa charged down the hallway. The gangster pulled his gun, but she batted it out of his hand with her baton, sending it skittering down the hardwood floor. Her next blow smashed him into a wall. He slid to the floor, unconscious.

Other doors flew open behind her. Armed shouting men emerged. She spun and sprinted down the hallway in a zigzag pattern. They opened fire.

Bullets whizzed past her. A couple struck her; they stung but bounced off. She jumped into the air to kick and bat at her assailants, and her blows landed with loud crunches. The men groaned and cried out in pain.

Some fell unconscious. Others only suffered the pain of broken bones.

There was only so much restraint Lyssa would show armed killers. Being damage-resistant wasn't the same thing as being immortal. Taking them down quickly was the best strategy to keep her from having to kill them, especially if a Sorcerer joined the battle.

Lyssa slammed an elbow into a man's nose. He screamed and grabbed the offended protrusion. She finished him off with a spinning kick that launched him into another man. Their tangled limbs set up an easy combo for one of her batons. Both men fell to the floor, groaning before losing consciousness.

A thug tried to jam a gun against her head and pulled the trigger, but she ducked, and the loud report rang in her ears. She repaid him by cracking his arm at the elbow. He screamed and dropped his gun, only stopping his wailing when her follow-up to his chin sent him backward.

There were plenty of enemies left. The gangsters had relied too much on surprising her and shooting her from a distance. Fear filled the faces of the remaining men.

Some men continued to fire. Others hesitated, unsure now that their enemy was in their midst. One brave soul tried to pistol-whip her. She parried the blow with a baton before kneecapping the man, then smashing him across the head.

"Remember, you're supposed to apply reasonable force," Jofi said. "That will improve your standing with the local authorities."

"If I was applying unreasonable force, they'd all be dead," Lyssa snapped.

A thug screamed and tried to tackle her. She met his face with a wide swing from both batons, knocking him to the side.

The sorcery trap continued to puzzle her. There was no Sorcerer to explain it. She suspected there had never been, which raised other uncomfortable questions.

Groans, screams, crunches, and cracks overlapped as Lyssa became a flurry of enchanted concussive force. She smacked and pummeled the pack of gangsters, who had been waiting to ambush wounded cops, not a combat-trained Sorceress.

The gangsters had been brave enough to sit in the rooms while sorcery went off, but that didn't mean they could win with the weapons they had. The growing frustration and terror on their faces proved that. They'd not done more than bruise her despite the advantage of a booby trap, superior numbers, and an ambush. Pathetic.

Lyssa hissed when a bullet struck her back. The round clattered to the ground, leaving a stinging ache. A jumping roll helped her avoid the next shot and close on the shooter. She slammed a baton into a man's stomach with a fierce jab, and he doubled over in pain. She finished him off with a blow to the head.

As best she could tell, she hadn't killed anyone yet. Seriously injured, yes, but not killed. Her sides, back, and chest ached. Rips in her regalia marked where she'd been shot. This job was beginning to annoy her.

"You can all just give up, you know," she shouted before bashing a gun out of a man's hand and introducing her knee to his nose with a leaping strike. "I'm Hecate! Look at my mask and know the truth. Look at your fallen friends. If you face me, you risk your death. Mercy is only for those who know their limits."

"You're more melodramatic than usual today," Jofi said.

Lyssa tuned out everything but possible targets as she kicked, bashed, and crushed anyone stupid enough to come near her. The numbers thinned. They didn't surrender, but their attacks slowed.

A man shook out his hand after losing his gun and drew a knife with his other hand. He lunged at her, and she blocked his stab with one baton before nailing him hard across the chest and knocking him to the ground.

Lyssa spun. "Oh, this is good."

There was no one left awake. She'd pacified the second floor. With the din of immediate battle and her pounding pulse receding, she could make out murmurs and barked orders from below, but nothing that sounded like anyone daring to come up the stairs.

"Something's wrong," she whispered after catching her breath.

"Why do you say that?" Jofi asked. "If you're worried, you can always use me."

"I think we'll get to that soon, but these guys should be more scared."

"They appeared scared to me."

Lyssa flexed her fingers on her batons. "*More* scared. Continuing to fight when you're getting your ass handed to you isn't the same thing as accepting that an unstoppable Night Goddess is beating you to a pulp even after you keep shooting."

She rotated her shoulder, wincing. Ice packs and some of Tricia's herbs would help when she got home. Her regalia would need to do the rest.

"I'm not going all-out on them," she continued, "but I'm not going easy, either. And why are their buddies letting me beat them up? They had that trap, but no follow-up."

"Many criminals are heartless," Jofi said.

"Sacrificial lambs, huh? Maybe."

Lyssa surveyed the downed men. Most were unconscious or semi-conscious. She had crafted a carpet of beaten thugs, and not one had acted like he thought he'd lose against a Sorceress. It wasn't as if she expected them to run in terror at the mere sight of her, but going hand-to-hand against someone in a death mask with a literal shadow aura took more than standard thug courage.

Maybe Jofi was right. A diversion? What would be the point? Even if they got away from her, half the Phoenix PD waited for them outside. Those cops didn't have enchanted batons and sorcery-enhanced defenses to keep them from going to lethal force sooner.

Lyssa looked down the hall at the stairs. No one had come up, which meant they were waiting for her.

They'd thought they'd caught cops with their blast, but her first victim had shouted that she was a Sorceress. The others must have put the pieces together.

"More traps," Lyssa muttered.

"A cautious approach might be prudent," Jofi said. "There was no explicit timeline mentioned by the lieutenant for job completion."

"No way. They tried to blow me up. I'm not creeping

around like I'm afraid of these guys, and I was in the middle of something when I got the message."

"You were in the middle of eating ice cream. I don't think that ranks highly among important human activities."

"It was *premium* ice cream," Lyssa said. "You don't appreciate that because you don't eat."

"I can't refute the logic in that sentence."

She didn't have time to argue with a spirit about the glories of ice cream, not with a whole other floor filled with murderous cartel thugs.

CHAPTER FOUR

Not every door on the second floor was open. Given how much pain she'd delivered without significant resistance, she now doubted a Sorcerer was involved, other than by handing over a dangerous toy. She didn't doubt it enough to risk getting hit in the back with a spell, though. Her regalia was far more vulnerable to sorcery than conventional weapons.

Lyssa rushed to a closed door and kicked it open. She found nothing but an empty bedroom with a giant TV and a gaming console connected. The starting screen for *Premier League Championship 2020* was there, along with a photorealistic graphic image of some pretty-boy soccer player who looked vaguely familiar.

Had they been playing games when the cops showed up? That didn't seem right. There were too many people in the house. They'd expected trouble.

Lyssa kicked in the other doors to reveal empty bedrooms and a bathroom. The other rooms were already open.

She crept toward the stairs, waiting for the pressure marking sorcery or a hail of gunfire. One side of the hall ended, replaced by an ornate railing that exposed the spacious living room below. She flattened herself against the wall and looked around the corner.

The gangsters had positioned themselves behind furniture, many of them pointing their weapons toward the windows and the front door. Her arrival hadn't cured them of fearing a SWAT raid. A small number of men watched the stairs, pistols in hand, looking nervous but not terrified. They swung toward her but didn't fire when she pulled back.

"Jorge Alvarez, are you here?" Lyssa called. "We don't have to do this the hard way. Your men up here experienced my power. It's painful, and survival isn't guaranteed. The more you resist me, the more you're asking to die."

Lyssa expected gunshots, but nothing came. Downstairs was eerily quiet, other than the heavy breathing of many large men and the scratches of their shoes and boots on the floor.

"Right now, I'm holding back," Lyssa continued. "And that's after you tried to burn me with a power you have no right to use. The police out there want you to survive to trial. I'm flexible on the matter."

More pressure built in her chest. Lyssa ducked back to avoid the anticipated explosion. Again, nothing happened. No bullets. No explosions. No lightning. Nothing strange.

Did they have a Sorcerer working for them and not just traps, after all? That might explain why they weren't as scared as she expected, but she had a hard time believing any Sorcerer would allow themself to get stuck in this kind of situation.

A trained Sorcerer could fight their way through police, especially if they didn't care about casualties, but they'd be forced to use their regalia in its true form. Public use of the regalia might not reveal their identity to the police, but it would guarantee the Society knew who they were.

Being a rogue Sorcerer was a futile quest that was almost guaranteed to end in death or imprisonment. If a Torch didn't take care of the problem, the Society would eventually send a dedicated anti-Sorcerer assassin, an Eclipse. Staying alive as a rogue Sorcerer or Sorceress mostly involved keeping out of sight, and that meant no massive unsanctioned public displays of sorcery against Shadows.

Lyssa shook her head. No, she'd been right before.

These idiots didn't have a Sorcerer working for them. They'd gotten their hands on shards, powerful arcane objects created with sorcery that were usable by anyone. The trap fit that description, but Lyssa didn't appreciate that no one had told her to expect shards.

"I'm beginning to think restraint is overrated," Lyssa whispered.

"Lieutenant Lopez wanted survivors," Jofi said. "Elder Samuel also highlighted the benefits of restraint during your last job."

"There are plenty of survivors on the second floor. And if I sit around too long, I'm going to have to beat them up again."

"I would think the current foes would need to demonstrate more inherent danger before you felt the need to resort to extreme force."

Lyssa scoffed. "Fine. Let's clear out the living room and let the cops point their guns at everyone who is left."

She darted toward the stairs. They weren't dark enough to use wall-walking, and it would leave her exposed for too long. She opted to bound down the stairs three at a time, trusting her enhanced speed and agility. The men guarding the stairs opened fire, leaving a trail of bullet holes in the wall behind her.

Once Lyssa made it three-quarters of the way down, she leaped over the rail. A bullet nailed her in the shoulder, stinging and tearing another small hole in her regalia before falling to the floor. She landed on top of one of the men guarding the stairs, and her quick roundhouse knocked another down. She clubbed the top of her landing pad's head to take him out.

Beating up a house full of thugs was better exercise than the *BollyX* her neighbor had made her do last week. All she needed was a catchy soundtrack.

Men hidden in the back popped up from behind their furniture bunkers to fire. Others turned from the front, suddenly more concerned about her than the cops.

The living room might have been large, but it wasn't a football field. She cleared the distance in seconds and became a whirlwind of unstoppable crushing and smashing pain. Her gangster victims collapsed to the ground, groaning and on the edge of consciousness if not out cold. Their loud echoing shots became less frequent as Lyssa continued her evil majorette routine until only the front guards remained. They'd ceased fire.

She faced them, smiling under her mask. That was one advantage of wearing a face covering. She never worried about the goofy faces she might be making in battle.

"I applaud your bravery," she offered, letting her enhanced voice do its work. "I'll remember you after you die."

The guards didn't open fire, just exchanged annoyed looks. Lyssa was about to congratulate herself on her intimidation when they all sprinted toward a large door that led to another room. The first man threw open the door, revealing a large rec room, complete with a pool table.

"Hiding in there isn't going to help," Lyssa shouted. "You're only delaying the inevitable."

Another hallway led deeper into the house, but only the rec room and the huge empty kitchen were connected to the living room. She suspected Alvarez was hiding in the back of the house. Running would place him right in front of the cops surrounding the place, which meant he probably had a final surprise for her wherever he was holed up.

Turning her back on a bunch of heavily armed men when she couldn't account for the sorcery she'd felt earlier was a good way to end up needing more than ice packs and herbs. She had to clear the rec room first.

"Come on, boys." Lyssa waved her batons. "Don't make me come in there."

Four men she hadn't seen before stepped toward the front of the rec room. They all held crossbows and were grinning from ear-to-ear. She widened her stance on the other end of the room, ready to engage. The pressure in her chest and the men's cocky attitude signaled that they weren't holding ordinary crossbows.

More shards. Now things were getting interesting.

Sometimes a man needed a reason to listen to his instincts. Lyssa didn't believe these gangsters could look at a room full of their beaten-down friends while a woman in a death mask and bloody shadow-covered batons fearlessly stared them down, even if they carried shard crossbows.

"You sure you want to do this?" Lyssa asked, infusing her voice with hostility. "You're not just asking for death, you're begging for it. You know who I am, right? I am Hecate, Sorceress and Torch of the Illuminated Society. The longer you oppose me, the more you risk your life. I've defeated every man you've sent at me, and I'm not required to spare your lives if you challenge mine."

The men raised their crossbows and chanted a phrase in Latin. A flaming bolt appeared in one crossbow. In another, a bolt made of dark stone materialized. The third weapon was loaded with solid ice ammo, while the fourth held a barely visible bolt made of swirling dust.

"He wants us to test these," Mr. Firebolt said, his body trembling with excitement. "We were saving them for the cops, but now we got ourselves a *bruja*."

"Having some toys doesn't make you my equal," Lyssa replied, her voice a growl.

"We got the magic now, bitch. You're nothing. You run away right now, and we will let you go. Everyone will know Alvarez and his boys beat Hecate."

Lyssa growled. "Okay. Fine. Bring it on, idiots."

CHAPTER FIVE

Mr. Firebolt shot his bolt. Lyssa cartwheeled out of the way, not eager to test her defenses against an enchanted weapon without more info. The bolt exploded into a curtain of flame behind her, setting the wall on fire. A wave of heat passed over her.

"Yeah!" Mr. Firebolt shouted in triumph. "You're gonna die, you *bruja* bitch!"

His friends nodded their eager agreement, spreading out but not firing. A long needle flipped up from the center of the crossbow. Mr. Firebolt stepped back and jammed a finger into it. Blood seeped from the wound, disappearing into the needle.

That answered one question. She could use the revelation to work their nerves.

"This is what you don't get about sorcery." Lyssa stepped back in front of the burning wall, twirling her batons in her fingers. "You can think of it as magic all you want, but there's no way to get something for nothing in this world."

"Does that include you?" Mr. Firebolt asked.

The other three men fired. Ready for the attack, she dove to the side. The enchanted bolts passed over her, the ice round striking the wall first. A sheet of ice coated the wall and quenched the flames from the earlier attack. It would save the fire department some work.

Mr. Stonebolt's shot struck next. It shattered the ice, showering the nearby area with small frozen chunks mixed with hard, sharp pieces of rock. A follow-up attack from the dusty bolt clarified its nature as a wild gust of wind burst from it, knocking Lyssa into an overturned table and scattering bits of stone, charred wall, and ice all over the room.

The instant storm forced the men back. They didn't keep both hands on their weapons, throwing up one to keep the rock and ice out of their eyes. A vase knocked over by the wind crashed to the floor and shattered.

"I recommend you make full use of your resources," Jofi said. "Including me."

"I've got this," Lyssa whispered. "The guys upstairs did a better job than the Four Horsemen of the Idiocalypse here. The real question is how fast they can reload and how much blood the shards need."

"You're going to die here, Hecate," Mr. Firebolt shouted. "We're going to shoot you and leave nothing but that mask, and Alvarez's gonna hang it up on his wall as a trophy, just like he has badges from all the pigs and feds he's killed."

Lyssa did her best not to look down on Shadows. Human society had accomplished brilliant and impressive things, including sending people to the Moon. But there was something galling about the punk standing there with an enchanted crossbow threatening a trained combat Sorceress. He needed a good lesson.

A flaming bolt formed slowly in Mr. Firebolt's crossbow, answering her earlier question and summoning a slow, cold chuckle from Lyssa. The other men stepped back, feeding their blood to their weapons. A weapon was only as good as the tactics supporting it.

"You're going to kill me?" she asked. "I am the night. I am fear. I am death."

"You're gonna be dead," Mr. Firebolt yelled.

Lyssa leaped over a couch and charged him, raising her batons. He rushed backward, grunting as he slammed into a wall. The other three men hustled to different corners of the room but kept their hands on the needles.

Mr. Firebolt's face twisted in an angry grimace as he raised the crossbow, the bolt not fully formed, and pulled the trigger. Nothing happened.

"You should have checked the manual," Lyssa said, arriving in front of the man.

She smacked the crossbow out of his hands with a double strike before bringing her knee up. The man groaned briefly before a backswing with her left baton sent him to the floor.

Lyssa spun to face the other men. "All things have limits."

Mr. Icebolt's needle lowered, and he offered her a grin as cold as his enchanted ammo. "Get down on your hands and knees and beg. Maybe we'll let you go."

"Do you understand the situation you're in?" Lyssa replied, holding her batons out at her sides. "You're a child holding a stick and pretending it's a sword against a real dragon."

"You're afraid." Mr. Icebolt laughed. "That's why you're being so careful."

"I'm being careful because the police want people they can question. If I come to believe there's a real risk to me, my concern over that goes away, idiot, and you die within seconds."

Uncertainty flicked across the thug's face, but he didn't drop his weapon. The other men maintained their positions. They'd improved their trigger discipline, but they were down a quarter of their force.

"I again recommend more extreme measures, including using me," Jofi said. "Them employing multiple shards increases the risk to both of us."

Lyssa ignored the spirit. She'd knock sense into the crossbow squad without her guns. Her pride was on the line.

She threw her left baton at Mr. Icebolt before charging at a nearby wall. He yelped and shot at her, and the bolt whistled past her into the rec room. It struck the pool table and turned it into a mini-ice rink.

Mr. Icebolt's two friends tried to follow her with their crossbows, frustration building on their faces as they failed to line up a clean shot. Lyssa jumped and bounded off a wall to launch toward the backpedaling first thug. She crashed into him and knocked him over, sending his ice crossbow flying. Two quick left jabs dazed him and she brought down her right baton.

"This ain't happening!" screamed Mr. Windbolt. "We've got the crossbows. She can't win."

Lyssa rolled over to collect her downed baton and hopped to her feet as he fired. She spun to avoid the bolt, but it caught the edge of her coat and caused another heavy gust that propelled her into the air. She smacked into a ceiling fan, bending a blade before falling to the floor with a loud thud. Somewhere along the way, she'd lost her batons.

She hissed. Her entire body ached, but she hadn't broken anything. There was nothing worse than a thug who learned quickly. That was the most solid hit any of them had landed on her during the entire raid.

"I did it!" Mr. Windbolt yelled.

Lyssa rolled out of the way and jumped to her feet before Mr. Stonebolt could line up an attack. She wasn't doing badly for someone who had been shot multiple times, nearly blown up, and slammed into a ceiling fan.

"I again recommend my use," Jofi said.

"Shut up," Lyssa snapped. "The situation is under control, and they're down to two guys."

Mr. Windbolt grinned. "Feeling nervous?" he asked, mistaking the target of her words.

His stupid grin annoyed her. He mistook one lucky hit for a win.

"I thought you magic types were supposed to be all special and badass?" Mr. Windbolt shoved his left palm against the greedy needle supplying his weapon and stomped his foot down on one of her lost batons. "But you're nothing once we get magic weapons."

Mr. Stonebolt looked more relaxed. He ran over to the other fallen baton and kicked it behind him. Mr. Windbolt nodded at his friend with an eager gleam in his eyes.

The poor, deluded souls thought they had the upper hand.

The problem with using guns, regardless of bullet type, was that it was a lot harder to avoid killing a man when you used them. However, no one had mentioned thugs armed with shard crossbows or enchanted traps during her briefing.

"You get your wish," Lyssa muttered, her gaze flicking between the men.

"You gonna surrender?" Mr. Stonebolt asked, sounding surprised. He didn't pull his finger off the needle. "You can run if you want. If we both miss, you might be able to get out of here alive."

"I wasn't talking to you, moron." Lyssa's hands inched toward her jacket. "I was talking to Jofi."

"Who the hell is Jofi?"

Lyssa yanked out both pistols and fired. Mr. Stonebolt dropped to the ground in a heap, blood pooling around him. The idiot hadn't even been wearing a bulletproof vest.

Mr. Windbolt shouted in rage and fired his newly reloaded crossbow toward her feet. Lyssa vaulted over a nearby downed table, and the blast of wind launched her toward her attacker. His eyes widened as she fired twice with both guns, putting four rounds into his chest before landing into a roll that set her back on her feet.

Loud clapping sounded from the hallway. Lyssa spun toward the source, her guns ready. Alvarez stood there in a blood-red robe covered with arcane sigils and glyphs. A gaggle of men surrounded him on either side, all armed with submachine guns.

"You're not a Sorcerer." Lyssa narrowed her eyes.

"You're a man with toys. I've been trying to be a nice girl here. Well, nice-ish? But that's over. Your choice, Alvarez. Final choice. Surrender, and I can guarantee you won't die. Fight, and you'll end up like your crossbow boys."

"I like you." Alvarez smiled. "I could use a woman like you in my organization. I don't know what they're paying you, but I'll pay more. And my bosses can pay you even more than that. You don't have to be full-time. We understand a woman like you doesn't like to be told what to do. We can respect that."

"You feed off human misery," Lyssa spat. "How many innocent people has your cartel harmed?"

"Don't act high and mighty, Hecate. You have your fancy costume, and you think you're all that, but how is your Illuminated Society different from my cartel? They're both about control and power. They call you a Torch. We'd call you a *sicario*. They send you to shoot and kill. We'd do the same." Surveying the unconscious and dead men, Alvarez sighed. "I'm not going to hold it against you that you killed some of my guys. We respect strength."

"Sorceresses aren't so easily bought. The Illuminated Society is older than all of your so-called civilizations, let alone your pathetic cartel."

Alvarez laughed. "You hear that, boys? She's a paid killer, but she can't be bought."

His thugs all laughed. They didn't look as tense as any of the other men she'd fought. Alvarez's robe radiated strong sorcery. Whatever it did, the outfit was a lot more powerful than the crossbows.

"Let's be real." Alvarez's smile vanished. "If your Society was clean, I wouldn't have all these toys, now would I?

Some *bruja* comes in here and thinks she's better than me because she wears a mask?" He gestured at one of the dead men. "I wasn't going to make you pay, but you made this easy. This robe has a cost, you know? The cost is life, and my boys' death has made me strong. Even in death, they're serving me and the cartel. That's loyalty."

Lyssa pointed the guns at him. "I didn't kill most of your people."

"What, you ask for mercy now?" Alvarez sneered. "Damn. You're nothing more than a weak chick in the end?"

"Mercy?" Lyssa scoffed. "Nope. I'm thinking if I kill you, there are still plenty of people for the cops and FBI to interrogate." She backed up slowly, keeping her guns pointed at Alvarez. "And I'd like to not damage the robe if possible. It'll help a friend of mine score some points when it's turned in."

"Kill this crazy bitch," Alvarez shouted.

Lyssa ran toward the rec room and out of the line of fire. That didn't save her when the thugs held down their triggers and released a hail of bullets into the living room. Bullets ripped through the front window, shattering them. The projectiles riddled the wall and door with holes.

Bullets struck up and down Lyssa's body, adding more damage to her regalia. Fiery pain shot through her thigh, and the layered defenses, including the enchanted mesh on her chest, could only do so much to dull the hits. She wore the Night Goddess, not the Stone Giant.

Lyssa backflipped off the wall, avoiding some of the shots as she returned fire. She ignored Alvarez, sweeping her arms back and forth and rapidly pulling her triggers.

Their boss might have a shard, but it wasn't going to save his men from the high-velocity rounds of her enchanted pistols ripping through them.

She ran toward an overturned table and slid behind it, firing the entire time. More men dropped to the ground with new holes in their heads. The idiots needed to understand she could survive being shot many times and keep fighting. They couldn't.

Bravery was overrated. Winning wasn't.

The sad part was she'd not even used any enchanted ammo yet. Each of her rounds tearing through the men was a normal bullet, though with Jofi residing in the pistols, the muzzle velocity was increased to the point where it was like getting shot with a high-powered rifle.

Lyssa fired through the table, emptying her magazines before ejecting them and reloading. No one else was shooting back.

Her heart pounding and sharp pain suffusing her leg, she rolled from the table to the couch, readied both guns, and jumped up. Alvarez was the only man still standing, though his robe now shone with a dull red light and his eyes glowed solid red.

Alvarez whistled. "You are one impressive woman, Hecate. I wonder what you look like under that mask. I'm thinking you're a badass *abuela* with a big scar across your face."

Lyssa kept silent. Everyone seemed to think she was old under the mask, but that didn't matter. The more ancient they believed she was, the better she could intimidate them. Sorceresses and Sorcerers could make use of the centuries of folklore associating age with power.

"Your men are all dead or out cold," Lyssa rumbled. "I'm still standing. Surrender, Alvarez, or die. Don't be an idiot."

"You are still standing." Alvarez looked her up and down. "You're shot up but barely bleeding. Your kind is special. You see all that on TV, and it makes you wonder, you know? They say all these special people are walking around, but most normal people won't ever meet one." He ran a hand over the robe. "This would have been enough to make me believe in your power, but now I've seen it. When I kill you, I'm going to become a legend."

"Enough of this crap." Lyssa fired both guns at Alvarez.

He jerked back before standing up straight, then poked his fingers through the new holes in his robe before kicking a crushed bullet out of the way. "I've got one of your costumes now."

Lyssa scoffed. "That's not regalia, it's just a shard. And you're not a Sorcerer. You have no chance against me."

He spread his arms out. "You just killed a bunch of guys and gave me power."

Alvarez charged at her. Lyssa kept firing, but he continued toward her. He swung a fist, and she dodged the blow with a quick jump. His momentum carried his hand into and through a nearby wall with a hardwood veneer.

"Damn." Alvarez yanked his fist out of the wall and shook off the dust. "It doesn't even hurt."

"I recommend using more powerful ammunition," Jofi said.

Lyssa sighed and tossed one of the guns to the ground before ejecting the magazine of the remaining weapon. "Agreed."

Confusion swallowed cockiness on Alvarez's face. He

frowned at the fallen gun. "Why not throw both away if you're giving up? You can't shoot me with an empty gun. If you're trying to trick me, it doesn't matter. I've got the robe, and you gave me the power. I'm in charge here."

Lyssa pulled an orange-tape-marked magazine out of a pocket and shoved it into her gun. Alvarez frowned.

"Who said anything about surrendering?" she asked. "I let myself get all shot up because of what the cops and FBI wanted, but I'm not going to sit here and let some idiot drug dealer with delusions of grandeur punch me through walls. You're not the only one with a reputation to maintain."

"Don't you get it?" Alvarez snarled. "You're nothing, *bruja*. I have your power now. You can't hurt me."

"You should be honored." Lyssa sucked in a breath. "This is expensive. And stop calling me a *bruja*. I'm *not* a damned witch." She gestured with her free hand toward her head. "See? I don't have the damned hat."

"You—"

Lyssa cut him off with a trigger pull. The bullet blasted through his chest with a bright flash, leaving a huge hole where flesh and bone had been. He opened his mouth to speak, but only a quiet croak came out. Alvarez fell to his knees with shock on his face before collapsing forward.

"Having a couple of toys doesn't make you better than a Sorceress," Lyssa snarled. She grabbed her other gun and holstered them both.

Her gaze lingered on Alvarez. The penetrator bullet had done its work well, enhanced by Jofi's passive power.

She sighed. "I'd say I earned some more ice cream."

CHAPTER SIX

Lieutenant Lopez spoke quietly with the newly arrived FBI agents, scowling at Lyssa between sentences. She ignored him as she talked to Damien and leaned against her bike, glad the mask protected her identity. The news locusts were out in force.

Damien's earlier antimedia efforts had collapsed before the power of First Amendment inevitability, leaving a street choked with news vans and reporters chatting in front of their cameramen. Three news helicopters now circled the area, along with tiny drones. Besides the professional reporters, twenty-something and teenage wannabe internet stars ran around the edges with their selfie sticks, trying to get reaction shots and fulfilling Damien's prophecy.

A huge crowd of curious onlookers only interested in watching the story unfold added to the chaos. The police had set up cones. Uniformed officers kept curious locals and reporters back with the occasional stern rebuke or threat.

Lyssa glanced at the sun, which had barely moved. That pissed her off. It was like the sun was mocking her.

All the tension and concentration of the fight inside didn't change that it had been a battle marked in minutes, not hours. It'd only taken as long as it had because of her restraint.

The conscious survivors of Lyssa's attack knelt on the lawn, cops on guard around them. Many of the criminals remained unconscious, bruised, and bloodied. EMTs walked up and down the rows of men to triage and apply first aid. Some were being carried on stretchers toward waiting ambulances, bandages on their heads or arms. Non-lethal force didn't mean harmless.

She didn't care. Even ignoring their other crimes, they'd had plenty of chances of surrender, but they'd convinced themselves the shards would help them win. The price of their arrogance was a trip to the hospital.

That covered the living. The police hadn't removed any of the dead bodies from the home, including Alvarez's. There were detectives and FBI agents already inside, inspecting things and looking for evidence.

She wasn't needed anymore. They hadn't hired her to investigate Alvarez and the cartel.

No one had taken a statement from her beyond a couple of quick questions. They expected Damien to file a report he'd pass along to all the relevant agencies. It cut down on the complications from both ends.

Lyssa's leg ached. She shifted position to take the weight off it.

Damien gestured at her leg. "Now that everything's calmed down, you want someone to take a look at that?

You've got a lot of holes in your outfit. They must have lit you up in there."

"I'm fine." Lyssa shrugged. "They got lucky a few times by throwing hundreds of bullets and some shards at me. Nothing big."

"If you say so." Damien's gaze lingered on the wound. "I've seen you get torn up before. You keep on coming back, but you're not immortal."

"Says you." Lyssa flexed. "People should learn not to mess with a goddess, and they won't get their asses handed to them."

"I'm not some hick. I know what you're capable of." Damien chuckled. "And I'd love to believe we had an immortal super-weapon on our side. Forget it. You cleared out a house filled with guns and shards and walked out. That's a lot better than we could have done without your help. And since no one's said it yet, I'll say it. Thank you."

"You're welcome."

Lyssa was annoyed at the wounds for a reason she didn't want to say out loud. Active healing spells were beyond her capabilities. Her regalia accelerated the healing process and would regenerate itself, but that just meant she'd have to keep it on for a while.

For all its disguise and shape-changing capabilities, there were limits to its power. There was no way it would feel as good as a nice, loose nightgown.

It would be a long night. She could supplement her healing with enchanted herbs, also courtesy of Tricia, but she'd taken too much damage to avoid discomfort for a day or two.

"So, uh," Damien began, "now that the thanks are out of

the way, there's something we need to talk about. Unless you have somewhere to go."

"Spit it out," Lyssa said. "I have an appointment at this lovely place called my house."

"Not the Hecate Cave?"

"Very funny."

Damien inclined his head toward Lopez with an uncomfortable look on his face. "The lieutenant's arguing you went overboard. The FBI isn't keen that you gunned down Alvarez. They really, really wanted to work him for their investigation."

"They've got plenty of people left alive." Lyssa shrugged. "And I was being attacked with shards. If you consider how many people were attacking me, I didn't kill a lot. The lackeys will know other higher-ranking guys and will have seen things."

"I know that." Damien looked uneasy. "But they wanted the big fish. I'm not saying I agree with them, but as a liaison, I'm trying to make the other agencies' positions clear to our Society contractor."

"Oh, I see." Lyssa folded her arms. "The FBI thinks I was supposed to sit there and let Alvarez cave my head in with his shard-enhanced strength." She shrugged. "Next time, make that clearer. I didn't realize Sorceresses needed to die to make sure the FBI has an easier investigation."

"It's going to be a lot of paperwork for them, and also for me. We have to justify it every time one of you kills someone, you know, contract or not." Damien gave her a pleading look. "I'm not denying that the government understands employing a Torch or an Eclipse has a high probability of ending in the use of lethal force, but I wouldn't be doing my job if I didn't communicate everyone else's concerns."

"Concerns? What kind of concerns would they have had if they'd been the ones in there dodging exploding crossbow bolts and super-punches?" Lyssa stepped away from her bike and dropped her arms. "Give me a damned break. I think the FBI and the lieutenant have been snorting whatever drugs Alvarez's boys sell."

"Come on. I'm—"

A handsome face and a bright smile weren't going to save Damien from her wrath. He was a liaison, yes, but that meant he also needed to communicate *her* problems to everyone else.

"I could have kicked in the door and killed everyone in there without breaking a sweat or getting more than a bruise." Lyssa gestured at the house. "Instead, I went in there with my batons and knocked most of them out." She pulled a baton out of her pocket and flicked it to its full length. "And I used sorcery to ensure that outcome instead of caving in their skulls."

Cameramen in the distance all focused on her. Some of the nearby cops looked uneasy, but no one went for a gun. One of the internet kids shouted excitedly. Damien gave her an exasperated look but didn't say anything.

Lyssa wanted them to watch. She wasn't their pet Sorceress. Everyone needed to remember that.

"The first thing they tried to do was blow me up with a shard, remember?" Lyssa flung her arm with the baton in the direction of some cops, who ducked and covered their heads. "And even after that, when they started shooting at me with their special crossbows, I tried to take them alive.

You ever been shot at with an elemental crossbow, Damien?"

"No, I can't say that I have." Damien sighed. "But I have been shot at."

"Oh, you've been shot at. It's totally the same thing. Wait, you ever been nearly blown up by a flame-blade trap? Hmm? How about that? Fought a guy in a robe that makes him stronger anytime somebody dies around him?"

"No, I can't say that's happened either." Damien averted his gaze.

"Then can we stop talking about this crap?" Lyssa frowned. "I didn't violate my contract."

"No one's saying you've violated the scope of your contract, but they wanted Alvarez." Damien shrugged. "That's all I'm saying."

"And I tried to get these guys to surrender a bunch of times." Lyssa collapsed her baton and stuck it back in her pocket. "But they thought they could win. That's the problem when non-Sorcerers get their hands on our toys. They don't know their limits."

"Yes, the shards." Damien gritted his teeth. "That was unfortunate."

Lyssa's heart rate kicked up. Damien had picked the wrong word. She could have let it go if she hadn't already been spun about her brother's anniversary and angry about the job.

"Unfortunate?" Lyssa snarled. "What's unfortunate is the tiny little detail where no one mentioned there'd be shard users in there. If I had known that from the beginning, I could have handled this differently, and maybe I wouldn't have had to end up wasting an expensive pene-trator round against Alvarez."

"I'm sure you'll finish ahead once you get paid."

"That's not the point." Lyssa took a couple of deep breaths, unsure if Damien was being obtuse or was just a standard-issue myopic government agent. "The FBI wouldn't have to complain about their suspect missing most of his upper body, either, but that's not the main issue."

"What is, then?"

A man that good-looking shouldn't be annoying her. She'd barely paid attention to the aftermath after calling in the cops and letting all the government people do their bureaucratic dance. The Phoenix PD and the FBI must have pitched a fit to wind Damien up like that. It was time he understood what was at stake.

"If a SWAT team had gone in there, or the FBI had sent in an HRT," Lyssa said, "there is a good chance you'd have a lot of dead cops and agents instead of a handful of dead gangsters. How would that look on the news? The first trap could have killed tons of guys. It might have killed me if I'd gotten hit."

Damien looked uneasy. He glanced over his shoulder at Lieutenant Lopez and the FBI agents. "I don't disagree fundamentally with anything you said, and you're right. There was an intelligence failure somewhere along the line, especially considering how closely the FBI and the DEA have been watching Alvarez. Somebody should have mentioned the possibility that he was smuggling shards."

"Something smells." Lyssa shook her head. "I can't be the only one who thinks so. Investigation's a sideline for me, unlike the detectives and FBI, but I know how to poke around."

"What are you suggesting?" Damien asked.

"It's not cheap to hire a Torch." Lyssa patted her chest. "And I have a hard time believing a random mayor would authorize it to clear out gangsters when he knew the feds were already on their way and eager to help. Sitting tight and letting the specialists do their job wouldn't have cost anything more, and it wouldn't look like they need a Sorceress to keep order."

Damien cupped his chin. "But if someone whispered in his ear about shards, then it makes a lot more sense. Dead FBI agents all over the news would make Phoenix look like a war zone, and everyone would be screaming about why didn't they send in a Torch to begin with."

"Exactly. I think someone somewhere along the line knew Alvarez had shards, and I think they decided to have me clean it up on the cheap." Lyssa leaned against her bike again, wanting to give her aching leg a rest. Getting shot could be inconvenient.

"I don't know about that." Damien shook his head. "You and the Society will still get bonuses because of what happened."

"It still ends up cheaper than contracting a Torch to deal with a sorcery-based threat, let alone going through all the trouble to get the Society to send an Eclipse to deal with a rogue Sorcerer."

Damien furrowed his brow. "These guys weren't Sorcerers. They were normies using shards."

A lot of non-Sorcerers were offended at being called

Shadows, but she thought normie was a more insulting nickname.

Lyssa's nose itched, and she wrinkled it under her mask. "I don't know. That part I'm not sold on, but there's no way I buy that no one knew about the shards."

"I'm not saying I disagree. I'm trying to figure out where we go from here."

"The simplest explanation is often the best. I think Samuel would have mentioned it if he knew. That guy might like his government connections, but he's still an Elder in the Society." Lyssa sucked in a deep breath. "Maybe I'm thinking too low-level on this. I wouldn't put it past the government to have heard and decide not to mention it. This wouldn't be the first time the EAA played a little fast and loose with their info."

Damien frowned and leaned close to her, almost touching. "Come on, Lyssa, you know me. Don't be like that."

"Don't use my real name *ever* when I'm in full-up Night Goddess mode," she snarled. She stared at him until he backed off, looking contrite. "And I need explanations and soon. The next time I walk into a situation that's supposed to be a bunch of *normies*, and I'm getting shot at with elemental crossbows and robes charged by death, I'm going to be a lot angrier. I'm not going to end up like..."

Like my brother, she thought.

"Like what?" Damien looked confused.

Lyssa frowned. "Forget about it. Just listen to what I said."

"Fair enough, and I understand why you're pissed." Damien sighed. "I'll do my best. There might have been a miscommunication somewhere, but I'm sure we can figure this out. I'll get you an update within a week."

Lyssa hopped onto her bike and started it. "You do that. I've got to go buy more ice cream. That's another thing this night ruined."

Damien blinked. "Huh? Ice cream?"

"What, am I speaking Lemurian? My ice cream melted."

Lyssa pulled away, leaving the government agent staring after her, his expression confused. Driving around town with a wounded leg seemed like a bad idea, even with her regalia and painkiller herbs. It was time for some good, old-fashioned delivery.

CHAPTER SEVEN

"Ninety-eight," Lyssa counted. "Ninety-nine. One hundred. One hundred and one."

Sweat poured off her brow as she continued doing push-ups. Her muscles screamed at her to stop, but at least she didn't feel any pain in her leg.

The wound was healed. A couple of days mostly spent in her regalia and Tricia's herbs had taken care of it.

Maintaining physical readiness was critical, given her aggressive and acrobatic combat style. Efficient delivery of pain and harm with minimal active spell use was what made her such a good Torch.

Not only that, but it was also as good a time as any to work off the nervous energy and all the calories from the pints of ice cream she'd downed while marathoning TV and recovering from her injuries.

Lyssa tried her best to ignore the shadow cast by tomorrow's anniversary of her brother's disappearance. While she always remembered it, she never observed it because part of her felt it'd be like admitting her brother was dead. It was easier to throw herself into TV and exercise.

During her time at home, she'd binged the entire first season of *Sensual Sorceress,* a reality show in which thirteen men thought they were being set up for a chance to convince a Sorceress to marry them.

The show's Sorceress was a Shadow actress. The featured sorcery was nothing but a lot of impressive timing and well-applied special effects.

For anyone with a taste for or knowledge of sorcery, everything about the show was a train wreck, from its take on regalia and sorcery to the ridiculous conceit that the alleged Sorceress on the show specialized in seduction magic.

This last led to a lot of painful melodramatic sequences of men claiming they were unsure if they loved her or were under her spell. Tight dresses, big boobs, and copious amounts of booze could be enchantments for the right sort of man.

Lyssa might have found the sorcery depiction ridiculous, but she proudly defended her self-declared trashy taste. She found the show strangely compelling.

In its way, it was a sociology experiment, exploring what Shadow men believed about Sorceresses. Contrived, yes, and edited for maximum entertainment, but the discerning woman could discover a nugget or two while watching a fake Sorceress who insisted she hadn't used a so-called make-out spell on a man who was trying to suck her face off.

Chuckling about the thought of a bunch of men competing for her love, Lyssa lost count of her reps and lowered her body to the ground. After rolling onto her back, she took deep breaths of precious oxygen and stared at her white ceiling. She needed something up there—a ceiling fan, maybe.

Her thoughts drifted back to *Sensual Sorceress*. The show made sense on one level. Sex and love were at the basis of human existence for both the Illuminated and Shadows. Sorcerers and Sorceresses would have gone extinct a long time ago if they never tried to find someone outside their tiny circle.

Despite recent increases, there were barely two thousand adult Illuminated in the world, a far cry from their numbers in ancient Lemuria when there were far fewer Shadows. They might not have good records of everyone with Lemurian blood since the Cataclysm had sunk the continent ten thousand years ago, but she wouldn't be surprised if there wasn't a little of Lemuria in every country.

Sex, love, dating? Even a Torch needed a life.

The Sorcerer dating pool was shallow, but the Shadow pool ran into the billions. The problem was finding a Shadow she could trust. How long would it be before there was no more separation between the two strains of humanity?

Lyssa stood and shook out her arms. Worrying about relationships could wait for the future. She was still getting established in Phoenix after years in San Diego, and there was at least one non-personal loose end fraying in her mind.

"I wonder how long it'll take," she mumbled.

"How long what'll take?" Jofi asked.

She'd almost forgotten he was there. That was dangerous. She should never allow herself to forget about the spirit.

"For Damien to turn up something." Lyssa sat on the couch. "I've been thinking about it. I'm half-wondering if that job was a trap."

"That's what you're concerned about?"

She retrieved a water bottle sitting on a small end table. After downing a quarter of it, she let out a sigh of relief.

"There are a lot of people out there I've helped take down who are still alive." Lyssa set the bottle back on the table. "Twelve years of being a Torch, and most of my targets have been the worst kind of trash. Some make Alvarez look like a saint."

"Are targeted assassinations of Torches typical?" Jofi asked.

She was surprised by the question, but she shouldn't have been. They didn't spend much time discussing Society business, but Jofi was always there to passively listen and observe when she received orders. Ultimately, his view of the Illuminated Society was narrow and shaped through the experiences of one young-ish Torch.

"No. I can't say they are, whatever you might think. There aren't a lot of Sorcerers and there are fewer Torches. On the other hand, it's not like the threat can be ignored. You might not appreciate the politics of all of it, but there's a reason Torches and Eclipses have to be careful about who knows their true identity. Soldiers and assassins are bigger targets. No one's going to go out of their way to screw with a Sorceress with healing sorcery and Earth Mother regalia."

"The mere possibility of an assassination isn't the same thing as verifying an occurrence," Jofi said. "There are many negative events that could happen but haven't."

"Such as?"

"A large meteor destroying a major city," Jofi explained, "like they spoke about on that show you were watching last week."

"True." Lyssa laid her head against the back of the couch. "The thing is, an assassination's far more likely than a killer meteor, and I feel like there's something here worth looking into. I want to know what it is before I stick my neck out."

"Are you sure you're not seeing connections that aren't there due to the incident with your brother and the anniversary? You've demonstrated emotional distress well beyond normal in the last week."

Lyssa jerked upright. "This isn't about that. Mostly. Besides, it doesn't change what I've said."

"Is there another possibility you can think of?" Jofi asked. "Something less pernicious that might make you worry less?"

Lyssa opened her mouth but closed it without uttering a single syllable. There were too many possibilities, and that was the problem. No one liked accepting that there were many different reasons someone might want to kill them.

"Let's not worry about it for now." Lyssa stood. "I'm going to take a shower, then go out to get something to eat. I've been ordering in too much."

"Will I be coming?"

"No, I think I can grab a chicken sandwich without

needing to shoot someone."

"You should take a normal weapon, just in case."

Lyssa smiled. "I'm not going to have a shootout at Emperor Chicken unless they've run out of chicken sandwiches again."

She waited for him to offer an additional complaint with a hint of guilt stabbing her. She wanted to be honest with Jofi. Her brother might not be the only reason someone might want to take a shot at her.

No. She wouldn't worry about the spirit. One crisis at a time. That was all she could handle.

***

Lyssa stopped in her garage and stared at her bike. She still planned to get food, but the shards and Alvarez snuck back into her mind.

Waiting around was adding to her agitation. She trusted Damien to get her information, but the EAA had its limits. They couldn't handle shards without the help of the Illuminated.

She ran her hands through her hair and groaned. "This sucks."

"What?" Jofi asked. "You've yet to leave. It seems premature to complain about your meal before you've eaten it."

"I'm trying to be patient about the shards, but I can't let it go." Lyssa shrugged. "It's been a long time since I've had a job where I got ambushed by something that unexpected."

"The rocket launcher incident in Sacramento didn't bother you as much?"

"No, because they told me ahead of time those terrorists might have weapons like that." Lyssa moved over to the bike and straddled the seat. "Knowing I'm in for a tough fight doesn't bother me."

"Then your primary concern in this incident was the lack of forewarning?"

"Sort of." Lyssa shook her head. "The trap alone wouldn't have bothered me. A single crossbow or the robe alone wouldn't have spun me up as much. But the entire package? It was too much."

"You survived with only modest injuries."

Lyssa snickered. "You were the one who wanted me to get rougher from the beginning."

"Due to tactical considerations, nothing more."

Lyssa thought for a moment and hopped off her bike. "I'm not going to sit around doing nothing."

"You're not going to the chicken restaurant?" Jofi asked.

"I am, but first, I need to get one of my spare phones out of the safe." Lyssa headed toward the garage door. "I need to give Reed a call."

"Didn't you threaten to kill him last time you talked to him?"

"Sure, because he gave me a bad tip." Lyssa grinned. "He's got a chance to make up for it now."

Lyssa donned her regalia before making the call. She'd long since learned faking her Hecate voice without her regalia was harder than she expected, and the last thing she wanted to do was provide a sleazy informant like Reed Peters any clues about her true identity.

She kept a box of burner phones she'd purchased all over the country, but in this case, there was no reason not to use a local number. Her identity might be a secret, but the fact that Hecate lived in Maricopa County wasn't.

"You're not going to visit him directly about this?" Jofi asked.

"That would require me to get near him." Lyssa wrinkled her nose. "And the less time I spend around that guy, the better. Plus, there's something that bothers me about his suits. The guy's not rich, but he can afford a suit that fits? It's crazy."

She dialed and waited patiently. There was no reason for Reed not to answer, given the time of day. Unless he was dead. That was always a possibility.

"Yeah?" Reed answered, suspicion thick in his voice.

"It's me," Lyssa replied, the gruffness of the regalia coming through. "It's a new phone."

Reed giggled. "Hecate, I'm not the NSA. You ain't got to worry about me tracing things."

"I'm not worried about you." Lyssa scoffed. "And I don't want to waste a lot of time with chitchat."

"You know me. I'm always up for a nice, well-paid chat. And you pay better than most."

"Is that why you haven't tried to sell me out yet?"

"That and you might drink my soul," Reed replied.

"Good, remember that. But let's get down to business. I've got an important place to be."

"Weren't you going to Emperor Chicken for a meal?" Jofi asked.

Lyssa put her hand over her phone. "Quiet, you. You're going to mess up my flow."

Reed coughed over the line. "Before we get down to business, I'm wondering."

"Wondering what?" Lyssa asked warily.

"Does it always have to be money?" Reed chuckled nervously. "Maybe you could owe me a fav—"

"Don't press your luck," Lyssa growled. "Jorge Alvarez. You know him?"

"Yeah." Reed sounded offended. "I ain't some idiot, you know. I knew about him before you kicked in his door and beat his ass. What about him?"

"He had shards."

"That's what they said on the news."

"Would you happen to know anything about that?" Lyssa asked.

"Ah, I got you." Reed chuckled. "I ain't got anything right now, but that don't mean I won't get nothing. Give me some time."

Lyssa hissed in frustration. "Everyone needs time, and no one knows anything."

"Whoa. Calm down there, Hecate. I'll find what you need. You want to know where he got them, right?"

"Yes." Lyssa ground her teeth. "Get me answers within a week, and I'll pay you twice as much as normal. The faster you get that info, the bigger the bonus."

She was more frustrated than she'd expected to be. Calling Reed crystallized the truth about what had happened the other day.

"Now that's what I call motivation," Reed replied. "I'll get what you need. Old Reed Peters ain't ever going to let you down."

"I hope not. For your sake."

CHAPTER EIGHT

Lyssa munched quietly on her spicy Szechuan chicken sandwich in the corner of the Emperor Chicken dining room. Despite her frustration, there was nothing to do but wait and relax by focusing on the mundane. Tomorrow, she had somewhere to go that would help distract her from the anniversary, but the only thing keeping her grounded for the moment was food.

Eating a chicken sandwich and sipping iced tea was about the most mundane thing in the world. No one would suspect that Hecate the Night Goddess would be at a corner Chinese-fusion fast-food place.

A TV hung in the corner of the dining room, blaring the news. She'd hoped everyone had moved on from the Alvarez incident, but it was still headlining broadcasts days later. A split-screen came up as the anchor introduced an alleged expert, a round-faced bespectacled man in a gray suit and a red bowtie.

She grimaced. She'd never met the man, but she recognized him from an article she'd read before moving to

Phoenix. He was a member of an anti-sorcery activist group.

"We're joined today by Grant Harris," the anchor said. "He's the president of the local chapter of the American Council for Sorcery Safety. Thank you for taking time out of your busy schedule to join us."

"It's my pleasure to be here," Grant replied with a smile. "I consider adding to public safety awareness the duty of every citizen."

"In that vein, we were wondering what your thoughts were on the recent raid in Phoenix on the home of reputed cartel member Jorge Alvarez." The anchor kept a serious expression. "The government brought in a Sorceress who goes by the name of Hecate. While the police, FBI, and EAA aren't being open with all the details, it's clear the alleged criminals present, including the now-deceased Jorge Alvarez, were in possession of multiple illegal magical items, sometimes referred to as shards."

Lyssa rolled her eyes. She loathed the word "magic."

It was a petty complaint. She could understand why Shadows didn't see a difference between magic and sorcery, but in her mind, sorcery was real, the result of careful training and study combined with the power of the regalia. It was ancient, older than Shadow science. Magic was something a guy in a top hat with a half-naked assistant did in Vegas at a super-cheap, way off-the-Strip casino.

The dictionary battle was lost, and her faction had been routed and humiliated. That was obvious to anyone. The day sorcery was revealed to the modern Shadow world was called M-Day, not S-Day. She'd have to get over it.

Grant steepled his fingers and nodded, his face grim. "The insistence by the government that this was a routine event is completely misleading, and I'm surprised that more people aren't terrified about what happened. That's one of the reasons I'm here today."

She hated agreeing with the man about the incident being more than it appeared, though her reasons were likely far different.

The anchor nodded slowly. "I see. Could you expand on your meaning for the people at home?"

"Of course." Grant nodded back. "The last time I checked, it was the job of law enforcement to apprehend criminals. Now, I have nothing but the utmost respect for our men and women in law enforcement, but hiring a witch to come in and do dangerous magic is not a good long-term solution to solving the problem of criminal threat inflation." He sighed and shook his head. "What if innocent people were hurt? It's my understanding that they didn't know about the shards beforehand, and the combination of this lethal woman flinging her powers around with these criminals using dangerous magical items? Well, we don't know the long-term effects or if a collision of their spells might have blown the entire neighborhood away. Do you want to trust your children's safety to a witch dressed like that?"

Lyssa rolled her eyes. She wasn't a witch, and the only people who could get away with bowties were college professors, guys who always went by three names, and English actors playing ancient alien time travelers.

The anchor nodded. "That's a big concern, especially with recent revelations about alleged accidents and dangerous occurrences that turned out to be the result of sorcery."

There were many mysterious explosions and dead bad people all over the world who'd been done in by Torches. Before M-Day, the leaders of the Illuminated Society hadn't been above trying to manipulate countries and societies both directly and indirectly. With greater numbers, they might have been more effective.

Lyssa took a sip of her drink. Grant Harris and his friends might be paranoid, but that didn't make them wrong. The problem was his people wanted to take down all Sorcerers.

"That's what led to the formation of the ACSS and our sister organizations across the world." Grant shook a finger. "It's important for everyone to remember that this Illuminated Society hid for thousands of years. Even if we believe their fanciful claims that they are descendants of people from a lost sunken continent, that doesn't change the fact it was an accident that revealed them to the world five years ago, not their honest attempt to reach out. I don't know about you, but if someone's been lying and hiding from me for a long time, it makes me suspect they're not being honest about a lot of other things."

"The Society claims they'd been intending to go public for a much longer time," the anchor replied. "They simply took advantage of that incident to come out of the top hat, as it were."

"Come out of the top hat?" Lyssa chuckled. She might not like the term "magic," but that expression was clever. She'd have to use it.

"It's obvious that's a lie." Grant furrowed his brow. "And

it doesn't change that these people didn't have a problem with hiding themselves for so long. It's shocking to me that the government maintains such a cavalier attitude toward them."

The anchor replied, "The Extraordinary Affairs Agency insists the situation is well in hand."

Grant guffawed before wiping away a tear of mirth. "I don't know about you, but hearing a government agency say, 'Don't worry, we've got this under control' worries me on the best of days, let alone when we're talking about sorcery."

The anchor laughed. Lyssa controlled herself. Unsurprisingly, growling at random TVs in public attracted attention.

"Given the range of magical abilities," Grant said, "we can't rule out undue influence on the government by the Society."

"Are you stating here, in public, that you believe the US government has been infiltrated or supernaturally influenced by Sorcerers?" the anchor asked, sounding surprised.

"I'm only noting it's a possibility we shouldn't ignore." Grant frowned. "I'm far more concerned about the local risks. Let's not ignore the other frightening aspect of this situation. Dangerous criminals had illegal magical items." He clucked his tongue. "Given how rare that used to be, it's obvious the Society isn't doing enough to keep their criminals in check, and now they're flooding our streets with their dangerous magical weapons."

"Isn't that more reason to hire Torches and other Sorcerers?"

Grant looked offended. "Don't you think that's convenient?"

"Convenient?" The anchor's eyebrows lifted.

"Dangerous criminals suddenly have magic items, forcing the government to rely more on the Society, but the only possible source of those items *is* the Society." Grant's smile became more of a smirk. "I'm not accusing the Society of anything. I'm only noting we have to keep all possibilities in mind when we're looking into the situation."

Lyssa clenched her jaw so hard it started to hurt. The extra-annoying thing was Grant was right. Alvarez wasn't a god. He was a cartel thug, and unless something awful had happened, there was only a single source for shards.

She didn't buy into Grant's convoluted logic of a dark plan by the Society as a whole, but there could be a Sorcerer at the end of the tunnel. That didn't fit with her paranoia about it being a trap, but a good conspiracy theory wasn't stopped by mere evidence.

"Also," Grant continued, his cheeks red, "we can't ignore that we don't even know where the capital territory of these people is. I continue to find that amazing."

"Isn't that Last Remnant?" the anchor asked.

"We know a name, and we know it's an island that is, by their admission, hidden by their magic somewhere in the Indian Ocean. But where exactly is it? Would you sign a treaty with another country if you didn't even know where they were? The Cold War didn't become World War III because the Russians realized if they nuked us, we'd nuke them. We don't have a similar balance with the Society."

The anchor looked concerned. "We're not at war with

the Illuminated Society, and we're not engaged in a Cold War either. Don't you think most people would say the situations aren't analogous? Sorcerers live among us."

Grant shook his head. "And doesn't that ever keep you up at night? You never sit in a restaurant and look around, wondering if someone eating a meal next to you might be one of them?"

An old man close to the exit slowly surveyed the restaurant. His gaze skipped right past Lyssa and landed on a Goth high-school boy wearing a t-shirt with a band logo so ornate and unintelligible it might as well have been in Lemurian. Dark makeup, all-black clothes, and guyliner fit the stereotype more than Lyssa, a pretty, dark-haired woman in a ponytail, jeans, a white leather jacket, and a t-shirt featuring Kawatsu-chan, a cutesy pink Japanese unicorn mascot character. Even her boots came off as fashion-conscious suburbanite rather than dangerous biker.

As Grant babbled on, she tuned out the television conversation to focus on her meal. Damien or Reed needed to come up with something for her soon. The quicker she found the source of the shards, the less chance there was of idiots like Grant Harris whipping up a panic.

She also needed the case to be over for her peace of mind. Accepting that she was letting the anniversary mess with her and having clear proof the job had nothing to do with her brother were two different things.

Grant's words stung because she knew people like him had the advantage in the war for the public's trust. The sad truth was, standing up and announcing who she was might empty the restaurant. Greater numbers of Illuminated or more open relationships between her kind and Shadows might make things different, but as it stood now, her kind were outnumbered and often not trusted. She couldn't even claim there weren't good reasons for mistrust.

Saying the Illuminated feared Shadow society might be going too far. Sorcery might not be infinite, but Lyssa had defeated an entire house full of armed criminals only a couple of days prior and was back to working out without ever hitting a hospital. Superior numbers ensured an unequal relationship.

A freckle-faced teenage employee barely old enough to work walked past her, trays in hand. He stopped to smile. "Enjoying your sandwich?"

She smiled at him, unsure of what this was about. "It's nice, yes."

"That bike is bitchin'." He nodded at the yellow Ducati outside. "I don't know a lot about motorcycles, but it looks cool and fast."

Lyssa laughed, her tension leaving with the sound. "I love my bike. It's cool, yes, and fast. Faster than you could imagine when I'm trying."

"Just surprised to see someone with a bike like that in here." He eyed her for a moment. "And you don't seem the type."

"Hey, sometimes a girl needs a chicken sandwich." She smiled. "And all sorts of people ride bikes."

"I'll get one someday, but right now, I've got to get all the trays." The boy laughed and lifted them. "The Man's always calling."

"You do what you need to." Lyssa waved at him as he stepped away.

Though she liked a good chicken sandwich, hunger

hadn't been the main force that sent her to Emperor Chicken. The truth was, sometimes she needed to get away from Jofi. It wasn't like the spirit could hear her thoughts, but she always felt his presence when she was close.

Sometimes she wanted to be alone. It was ironic that going to a fast-food joint filled with people would make her feel more that way than sitting in her house. There were too many secrets in her life, too many mysteries.

It was pointless to worry about what she couldn't change. She'd been born into the Corti family and come into true power. That might not mean she had a destiny, but she had a responsibility.

She offered her tray to the boy and glanced at the TV again. The interview was coming to an end.

"I think every normal person out there should remember what we're saying and not let our opponents mischaracterize our stances." Grant adopted a stern look. "Whether the Society wants to call it magic or sorcery, it's all the same. There is a group out there with powers beyond normal limits. Many of these people don't even do us the courtesy of showing us their faces. If you have nothing to hide, Hecate, why do you wear a mask?"

"Screw that guy," the busboy said, sweeping by Lyssa to grab her tray. "I bet Hecate is hot. That's why she wears the mask. She doesn't want guys always hitting on her."

Lyssa laughed. "You think so? You don't think she looks like an old lady?"

"No one who kicks that much ass looks like an old lady." The boy left with his trays.

It was nice to know not every Shadow was against her, but she was concerned about adults like Grant Harris. The

Society needed to clean up to keep his influence from growing.

Alvarez hadn't conjured his shards out of thin air. There was a good chance that somewhere, a Sorcerer had gotten greedy. Whatever else it had to do with her, someone needed to go down.

CHAPTER NINE

Lyssa groaned when her cell phone awakened her the next morning. She rolled toward her nightstand and groped for the offending piece of technology, then opened her eyes enough to hit the accept call button. It wasn't until she'd done so that she realized it was from an unknown number.

There was silence, then a click on the other end. She muttered, awaiting the stupid computer voice attempting to sell her an extended warranty on her bike or claim she owed the IRS millions of dollars. Who needed sorcery when there were so many ways to con people?

A single word came over the line, the voice distorted, not male or female, but with familiar diction. "Chartreuse."

Lyssa's stomach tightened. The universe was trying to screw her over by making everything come at her at the same time. Before she could even think to reply, the call ended. She had no choice now but to take a little trip.

"I'm going to grab a bite to eat," she announced. "I'll just be going around the corner. No reason to get you out."

"If you're sure," Jofi replied. "I'm surprised to see you eat so early."

"Sometimes you're hungry."

Sure? No. This was one thing she'd never be sure about.

Lyssa sped north on I-17, appreciating the light morning traffic. She didn't bother with her regalia. That meant she couldn't go any faster than normal and needed to avoid speeding, but the caller wouldn't have contacted her if he wasn't close. She'd been riding for about an hour, and she knew she was almost there.

More importantly, she hadn't brought Jofi, instead packing a similar-looking 9mm. It couldn't handle enchanted ammo, but it would do in a pinch if she needed to shoot someone in the head.

The problem was the spirit could hear and see near his physical form, even through walls. This was one meeting she couldn't risk him overhearing. As far as she could tell, less than twenty yards was his normal range.

"Jofi?" she asked to be sure. She wasn't surprised by the lack of response.

The stray thought of an ambush came into her head. Without her regalia, her sorcery was far more limited, but her combat training and experience remained.

"It's the anniversary, huh?" Lyssa scoffed. "Try and take down two different Cortis on the same day?"

Why was she thinking like that? Her brother wasn't dead. It wasn't like her family was cursed. Her parents had died on different days.

This had nothing to do with her brother. The code word Chartreuse had confirmed that. She went weeks at a time, sometimes months, ignoring where she'd gotten Jofi and why, but that didn't mean it had changed. The man who'd contacted her was interested in the spirit.

A jade necklace was snugged securely under her white leather jacket. She'd grabbed it from her safe before heading out. While she wore it, she intuitively knew the right way to go.

She was getting closer to the target. I-17 fed into a state road, and an exit was coming up soon.

Lyssa took the exit, not spotting anything notable other than a sign warning her of no services at the next stop. That warning wasn't unusual in this part of Arizona. More than a few ghost towns dotted the highways between the major cities. The desert didn't forgive the weak.

She kept driving, and the necklace directed her toward another side road. After slowing, she continued for a couple of minutes.

The side road gave way to a dirt path no one would call a road. She didn't worry. Her fancy racing bike might have problems if she tried all-terrain driving without sorcery too often, but it would survive for a couple of minutes. She all but coasted, following the path of a dry creek bed until she stopped.

Her chest tightened, and the enchantment on the necklace kept her focused on the center of the creek bed. There was nothing there, and nothing seemed wrong, other than the increased pressure in her chest marking sorcery.

She stopped the bike. A man appeared out of nowhere.

No, that wasn't right. It wasn't that he'd appeared; more

that he'd been there all along, and she'd just noticed him. She'd encountered that kind of spell before from this same man.

The Sorcerer stood in the road in full regalia, green and red robes with elegant dragon figures stitched up the sides. The man wore no mask, but an elaborate golden headdress topped his head.

She knew he didn't need a mask, although she couldn't be sure she knew his true appearance. She thought he was a shaven-headed Chinese man in his mid-forties. At least, he had the skin of a man in his mid-forties, but trusting one's senses around a Sorcerer with a mind essence was dangerous.

He currently wore the Imperial Sage regalia. Embodying the concept more completely might have included having other people see something more appropriate for tenth-century China than twenty-first-century America.

Lyssa lowered her kickstand and slid off her bike. She nodded at him before pulling off her helmet and setting it on the seat.

"It's been a while, Lee," Lyssa said.

"Yes, it has been, Miss Corti." He watched her with a faint look of disapproval. "Some things came up, but since I was in the area, I thought it would be best to check with you directly. You should have anticipated that your move from San Diego would result in an earlier visit."

"I moved because Samuel told me to." Lyssa shrugged. "But getting down to business, Jofi's secure. You didn't need to come all this way if he's what this is about."

"*It*, not he," Lee replied. He folded his hands behind his

back. "As a reminder, I represent all the relevant parties in this regard. What I say is the unified voice of many. You don't always appear to understand that."

Lyssa snorted. "I get it. I don't see the problem. I'm doing my part to keep Jofi's seal intact, just like I have been for the last six years. You do your little mysterious visiting stranger thing every few months, and it's the same every time. Don't you ever get tired of it? If you were anybody else, I'd think you were getting off on it, but you're as annoyed with it as I am."

She'd only participated in the ritual to seal Jofi because she'd been ordered to by Samuel. At the time, he and the others had insisted it was for the safety of the world.

"Yes, annoyance covers it well." Lee narrowed his eyes. "I was tired of it a long time ago, Miss Corti. Your involvement was a fluke, and I remain undecided about whether that's a good thing. However, your unusual traits were useful at that time."

"But what about the others?" Lyssa grinned, injecting all her sarcasm and defiance into the expression. "If you all came at me seriously, I couldn't stop you. To be honest, I used to worry about that. Worry that I'd screw up somehow by your standards, and the next thing I'd be doing was fighting off a half-dozen Sorcerers bent on killing me."

"We have no wish to harm you. Don't misinterpret my distrust of you as a steward as a desire to hurt you."

"But you would hurt or kill me if necessary."

"Yes, if necessary."

They watched each other in silence as a light breeze blew grass and twigs down the arroyo. Farther up it, blackened ground marked the edge of recent summer fires.

"As a group," Lee continued, "we remain committed to it being bound to your weapons and feel that is the best solution with the least risk at this time." His nose twitched. "But I've become concerned, especially since your activities are now more high-profile than when it was bound. The group thinks it's appropriate for me to increase the frequency of my visits until the situation stabilizes."

"Stabilizes?" Lyssa scrubbed a hand over her face. "You're going to be up my ass until, what, you discover a way to destroy Jofi?"

"If necessary." Lee's expression didn't change. The man didn't need a mask. His face *was* a mask.

"Give me a break. The sealing happened before M-Day. High profile? Haven't you heard? We're all out of the top hat now." Lyssa shrugged. "And let's face it. The Shadows might like the occasional healer to help them out, but there's nothing easier to understand than how to use something or someone as a weapon. It's no big surprise that Torches are getting decently well-known. That's not going to lead to any problems. They barely understand what regalia is. They aren't going to figure out anything about dangerous spirits bound to guns."

Lee's gaze flicked to the ground as a small bark scorpion scuttled past. He lifted his foot and crushed the insect under his heel. It took all of Lyssa's self-control not to laugh at the obvious symbolism.

"I have my concerns." Lee inclined his head at her. "Your powers would be reduced without it. You can't deny that."

"I'm not a Shadow running around with shards." Lyssa shrugged. "Yes, I can pull off a lot more stunts with Jofi's help, but that's not the same thing as being reliant. I rarely get even close to drawing on his full power. Besides, what do you care about my ability to do my job?"

"You misunderstand my concerns. Or you're purposely missing the point."

Lee made a quick series of elaborate hand gestures. A shadowy figure appeared in front of him, roughly humanoid but wavering and shifting constantly.

"Your concern is sorcery-enhanced puppet theater?" Lyssa asked. "You should move to Bali with that. We need more Sorcerers working the entertainment circuit."

"Your involvement with it was necessary because your essence is darkness and your regalia is the Night Goddess. It was a unique combination of factors at a time that meant rare effectiveness against the grand emptiness spirit. It wasn't like we had time to hunt for a lot of help when binding it. The fool who brought it to this world had no idea what he was doing. If he hadn't already paid for it with his life, we would have punished him ourselves."

"Sounds like I'm a hero," Lyssa joked.

"Don't forget it's not defeated, only sealed and limited. There's still a risk of it breaking free of the binding, especially if you draw too much power too often." Lee strolled toward her, his hands behind his back. "Power is seductive, isn't it? It's the thing every Sorcerer wants. In the end, age brings refinement, not true extra power, but you might have found a way around that and think to take advantage of it. This is, after all, a time of great change. Certain factions are selfish and think more in terms of years than centuries."

Lyssa stepped forward and squared her shoulders. "Here's the thing. I'm not interested in Society politics. I don't care what a bunch of fossils sitting around pretending this is 4000 BC say or do. I'm not a member of some faction seeking power."

"It sounds like you'd like to change things. A devotion to changing the status quo is a de facto faction, Miss Corti."

"I'm too busy with my own life to worry about the Society." Lyssa stepped back and wondered if she could get away with punching him. "Jofi's fine. He helps my work, and my work helps the Society and feeds him what he needs. Win-win-win."

Lee's eyes bulged. "Stop using the word 'he,' girl," he shouted. "That thing isn't human. It's an emptiness spirit and an extremely dangerous one at that. The only reason we haven't destroyed it outright is that we can't risk losing people in the process or have it break free and go on a rampage. The more you pretend it's a friend who thinks and feels like a person, the greater risk you take. It's nothing more than an embodied concept, and even if we've tricked this one and stripped away what it once was, that doesn't mean it's gone. It's waiting beneath the seals, ready to be released."

"You think I don't know that?" Lyssa scoffed. "Screw you, Imperial Sage. I've got the situation under control."

"Because of your violent lifestyle?" His tone dripped condescension.

"Partially. I think I've got a nice balanced way to feed Jofi without risk. What's your plan without me? Toss sacrifices into a pit every few months and hope the angry god doesn't wake up? As it stands, he's been fed enough by my Torch work to not awaken for a long time, and that's with me going out of my way *not* to kill people half the time."

From what Lee had told her, Jofi took sustenance from the death of intelligent beings, which was a twisted aspect of its nature as an emptiness spirit. It wasn't that it was absorbing their lifeforce as much as the resonant metaphysical energy of the transition between life and death, a ripple from the soul leaving the body.

Lyssa had worried enough about the implications of Jofi's feeding not to agree to the ritual until another Sorcerer's truth spell had verified Jofi wasn't feeding on anyone's souls. There were things far worse than death.

"It's not a god!" Lee yelled. "It's nothing more than a spirit."

"Whatever. I'm not the one freaking out." Lyssa shook her head. "I think after all these years, you'd trust me a little. I've not once damaged the seals or risked Jofi waking up. Not for a second, even when my life was on the line."

"You'll die rather than risk releasing *it?*" Lee asked. "It won't believe it's a gun spirit forever. You might not be able to escape."

"I'll do what it takes to protect people." Lyssa glared at him "I'd feed myself to Jofi if that's what it would take. That's what it means to be a Torch."

"There are ways to enforce that oath."

"Screw you." Lyssa sneered. "There's no way I'm letting one of you freaks control me with a spell, and besides, you're the one who told me it would risk messing with the seal and Jofi's connection to me."

Lee stared at her for an uncomfortably long time. Lyssa stomped on all the sarcastic replies floating to the tip of her tongue. She didn't like the man, but she could understand his concerns. The problem was he needed to show her the same respect.

"I get it." Lyssa sighed. "You're all in paranoia-land because of what happened a few days ago."

"All Sorcerers should worry when our gifts are misused by criminal Shadows."

"Did you miss the part on the news where I raided their hideout and took them out?" Lyssa raised her brow in challenge. "And the EAA took all the shards into custody?"

"Serendipity is a curious thing. What are the chances of a Torch being in the same city as a group of criminals with such items? How often have you been sent to your home city during your career as a Torch?"

"Technically, I live one city over from the house I raided." Lyssa rolled her eyes. "You've got a complicated theory there, but I heard an idiot on the news lately that put me in the right headspace to interpret. Let's see. I'm supplying gangsters with specific shards that somehow have powers well outside the scope of my essence, then I'm waiting for the Society to call me and tell me to take them out. That about sum it up?"

She didn't feel the need to give Lee any ammo by suggesting any of her other paranoid theories about what might have happened. He might accuse her of being mentally unstable. He had in the past.

"According to news reports, it was hoped you'd take the leader alive," Lee said. "His death was convenient if one was attempting to cover up where he'd acquired his shards."

Lyssa flipped him off. "That's what I've got for you, Lee. This is ridiculous." She stomped toward her bike. "I'm a Torch. I blow things up and kill people when the Society needs me to. This time that happened to be in my backyard, but I'm not going to stand here and let you accuse me of anything."

"We're not finished," he spat.

Lyssa slammed on her helmet, straddled her bike, and pushed up the kickstand. "Yeah, I think we pretty much are because you're being an ass, and I'm not sure you haven't been corrupted by the Grand Spirit of Asses. You might want to talk to the others and get that checked."

Lee bared his teeth. "If the seal ever breaks, it'll be too late, Miss Corti. You realize that, don't you? Others will die, but so will you. Unlike what you're doing now, souls will be at risk, not only lives."

She started her Panigale, the mild rumble of the engine soothing. "Don't worry. I won't take it personally if you all come and kill me when I'm a soulless shell for a corrupt spirit abomination. Before then, let's not waste my time, okay?"

"We'll always be watching." Lee gave her a cool look. "You understand that?"

"It's good to have hobbies. I don't judge." Lyssa pulled forward and spun her bike around. "Just stay out of my way until it's time to kill me."

CHAPTER TEN

Lyssa took off her helmet and hung it on a hook in the garage. She didn't bother to put the necklace away yet. It was invisible to Jofi, an artifact of the sealing, but she didn't normally have it out because she didn't want someone else to see it and accidentally remark on it.

The meeting with Lee had left her unsettled. After six years, she'd hoped their meetings would have become routine, but somehow the man always managed to get under her skin with his accusations and dirty looks.

No, that wasn't it. He'd always been a suspicious ass, and she hadn't gotten offended. She was on edge because of the shards and the anniversary.

A familiar presence pushed at the corners of her mind, Jofi. His omnipresence normally made it easy to tune out, like living next to a waterfall and forgetting about the sound. It was only after she was gone for a while that it stood out upon her return, unnerving and comforting at the same time.

"Was your meal unusually delicious?" Jofi asked.

Lyssa stepped through the door. "Huh? Why would you ask that?"

"You were gone a long time. I assume that means your meal was delicious. You don't tend to drink during the day, though I did consider the possibility, given your current stress levels."

She needed a better cover story next time. The anniversary had put her off her game.

"Yeah, I'm not that much of a lush." Lyssa closed the door. "But that whole idea is strange to you, isn't it? I don't think about it enough. You can hear and see in your way, but I always forget you can't smell, touch, or taste. Delicious food is an abstraction to you."

"Understanding the experience isn't necessary to understand you enjoy it on some occasions and dislike it on others."

Always the same calm, even tone. That was what she needed and wanted. That was what Lee and the others he represented wanted. A relaxed Jofi would stay in the guns, thinking he was a gun spirit. A relaxed Jofi would never question anything.

That didn't make Lyssa feel better about it. They were partners of sorts. Lee insisted he was nothing more than a spirit, but not being human wasn't the same thing as being mindless. The truth wouldn't set him free, though. It would obliterate the Jofi she knew and replace him with a homicidal stranger hell-bent on spreading chaos and death.

She'd been in the wrong place at the wrong time with the wrong essence six years ago, but she couldn't change it now. All she could do was try to make sure she helped people with his power.

Lyssa shook her head. The fewer lies a woman told, the easier it was to keep track of them. Wrap the lie up in a nice truth, and it became trivial. "I met an old acquaintance."

"You don't like this person, do you?" Jofi asked.

Lyssa pulled off her jacket and holster and hung them up. "Why do you say that?"

"You look and sound tense. You looked and sounded the same when you left. Your face and voice."

"I'm not a huge fan of the guy, no, and he's not a huge fan of me, which is why he's an acquaintance and not a friend."

"But not an enemy?" Jofi asked.

"You need to try to kill me at least once to qualify as an enemy."

"A useful schema."

Lyssa dropped onto the couch and laid her head back. "If only I was born with a healing essence instead of darkness. I probably wouldn't have ended up a Torch, and I wouldn't have ended up with so many complications in my life."

"Do you believe that?"

Lyssa lifted her head and frowned. "What's that supposed to mean?"

"I would have assumed your family history was your primary motivation for your choices rather than your essence. There's no inherent non-dangerous essence. You could invert healing spells to harm. Your combat style and tactics might be different, but you would have ended up a Torch."

"I don't know about that." Lyssa's heart rate increased,

and she let the other comments slide. The last thing she wanted to talk about was her family situation on that day of all days.

"Your past informs your future," Jofi said. "I know your brother's disappearance bothers you."

"Enough," Lyssa snapped. "I don't want to talk about *that* right now. Sure, I've got a lot on my mind, but don't worry. I'll work through it. I always do. I'm sure Damien will find something useful, and I can busy myself taking down shard smugglers and not have time to think about anything else."

She grabbed a remote off her end table. Some mindless TV might get her mind off the feelings Lee's visit had stirred up. She pressed the ON button and hoped to avoid any anti-sorcery propaganda.

The noon news played, and fortunately, there was no sign of Grant Harris. A bright chyron at the bottom highlighted something she'd stopped worrying about in June.

A Reflection on the Post-Summer Anniversary of M-Day.

"Although many people take it for granted," the anchor announced, "it's hard to believe that it was only five years ago the truth of magic and sorcery came out. Although Sorcerers remain rare and the average person is unlikely to have a direct encounter, we can all agree that the world is no longer the same place it once was. It all started with this one spectacular incident."

Camera footage appeared, showing a royal procession in London with the Queen of England in an open horse-drawn carriage. The elderly monarch sat with a smile in a powder-blue outfit and a matching broad-brimmed hat with her husband, the Prince. Mounted guards in red preceded and followed the royal couple, along with carriages filled with other members of the British Royal Family. Commentators chatted about the dignity of the queen during her part of the opening ceremonies for the event, a horse-racing cup.

Lyssa watched, even though she, like everyone else on the planet, had burned this video and others taken from different angles into their minds. The current video, shot by a team from an American sports news channel, was among the most famous because it provided the clearest view of the events to follow, the events that had changed modern history.

Four men ran toward the carriage from either side, pistols in hand. Screams erupted. They began firing, dropping nearby guards. The Prince and the Queen sat, unflappable, their smiles gone and their expressions hard. No one was surprised that the two royals didn't immediately hop out of their carriages.

The first major anomaly wasn't pointed out for two days after the video hit the net. Horses in front and behind the first carriage lost control, charging away when the gunfire started, but the Queen's horses stayed unusually calm and didn't move. The video had been picked apart by internet sleuths and news organizations, including showing frame-by-frame where the would-be royal assassins had emerged on camera and the first clear piece of evidence of something being wrong: two fleeing birds at the edge of a frame.

One of the Queen's Guard who hadn't been hit jumped off his horse, his uniform shifting and growing around him. He pulled out what looked like a simple bandana and pressed it to his face. His appearance wavered for a moment, and the red-uniformed Queen's Guard was replaced by a man in close-fitting black and red metal armor, complete with a solid red mask that extended to his chin.

It was the first publicly identified regalia, the rather appropriate Royal Knight. It belonged to a sergeant in the Queen's Guard, Gareth Smith. The closeness of a Sorcerer to the Queen would later fuel conspiracy theories about how extensively Sorcerers controlled the world. The revelation that they belonged, by their admission, to a group they called the Illuminated Society had done the rest.

The Society had only done so much to squash the link between the Illuminati and themselves, partially because they couldn't. The truth was the Society had interfered with politics, and some of that had become indirectly known and exposed through conspiracies related to the Illuminati.

All of that had come later. The glory of sorcery had dazzled people during the attempted royal assassination.

Sergeant Smith thrust out his arms, and protective walls of dirt had shot up on two sides of the royal carriage. The assassins paused for a couple of seconds at the strange sight before charging toward their targets, firing freely at the royals. The thick earthen shields absorbed their bullets.

Two of the assassins opened fire on the armored man, but their shots bounced off his armor. When he twisted his palms, coils of dirt and stone shot out of the ground and wrapped around the men before enveloping their guns.

An earthen arm whipped toward the remaining assassins, sending them aloft. They tumbled through the air before crashing into the ground. The arm lifted again, preparing to crush the assassins, but stopped feet from their bodies.

The camera shifted and focused on the Queen. She stood, her expression stern and her palm out. She shook her head.

Sergeant Smith backed away as police approached cautiously, eyeing the Sorcerer and the terrorists with equal concern. The Queen gestured at the sergeant and began clapping. Soon, the entire area was filled with cheers and applause.

From what Lyssa understood, the Queen was aware of the existence of the Society, but she hadn't realized that one of her guards was a Sorcerer. Even though she was a Sorceress, there was a lot Lyssa didn't know about the incident.

The convenience of Sergeant Smith having the Royal Knight regalia didn't bother her. Beyond compatibility with essence, the more an Illuminated embodied the concept of the regalia through their actions and influence on others, the more power they could draw. It made perfect sense for the Royal Knight to be guarding a queen.

She turned off the TV. Sergeant Smith didn't need sorcery to stop the assassins. The Society would later claim they'd received a tip that shards would be used in the attempt, which was why the sergeant had gone straight to sorcery, but given that the Society was the only organization capable of investigating at the time, along with limited personnel in the know in governmental intelligence agencies, no one could confirm their claim.

Most people, including Lyssa, doubted the official story. The Tribunal who ruled the Society and their handpicked Elders had wanted the Society to stop hiding from the rest of humanity. She wouldn't be surprised if they'd somehow concocted the assassination attempt.

The would-be regicides' bizarre motivations only added to the mystery. They weren't with any of the usual terrorist groups one would suspect of sowing discord in London. Instead, they claimed to belong to the New Cromwellian Freedom Army, a group dedicated to the violent overthrow of the monarchy despite the modest and mostly ceremonial power of the institution. Interrogation revealed they were a group of disturbed young men who had planned the attack in intricate detail for months and had no links to other terrorist organizations.

The Society took advantage of the positive press to fully admit their existence to the public and governments of the world, reestablishing the ancient patterns where the Illuminated and the Shadows openly acknowledged each other. The Society tried to downplay their manipulation of history, including Sorcerers posing as gods in the far past.

"We opened up to go backward." Lyssa frowned.

"I don't understand," Jofi said.

"The Society." Lyssa stood and licked her lips. It was going to take her a while to get used to the dry heat of Arizona. She needed better humidifiers. "Sergeant Smith had to leave the Queen's Guard after that. All the different governments insisted that Sorcerers involved in high-level positions be identified. Now, they might hire Torches and Eclipses through the Society, but the idea of someone like

Sergeant Smith serving directly freaks people out. The guy saved the Queen, though!"

"Does that anger you?"

"It's more that it confuses me." Lyssa laced her fingers together and stretched them over her head. She needed to work out the tension in her muscles from the long ride and being around Lee. "The Tribunal and Elders don't tell us rank-and-file Sorceresses what they're thinking most of the time. We didn't get a lot of warning before they announced us to the world. I'm lucky I wasn't that deeply embedded in Shadow society. A lot of people got screwed in the aftermath."

"Do you want to go back to secrecy?" Jofi asked.

"It doesn't matter." Lyssa shrugged. "You can't put the rabbit back in the hat so easily."

Lyssa had hated the Society's secrecy when she was younger. She'd attributed it to the hubris of ancient fossils stuck in their ways, idly pining for a Golden Age of Sorcery, which had been over for thousands of years. Now she wasn't sure they hadn't been onto something.

The public confirmation of the existence of sorcery meant the worst scum of humanity now knew there was a previously untapped power they could seek, both from rogue Sorcerers and lost shards. It wasn't as if rogue Sorcerers hadn't always existed, but they'd had to keep a much lower profile in the days when any odd public occurrence might lead to a Society investigation.

Shadowy hands clawed at the edge of her vision, and a chill seeped through her body. Lyssa's perimeter alarm might not be loud, but it was hard to ignore.

She spun toward her front door, narrowing her eyes.

She didn't grab her gun from her closet or go for the safe and Jofi. Her alarm spell might have been tripped, but she didn't feel active sorcery. Many of her neighbors might like their guns, but pulling a weapon on a Girl Scout selling cookies or a member of the HOA wouldn't fly. Mostly.

She hurried to the door and the peephole before frowning. At least Damien'd had the common sense to wear casual clothes and a hat, but how the hell was she supposed to maintain her secret identity if EAA agents started showing up on her doorstep?

Lyssa threw open her door and gestured him inside. "Get in here before somebody sees you."

CHAPTER ELEVEN

Damien offered a sheepish smile to Lyssa as she slammed the door behind him after looking around the street. "You seem pissed."

Lyssa snorted. "You're not exactly giving interviews on camera, but it's not like someone can't look you up." She pinched the bridge of her nose. "Showing up at my house in the middle of the day means someone might ask why an EAA agent is here, which could lead to me losing any chance of keeping my identity a secret. I've just started getting comfortable here, even if those HOA women keep sniffing around, asking me to participate in their stupid block party fundraisers."

"Sorry." Damien chuckled. "I'll try to arrange a meeting elsewhere next time. There are complications to meeting at my office, and I'm still getting used to my new coworkers. Besides, we used to meet at your house before you moved."

"I lived on a cul-de-sac with a bunch of trees and no one else around." Lyssa rolled her eyes.

"I circled the block to make sure no one was watching."

Damien shrugged. "But sorry. You're right. I apologize for any inconvenience."

Lyssa waved a hand dismissively, not in the mood to let herself get angrier. "It's fine. Just remember for next time." She nodded at the couch. "Take a seat. Sorry about the lack of chairs. I'm getting some delivered soon."

Damien watched her warily as he sat down. "You sure you're okay? You were real spun up at Alvarez's place."

"It depends on what you have to tell me." Lyssa sat down, not wanting to get too close to Damien. "I hope you didn't come here empty-handed. I can let showing up in broad daylight at my house go, but I'm still irritated about the whole ambush thing and the EAA not having a clue."

"You got out okay." Doubt tinged Damien's voice.

"Would you be fine with being shot at as long as you got out okay?"

"I see your point."

Lyssa frowned. "I don't mind going after shards or thugs using them, and it's not like every rogue bit of sorcery out there needs to have an Eclipse sent to handle it, but I want to go in prepared whenever I'm hired."

Damien nodded. "Fair enough. And let me make it clear: I don't disapprove of how you handled yourself."

His gaze lingered on her for a moment, an outright stare. Lyssa scooted farther away, her cheeks heating.

Why was he doing this? Not that she wasn't flattered, but anything other than the job was way down the list right now.

"What?" she asked. "Something on my face?"

"No." Damien looked away. "I'm so used to dealing with you as Hecate that I forget that's not your face."

"You don't like my face?" Lyssa ran a hand over her cheek.

Damien shook his head. "You've got a great face. One I don't mind looking at." He grimaced. "I'm saying you're not unattractive."

"I'm not unattractive?" Lyssa asked. "Ouch. That's the bare minimum praise."

What the hell was she doing? She'd been pissed at him for flirting, and now she was?

"You're attractive," Damien sputtered. "Completely. Affirmatively."

Lyssa tilted her head, unsure of how to respond to that. Damien had never said anything like that about her mask before, but he was right. Ninety percent of the time when they dealt with each other, she was dressed as Hecate the Night Goddess and sounded like a sailor who'd spent twenty years smoking.

Damien, in contrast, got to show off his handsome face whenever he wanted to. She wouldn't say it was unfair, given the power granted by the regalia, but it did make the conversation awkward. She could understand how he might almost see Lyssa and Hecate as two different women.

"Okay." Lyssa looked away. "Enough about my face. You're here about the shards, right?"

Damien's smile faded, and serious concern settled over his face. "Yes. I've been looking hard into the situation with Alvarez. We don't have the deep personnel bench and resources in the local office that some of the bigger offices do, but that doesn't mean I don't have pull."

"Okay," Lyssa replied. "I'm glad to hear you're doing your job, but I'd prefer to hear about the results."

"How about information?" Damien asked.

"Same thing. I've quietly asked around on my own, but I'm still waiting to hear back."

Damien looked down for a moment, his brow furrowed, before speaking. "I pressed a little deeper, and the mayor's call for a Torch doesn't seem like it had much to do with testing you out. I don't think Lopez lied. I think he was fed a line."

Lyssa hopped off the couch and pumped her fist. "I knew it!"

Damien eyed her with concern. "Yes, you were right that day. I checked into local procedures, and it's clear that if they have any reason to suspect shards or Sorcerers, their first step is to coordinate with the EAA to request a Torch or an Eclipse."

"And they didn't do that?"

He shook his head. "That only happened because the mayor pressed the Chief, and he got the ball rolling. It didn't come from the police side of things, which is where we'd expect it in this kind of situation."

"Then why are you so sure this wasn't just the mayor wanting to test his new pet Sorceress?" Lyssa asked.

Damien frowned. "I thought you were the one who thought all this was suspicious. I bring you evidence, and you're trying to poke holes in it?"

"Don't get me wrong; I'm completely dedicated to my paranoia hobby." Lyssa folded her arms and flicked her wrist. "But I also want to make sure we're following actual evidence and not phantom leads. It'll make it easier when I need to ride somewhere to shoot someone."

Damien blinked at her answer before nodding slowly. "I got my hands on an internal email from the mayor's office. In it, the mayor references 'a message from our friends at the Bureau' before telling his chief of staff to get a Torch for any potential Alvarez raid. That email was written earlier that day, before Alvarez was spotted returning to his home."

"Who are these friends at the FBI?" Lyssa asked.

"Nobody knows." Damien shrugged. "I asked around the mayor's office, and they're arguing I misinterpreted the email, and I wasn't supposed to have it anyway. They threatened to make a big stink about it. They also pointed out that hiring a Torch via the EAA is the proper procedure, so it's not like they did anything wrong."

Lyssa returned to the couch, scowling. "But why all the secrecy?"

"They were acting so offended it made me more suspicious. I thought the cost might come off as extravagant, and maybe they were worried about justifying it, but I think this is more about maintaining relationships." Damien inclined his head toward the window. "It's the same reason the EAA sent me and a couple of people here from California to follow you. I think the locals are still getting used to the idea that they have a Sorceress living openly among them and trying to figure out how they can use that politically and otherwise."

"How does that translate into the FBI and their leads?"

Lyssa didn't understand or care much about the fine details of politics. She could barely bring herself to care about Illuminated politics, and it was all but impossible to muster any interest in Shadow politics. She dealt with assignments involving discrete targets and harbored no interest in working her way to an Elder position, let alone the Tribunal.

For now, she needed flexibility if she wanted to achieve her long-term goals, including finding the truth about her brother. But not caring about politics wasn't the same as not having them affect her. If the mayor had indirectly set her up because someone at the FBI had told her something, she needed to understand why.

Damien leaned forward and lowered his voice. "It seems like there's been a major spike of illegal shard smuggling in the US in the last couple of weeks, particularly in the Southwest. I don't think you appreciate that we're still working out the fine details of handling all this."

"As in, the government?"

"Exactly." Damien nodded. "Technically, the illegal transport and import of any sorcery-based object should be handled by the same organizations handling all black-market smuggling, but the practical truth is, the FBI, the Coast Guard, the DEA, and just about everyone else doesn't want to get near sorcery. They try to shove as much of it as they can onto the EAA, but we're stretched thin, and we don't have the depth of experience or the personnel to handle that kind of thing." He averted his eyes. "There are other considerations."

Lyssa stared at him, trying to read his face. She'd only known Damien for a few months. He'd been a welcome relief after the uptight idiot who had been her previous primary personal liaison, but that wasn't the same thing as always understanding how his mind worked.

This time, though, she could see it right on his face—the shame. The rest worked itself out quickly.

"You don't always want to come to the Society hat in hand," Lyssa murmured.

"It's more than that. If a fox eats a bunch of hens, it's crazy to hire another fox to hunt them down. No offense."

"It sounds more logical than hiring a bunch of hens. *No offense.*"

Damien met her gaze with steely determination. "You saying you think normies are a bunch of hens waiting to be eaten?"

Lyssa rolled her eyes. "Dial it down, Damien. Remember what you told me the other day? It's me you're talking to, not some fossil Sorcerer who thinks he's inherently better than all Shadows."

He gave a shallow nod. "You're right. Sorry. But yes, the more we depend on Torches, let alone Eclipses, the more the higher-ups are concerned that it makes normies look weak. I don't think you always appreciate how deeply people are afraid of you."

"The ratio of Shadows to Illuminated is, like, four million to one." Lyssa shrugged. "If we were all-powerful, I don't think the Society would have gone public after M-Day. They would have found a way to blow it off."

"I'm not saying I buy into all the conspiracy theories. What I am saying is that the federal government, at both the law enforcement and military levels, is very, very paranoid about what would happen if the Society decided the treaties are nothing more than pieces of paper. Things like shards flooding the black market don't make them feel calmer."

"I'm not going to defend every Sorcerer, but I know the Society can't be happy about this either. I'm waiting to hear back from Samuel, but you know how that guy is. The question is, if the FBI knew about the shards, why didn't you? Shouldn't they have wanted to shove the investigation off on you EAA boys?"

Damien looked grim. "Normally, I wouldn't have to ask. I'm still trying to figure that out, but for now, we need to proceed on the assumption that the best solution here is to send a fox after a fox. For now, I'm authorized to hire you to front a longer-term investigation into the shards, though it seems only Alvarez knew where he got them from."

Lyssa grimaced, regretting blowing a hole through the criminal. "Really?"

"They're following up with their phones and computers and the others, but I don't think the FBI or the police are going to find out. I'm going to do what I can on my end too, but I'm not convinced I'll get far. Too much ass-covering and not enough resources. I'm also going to keep my distance on this for your benefit."

"More politics?"

"Exactly." Damien nodded. "There's been more noise than I expected about the alleged excessive force of the raid."

"Hey." Lyssa glared at him. "Do you expect—"

"No." He shook his head. "After reviewing all the facts, I think if anything, you were restrained. But what I think and what the people above me decide aren't the same thing. You've been working with us long enough to understand that."

"By Society laws and Society treaties with the US, I have the right to defend myself with full sorcery, up to and including lethal force." Lyssa clenched her hand into a fist. "If they think I went overboard, they should take it up with Samuel and the Society. They can try to get an Eclipse after me."

"I don't think anyone's interested in doing that, and it's not like your people would hunt you for taking down a criminal with a bunch of shards. I'm just trying to communicate that I don't put it past some ambitious types to try to use this situation—and you—to advance themselves."

"Screw them." Lyssa hopped up and shadowboxed the air. "If they want a piece of me, they can come at me."

"You're a tough chick." Damien's voice trailed off, and he stared at her chest.

Lyssa blinked. "Is this the time to be checking me out?"

Damien winced. "I wasn't doing that." He gestured at her shirt. "Tough chick, but you're in that."

Lyssa looked down at her shirt. More Kawatsu-chan. Toughness and cute unicorns didn't go together.

"You've seen this character before." She shrugged.

"I know." Damien laughed nervously. "It's just the situation. Anyway, forget it. The point is you're not untouchable. If you resolve this incident quickly, they won't be able to do much without looking like the snakes they are."

"Fine, fine." Lyssa smiled. "Get the contract set up on your phone, and let's do the signing. Maybe my info will come in before that, but I've got something personal to take care of later tonight."

Damien didn't know it was the anniversary of her brother's disappearance. She didn't feel the need to mention it or talk about where she went every year at this time.

"Sure," he replied. "You do what you need to, but the sooner you finish—"

"The sooner everyone stops being asses."

CHAPTER TWELVE

A white-jacketed rider on a yellow Ducati Panigale screaming down a highway at hundreds of miles per hour would, under most circumstances, attract the attention of the highway patrol, as well as more dangerous people. That meant that when Lyssa took full advantage of her abilities to maximize her speed, she needed to hide from prying eyes.

On a day when she wasn't pressed for time and was looking to relax, she could have kept to the speed limit, or near-ish, and hit San Diego from Scottsdale in around five hours. Zen-like calm accompanied a long bike ride. It was one of the reasons she preferred her motorcycle. She liked being exposed to the elements as she tore across the land. Freed from the cage of a car, she felt like she could become one with the road.

Today her schedule removed any chance of a relaxing trip. Tomorrow she needed to start her new contract. The timing meant it was even more important that she finish her personal business that night. That translated into getting to San Diego as quickly as possible with the help of sorcery spells and rituals. She had started by using her standard package of spells to escape her home before driving west as Hecate.

Focused on splitting her attention between mental imaging and chanting as she prepared her long-distance travel spells, along with driving, she didn't mind the looks and occasional honks as she made her way along surface streets to the highway.

Once she hit the highway, a group of bikers cruised in formation with her for a while, but no one dared get too close to the dark rider. Once she'd hit AZ-85, the long minutes of chanting under her breath and her mental images of strings of shadow and dark twins layered in intricate patterns took effect, turning her sorcery from mere potential to an alteration of reality.

Lyssa pulled away from the bikers with a wave, not wanting to startle them into an accident. They offered respectful nods.

Once she'd distanced herself by hundreds of feet, she finished the last portion of the ritual. The melodic Phrygian flowed with ease, each syllable spoken in time with a specific mental image precisely memorized over years of practice. When she'd learned the ritual, she'd never imagined using it on a motorcycle.

That kind of flexibility was what the Society needed. The combination of technology and sorcery represented the future of humanity.

The Phrygian wasn't her choice, but she didn't mind. Every Illuminated had their own methods of calling on their power, linked to both family and essence traditions.

In a sense, every language was sacred and could bring out the power of a Sorcerer's soul. Lyssa used the ancient Indo-European language as part of her efforts because her mother, the last bearer of the Night Goddess, did so.

Specifics didn't matter as much as finding what resonated within. All the pointless squabbles of the past where different factions obsessed with their paths warred with each other represented a fundamental misunderstanding of sorcery.

Lyssa spared a brief thought for how she'd inherited the Night Goddess indirectly. That had caused trouble with another family, the Khatris, who had previously controlled the regalia, but such was the way of the capricious enchanted garments.

Her grandfather, though a user of different regalia and essence, also made use of the language, and so it had been for generation after generation of Corti before their family blended in with lost ancestors. Since getting Jofi, Lyssa typically only needed the language for powerful, lasting rituals.

With the ritual complete, the bike and rider were an all-but-silent, ghostly, intangible wraith form. She was barely noticeable unless someone was close, but the power of the vehicle remained. She jerked as the Ducati ripped down the side of the road, barely touching it. The maxed speedometer was useless. She knew from experience that her bike had reached four hundred miles per hour.

Lyssa took slow breaths, the spell helping her breathe evenly. Driving on the side of the road, combined with her spells, would help her avoid a serious collision. The worst-case scenario would involve a sudden stop and her wraith form failing.

In the past, she hadn't always been able to perform the complicated ritual she'd dubbed Tenebrous Air successfully. Darkness wasn't an essence that lent itself to quick travel, but once she'd acquired Jofi, things had changed. She'd been able to maintain spells and rituals that had seemed far out of reach when she was younger.

It wasn't relaxing, for sure. The trip required heavy concentration, but there was a lot to be said for being able to get around quickly and not having to leave the ground.

Lyssa could do Phoenix to San Diego in less than an hour on a single tank of gas. An alert driver might notice the slight wake of her passage on the ground, but it wasn't like anyone dared chase a shadow going hundreds of miles per hour. Not only did Jofi grant her the extra power she needed for the spell, but the spirit also helped guide her driving, even beyond the enhanced reflexes her regalia granted.

The nearby road and countryside became blurs, but the mountains in the distance provided a stable measuring point. Her fingers and arms flexed with movement, both her own and the slight tug by Jofi. This would be her first trip back to her stomping grounds, the San Diego area, but it was almost a straight shot west after the beginning.

She was now passing Yuma. She could stop at her informant Reed's place, but there wasn't any point. The snake would call her when he had something useful.

"Thanks for your help," Lyssa said once she hit I-8.

"You're welcome," Jofi replied.

Her fingers tightened on the handlebars. She slowed

her breathing and focused on making it rhythmic and drawn out to help maintain the ritual.

"You were quiet earlier," Lyssa murmured.

"I'm often quiet."

"When I was talking to Damien, I mean. I'm surprised."

"I had little to add," Jofi replied. "When we're close, I see what you see. I hear what you hear. Your thoughts may be your own, but we share everything else."

The spirit delivered the words in the same calm tone he always did, but the implied threat almost broke her concentration. She didn't respond immediately, letting the rumble of the bike massage her worry away. A long-buried paranoia poked her calm. That idiot Lee shouldn't have bothered her.

In Lyssa's experience, the best way to bury a concern she didn't want to deal with was by focusing on a more immediate threat. It wasn't a bad strategy in her line of work.

"There are too many loose ends on this." Lyssa zoomed past an eighteen-wheeler. "Too many people who should know more don't know enough. I don't mind doing the legwork, but I'd be more comfortable if I didn't feel like I was being hung out to dry."

"You still suspect conspiracy and assassination?" Jofi asked. "A targeted conspiracy?"

"Conspiracy's too strong a word. And I'm not sure this is about me directly, but I don't want to dismiss the possibility. What do I suspect? At a minimum, I suspect good old-fashioned corruption."

"What's the difference between corruption and conspiracy?"

It was almost cute when he was naïve. That didn't make the question easy to answer.

Lyssa thought about her response before offering it.

"Conspiracy's about a complicated plan and changing the situation with the plan. Corruption's about taking advantage of the situation that's in place. Active versus passive."

"Who do you think is corrupt?" Jofi asked.

"That's the big question. I've got a lot of suspects, but no one I'm willing to accuse yet."

Lyssa stared ahead, thinking about the answer. While under the effects of the Tenebrous Air, the world around and in front of her turned into a hazy monochrome mist, much the way she appeared to others. She had no trouble making things out since she was used to the blacks, whites, and grays, all distinct to her eyes.

Every sound around her except for Jofi's voice and her own came to her ears as muffled and remote. The mighty Ducati engine continued to vibrate, but the spell quieted its voice from a tiger to a kitten with the strength of a tiger.

"I hate to say it." Lyssa took a long, deep breath. "No matter how much I think about this situation, it doesn't smell like something pushed by the Shadows. They might be able to get their hands on a shard or two, but Damien made it sound like it was about a lot more than just Alvarez."

"You worry about a rogue Sorcerer being involved?" Jofi asked. "And you don't believe this just because of the anniversary?"

"The evidence points to a rogue Sorcerer, and not just because of my personal feelings." Lyssa frowned. "Some people say, 'Don't attribute to malice what you can attribute to incompetence.' I say, 'Don't presume incompetence until you have proof that there is no malice.'"

"How cynical," Jofi replied.

"Pragmatic. I have a hard time believing an Illuminated would screw up and accidentally flood the southwest United States with shards, and if a major cache had been raided, Samuel would be screaming at me about it. If he wasn't, the Society would be screaming at him until he started screaming at me." She watched a mountain recede in the distance as she moved farther off the road, the spell making that far less of an obstacle than during normal driving. "Which is what has me so worried. The radio silence on this makes me think someone's trying to keep something from me, and that makes me circle back to wondering if it's about me."

"You believe Elder Samuel is conspiring against you?"

Lyssa laughed. "The Colonel?"

"Doesn't he prefer 'Elder Samuel?'"

"It goes with the herbs and spices joke. Forget it. I'm saying I might not like the guy, but I trust that he's not corrupt in *that* way. He'd consider it not genteel enough." Lyssa furrowed her brow. "If someone's trying to screw me, it's not him, but that leaves the question of who it might be."

"Relying on aesthetics to ensure appropriate behavior is an interesting approach."

Lyssa never bothered checking for tails when she was traveling so fast. Even with Jofi's help, it wasn't like she could spare much attention. She relied on the rarity of threat sources and the difficulty of shooting fast-moving targets under normal circumstances.

"Just saying, Samuel may get on my nerves, but he's okay." Lyssa managed a smile.

"But you worry he hasn't contacted you."

"Yeah, but this wouldn't be the first time he waited a while so he can figure out some BS way to make the Society look better out of it. It's political garbage making my job harder."

"If there's a rogue Sorcerer, there's a good chance they'll send an Eclipse to handle them."

"They have to know who it is first. Until then, they'll be happy with a Torch." Lyssa thought about the various potential outcomes of the job. "We might not be able to wait that long. I want to get this solved, not sit on my hands while the Elders debate how best to impress politicians."

"Are you worried?" Jofi asked.

"About the Society?" Lyssa replied. "Yes. I'm always worried about those fossils."

"No. Are you worried about having to fight another Illuminated?"

Lyssa chuckled. "A rogue Sorcerer isn't Illuminated. That's what the Elders say."

"Then you're worried about having to fight a rogue Sorcerer?" Jofi asked.

Lyssa didn't answer for a long time, content in the knowledge that Jofi wouldn't follow up until she was ready. She'd been involved in more than her fair share of deadly serious incidents during her twelve years as a Torch, including taking on terrorists in her first year, long before M-Day. Her techniques and experience had been honed over those years. She wasn't going to claim she could beat every Sorcerer out there, but that didn't make her less lethal.

"No." Lyssa nodded. "I've fought more than enough of my kind, even if I haven't had to kill any yet. I'm not crazy about cutting down the number of Illuminated in the world, but I'm not naïve enough to believe that doesn't mean some of our people would be better off dead. But it doesn't matter anyway."

"Why?"

Lyssa moved closer to the road. There wasn't anyone else on it for miles.

"Because I can't kill someone until I've found them. And for the rest of the day, I'm going to try not to worry about it."

CHAPTER THIRTEEN

By the time Lyssa rolled into the San Diego area, she'd adopted her disguise, now a white-jacketed woman on an expensive yellow motorcycle. That earned her approving looks from men in nearby cars, but no one tried to follow her.

Lyssa continued down the highway, passing through San Diego proper and reaching the beach-hugging community of Cardiff. Once in Cardiff, the streets and roads called to her, telling her exactly where she needed to go. She was headed for a house she'd lived in from her middle teens until her twenties, when she'd moved to San Diego. More than that house or her place in Scottsdale, her current destination was the closest thing she had to a home.

She climbed a hill and turned a corner, finally arriving at a modest Spanish ranch house overlooking the ocean, the gentle waves striking a beach below. Exquisite rows of carefully arranged beautiful flowers in a dazzling array of colors lined the narrow driveway. The packed trees surrounding the house and the ocean view produced a feeling of solitude despite all the nearby houses.

The place never changed. That was why it was so comforting.

A person with a careful eye for detail, if they ignored the color, might be able to pick out some of the sorcery glyphs traced by the flowers. Any Illuminated could sense the constant pulse of background power. This garden was a powerful artifact, as much a shard in its way as Alvarez's robe. A constant, living ritual.

Lyssa slowed to a stop before lowering her kickstand and killing her engine. She pulled off her helmet, shook out her hair, and inhaled deeply, enjoying the complex interplay of the floral and salty scents.

By the time she was at the door, it was open, and a smiling middle-aged woman with dark hair was on the other side. Her floral-patterned apron and dress added to her motherly aura. The woman's true age was a good two decades higher than her apparent age. Tricia Bennett was a welcome sight after Lyssa's recent stressful days. It was good to be home with her foster parents.

The woman pulled Lyssa into an embrace. "It's been too long."

"Sorry, Tricia." Lyssa hugged her back. "I've been busy between the move and work."

"Work." Tricia puckered her mouth with displeasure. "I've heard. Your alter ego is becoming famous."

Lyssa smiled. "Listening to the news, huh? That's bad for your heart."

Tricia motioned her inside. "It's good to keep aware these days. Things were a lot easier before M-Day."

Lyssa entered the living room to find a huge man sitting on a couch, watching a NASCAR race. "Hey, Fred."

He looked at her and smiled. "Hey, sweetie."

"I'm thirty now." Lyssa rolled her eyes. "I think I'm a little old for 'sweetie.'"

Fred shrugged. "You said the same thing when you were fifteen. You say the same thing every time you visit, but I'm still older than you."

"Okay, you got me there."

A rich, earthy scent wafted from the kitchen and ambushed Lyssa's nose. Her stomach rumbled.

Tricia gave her a knowing look. "I have mushroom soup almost ready." She held up a hand. "And don't worry. I didn't use a new recipe this time. It doesn't change its flavor with each bite."

"Good." Lyssa removed her jacket and the holster and moved to the coat rack. She hesitated for a moment before taking a deep breath and hanging them up. Disguised regalia or not, this was one place she didn't need to be on guard. "I'm more than happy to have some soup."

Tricia eyed the guns with a slight frown. Her expression twitched into a smile as she turned to her husband. "I'll never understand what you see in that racing, and what about the parade? You promised we could watch it."

"That's not until tomorrow," Fred replied, "and racing is the ultimate combination of technique and technology." He shook a finger. "The Society should start up a sorcery racing circuit. People would pay good money to watch that. I'd never get out of my chair if I could watch that."

Lyssa snickered. It sounded absurd on the surface, but it wasn't a half-bad idea. The Elders and the Tribunal were so obsessed with supplying soldiers and assassins to the governments of the world, they'd forgotten how impressive soft power and cultural influence could be. Humanity had enough weapons. They could always use more joy.

"What parade?" Lyssa asked.

Time had flown by in recent weeks, but Labor Day had come and gone. She couldn't think what else might be happening in September that would be worth watching on TV, not that she paid attention to much other than the news and her reality shows.

"The First Annual Sorcerer Appreciation Day parade in downtown San Diego," Tricia said with a warm smile. "Originally they wanted it to be on M-Day, but it got delayed for various reasons."

"'Sorcerer Appreciation Day?'" Lyssa tried to picture what that might involve but failed. "What's the point? There's only a handful of Sorcerers in all of California, and it's not like most of them, including you, would publicly reveal their identity. They might get lucky and get one Sorcerer to show up in regalia."

"It's pointless." Fred gave a firm nod. "A waste of money."

"It's not pointless, dear." Tricia wagged a finger. "Somebody needs to say something nice. I think it's good we have that sort of thing, especially after all those ACSS protests in the last few months." She laughed. "And I think a lot of people just like dressing up in costumes. They do that at that big comic convention anyway, and have been doing it since long before M-Day. Why not take advantage of the spirit of fun to get more people on our side?"

"I'm not going to stick around for the parade." Lyssa offered her an apologetic look. "I've got work."

Tricia squeezed her hand. "We'll always be here for you on this day. You know that, Lyssa." She smiled. "We're going to watch the parade on TV anyway. But if you're not staying the night, let's make sure we spend as much time together as we can." A timer dinged, and she looked toward the kitchen. "Time to eat."

The three sat at a small dining room table, working on the soup and drinking strong sweet wine. Fred watched both women as Lyssa chatted about adjusting to life in the Phoenix area.

Glorious umami packed the soup. Each mouthful offered balanced seasoning, and although Lyssa discovered new subtle hints of flavor with each bite, there was none of the bizarre experience from her last visit, where one of Tricia's experiments had ended with a fruit salad that changed from tasting like lemons in one bite to spaghetti in another.

"The temperature's the big adjustment over there." Lyssa grimaced. "I know it's not going to be so bad in a few months, but it's hard to spend so many years here and then go to a place where it's hot even at night. I've set up spells to cheat a little, but it's still annoying."

Tricia chuckled politely. "You could always move back. We'd love to have you closer. It's nice not to have to use a ritual when you're trying to stop over for a quick bite."

Lyssa shook her head. "It was better to get away from

California. I've annoyed too many people here, and remember, it wasn't exactly my choice. Samuel all but ordered me to move. I think it's about overall coverage."

"Coverage?" Tricia looked confused.

"He doesn't need as many Torches in California," Lyssa explained. "You know how it goes."

Tricia's smile dimmed for a second. She never could fully accept Lyssa working as a Torch, but she never tried to forbid her, either. It didn't matter if she wasn't her mother or Fred, her father. They were the closest thing she had to a family after being left alone at fifteen.

Lyssa ladled more soup into her mouth, taking time to savor the flavor and let some of the tension from the last comment fade. Jofi was always silent when she visited the Bennetts. He'd answer if called, but he appreciated what spending time with the couple meant to her.

At least, Lyssa assumed he did. She'd not asked him directly because it had never occurred to her to do that, and the less Tricia and Fred knew about Jofi, the safer it'd be for them.

Lee's words lingered in her mind. He'd been right about one thing. Jofi might "talk" to her, but that didn't make him human. No matter how human a spirit seemed, it was a fundamentally different entity—a crystallization of a concept, not a lifeform.

"Your flowers and trees are looking nice," Lyssa said, trying to distract herself from her brooding.

Tricia's bright smile returned. "I always feel bad when we get a visitor and they ask me to share my gardening secrets. I feel so devious."

"It'd blow their mind if you told them you're a

Sorceress with a plant essence." Lyssa grinned. "Though that sounds a lot less threatening than living next to a darkness essence."

"Our essences don't define us."

Lyssa laughed. "Sorry, Tricia. Of course they do. That's why they're called essences. It's also why I have the Night Goddess regalia, and you have the Sacred Flower Bearer."

Fred grunted in slight disapproval. Lyssa offered an apologetic smile, but her point stood. Her foster parents lived a different lifestyle from her.

Tricia looked away. "Never mind."

Fred set his spoon down. "Thank you for the food, honey." He departed without another word, escaping not into the living room but to a bedroom.

Lyssa tensed. Fred didn't like conflict, especially between Lyssa and Tricia. It made sense because he wasn't a Sorcerer.

Having been raised in an all-Illuminated family, it had taken Lyssa a while to understand how uncomfortable Fred was with inserting himself into their arguments. He couldn't even claim any hint of Lemurian blood.

Pure Shadows marrying Illuminated was always difficult, even post-M-Day. The Society preferred to strengthen what little of the Lemurian blood was left, even if it meant relying on old bloodlines that hadn't produced a Sorcerer in generations.

While it hadn't been forbidden for Illuminated to marry pure Shadows for millennia, a stigma remained. Lyssa hadn't cared about it, but she knew both Fred and Tricia had been forced to deal with dismissive Sorcerers.

"Just say it, Tricia." Lyssa exhaled. "I don't want to leave here with you upset. I've got a lot on my mind, and I need a clear head going forward. If you have something you need to tell me, go ahead. I came here because I wanted to be with family on the anniversary. Because I know you two give a damn about me, at least."

"I've said it before." Tricia shrugged. "Does it matter?"

"Yes. Come on. We both know words have power." Lyssa set her spoon down and waited. "So, spill it."

"I worry about you, Lyssa." Tricia blinked and looked down, a hint of tears threatening her eyes. "You're a Sorceress. If you're careful, you could live two hundred years, but…"

Tricia was right. They'd had this conversation before, but maybe it didn't have to end in hurt feelings.

Lyssa nodded slowly. "It's not like the Society's keeping stats, but the average Torch or Eclipse doesn't make it that long."

"Yes." Tricia gave her a plaintive look. "Your mother and father both died so young. I know you think there's a special meaning in the fact that you inherited the same essence as your mother, but that was just chance. Nothing more. Don't let your life be defined by chance."

"I can't say if it's chance or fate." Lyssa shrugged. "But I'm one of the few Sorceresses alive with the same essence as a parent. That might not be true fate, but it locked me into a path. When it was time to go to the Vault of Dreams during my Initiation, I knew I would take the Night Goddess."

Sorcery didn't manifest until puberty. Full membership as an Illuminated in the Society followed three years after that. Until then, all Illuminated raised their children under the assumption that they would come into power. Her parents were unusual in that both their children had done so.

"But you don't have to be a Torch." Tricia rested her hand on her chest and took a deep breath. "You don't have to risk your life fighting. Things are different than before."

"How?" Lyssa gave her a defiant look. "How are things remotely different? There are always dangers out there, and there always will be. Sometimes force needs to be met with force. Violence and cruelty aren't going away, and I can do my part to remove corruption from the world."

"M-Day is what's different." Tricia let out a nervous laugh. "We have an opportunity to live as a true part of humanity. We don't have to convince them to value us as weapons. Think of the parade. I know you and Fred think it's a silly little game, but it means something. We've gone from conspiracy theories and witch hunts to parades. All we had to do was be honest."

"A bunch of Shadows partying doesn't mean we're accepted by them," Lyssa snapped. She immediately regretted it after seeing the hurt look on Tricia's face, and she softened her tone. "I'm just saying, Tricia. We can't all sit in our flower gardens pretending evil isn't out there."

"Oh, honey. I know all too well there's evil out there, and I also know this isn't about that."

"What's it about, then?"

"I didn't want to argue about it, but..." Tricia shook her head, the pity in her eyes almost palpable. "You need to stop torturing yourself. I know you loved your brother, but he's gone, just like your parents. You need to accept that."

Lyssa shot out of her chair, rattling the table. The chair

smacked the floor hard. She glared at Tricia, her jaw rigid, taking short, ragged breaths. Tricia looked back as softly as before, not concerned by the sudden movement

The purpose of the trip was to be around people Lyssa loved on a day of pain. Some mention of her brother was inevitable, but she didn't want it to be like this.

"You don't know that." Lyssa's voice came out low and hostile. "He's not dead."

"It's been fifteen years." Tricia shook her head. "When you were younger, I never wanted to take your hope from you. Now I wonder if I did the right thing by not trying to get you to give up earlier. When you came to us, you were a sad, broken young woman. You'd suffered so much tragedy. I know he was your last real family member, but after all this time, we must face the truth. If he were still alive, he would have tracked you down. If not before, then after M-Day."

Lyssa crouched and picked up her chair, her heart thundering. Rage and bitterness swirled in her, but she couldn't vent them on the woman who had treated her like a daughter for fifteen years.

"You're my family, too," she murmured and sat. "But that doesn't mean I don't want him back. It's not like my parents. They're dead, and they aren't coming back. He's missing. He could come back. He will. Or I'll find him and bring him back."

"Tracking sorcery has failed repeatedly, both from the Illuminated we contacted and those you approached." Tricia kept her voice soft. "You need to let him go. You can't carry around that kind of baggage and not have it hurt you. The past is the past."

Lyssa stood slowly. This time she stepped away from her chair and pushed it in before spreading out her arms. She took a deep breath and pictured her normal regalia in her mind. Her form wavered and shifted, and her light clothing turned into the familiar dark leather. The jacket hanging on the rack in the other room shifted to a long overcoat.

Tricia watched her but didn't speak. Lyssa was determined to make her foster mother understand.

"He can't be dead for the same reason I can change this." Lyssa slapped her hand over her chest. "If he were dead, then why isn't the Northern Trickster regalia back in the Vault of Dreams? I've been there. You've been there." She threw up her arms. "I've set it up so they'll contact me if it returns." She held up a dark-gloved hand. "Tell me, Tricia. Have you ever heard of a regalia not returning to the Vault after the Sorcerer died? Sure, delays happen, but fifteen years? That'd be unprecedented."

Tricia stood with a concerned look. "I think you already know the answer to that. I don't think it matters. We could go all the way to Last Remnant right now, and you could scour that entire island. Even if you found his regalia, I don't think you'd believe he was dead. And we're Illuminated. Our lives are steeped in ancient sorcery. Rare things happen all the time. You sharing your mother's essence is an example of that." She walked over and embraced Lyssa. "I don't mind hope. It's a beautiful thing, but I don't want hope to become an obsession that destroys you."

Lyssa pulled away and brushed her hair out of her eyes. "I didn't become a Torch to find him. Not completely, anyway."

Tricia gave her a dubious look. "Really?"

"I would have become one even if he had not disappeared," Lyssa continued. "I think that was inevitable since I came from a family filled with them."

"Maybe." Tricia patted Lyssa on the shoulder. "It's okay to start living for yourself. Promise me you'll at least try."

"Hey." Lyssa forced a smile. "New city, new opportunities, right? I *am* living for myself."

"I hope so." Tricia headed back to the table. "Please go get Fred and bring him back before the soup gets cold. I don't want to lose him to his silly cars again."

"I will." Lyssa walked out of the dining room.

Tricia was right. That was what any logical person would say. For all Lyssa knew, her brother's regalia had returned to the Vault of Dreams, and no one had bothered to tell her. Like most non-politically-minded Illuminated, she didn't go out of her way to make a trip to their hidden island in the Indian Ocean. She hadn't been to Last Remnant in ten years. A smart Sorceress stayed the hell away from the Tribunal and their machinations, and it wasn't like they let people come and go on a whim anyway.

The problem was she couldn't let her brother Chris go so easily. Tricia could be right. Lyssa's current obsession with trying to link him to the smuggling case supported her foster mother's theory. Lyssa had no reason to believe he was involved, but she desperately wanted him to be.

She took a deep breath and let it out slowly. She might be there because of the anniversary, but she wouldn't miss the opportunity to relax with her foster family. With her officially being on the job, she might not have another chance to relax for weeks.

Her second phone buzzed with a message, and she made a face. That phone ringing meant one thing: the call was from Reed. Working with informants didn't always mean liking them. She checked the message.

I should have something for you by tomorrow night.

Lyssa's brows went up. The universe was pushing her along quicker than she had anticipated. This called for a resupply trip to Las Vegas before she headed anywhere else. It'd be easy enough to handle the next morning with a detour on the way home.

There would be no difficult emotional webs to navigate in Las Vegas. There would be nothing to worry about on a simple supply run.

Lyssa headed back to Tricia. "How about I stay for the night? The job looks like it won't be happening until tomorrow evening at the earliest."

CHAPTER FOURTEEN

Lyssa found a good spot in a parking garage that put her close enough to walk to her destination, but not so close she couldn't throw off a potential tail before arrival. She doubted anyone had managed to follow her from her foster parents' house given her layered spells, but now that she'd left the Bennetts' home, classic Corti paranoia had returned.

After parking her bike, Lyssa went down the stairs of the garage and emerged on the street. A huge casino stood on one side of her, the signs beckoning visitors inside.

Shortly after M-Day, Las Vegas casinos started making big offers to Sorcerers. They wanted true supernatural entertainment to offer to their guests. Lyssa knew at least one Sorcerer who performed in Vegas but still maintained his secret identity. No one had taken any offers publicly, and she wasn't interested in changing careers, whatever temporary ideas came to mind about An Evening with the Night Goddess.

Across the street, a dull-looking storage facility formed an amusing dichotomy with the casino. The contrast between the prosaic and the glamorous was the case for much of the street, including its shipping offices and other such businesses. Even a glittering heart of tourist consumerism like Las Vegas needed the mundane to survive.

She continued along the street. When she turned the corner, a busty female mime in a flesh-colored leotard and a bowler hat surprised her. The mime engaged in some hurried climbing of invisible stairs with only a curious old man in an I LOVE VEGAS t-shirt watching her.

The higher-level weirdness was concentrated farther east on Fremont Street near the canopied pedestrian mall, but that didn't stop colorful characters like the climbing mime from leaking into the surrounding area. Lyssa wasn't surprised to see a performer so early in the day. Showing up any later would have almost necessitated sorcery to carve through the thicket of entertainers filling the streets.

The last time she'd visited the area at night, she'd had to fend off leather-clad dominatrices with whips and two different guys in bear suits offering to twerk for money. The presence of a mild violin or a singing busker seemed strange in comparison, but even Vegas couldn't be freaky twenty-four/seven.

No twerking bears ambushed Lyssa this time. She managed to make it down a side street before crossing the road. The freak concentration dropped to near zero, and after a couple of minutes, she closed in on a bronze anvil sign hanging on a building standing next to a bar. Elaborately twined black metal spelled out *Serafina's Gallery.*

Heavy pressure in Lyssa's chest built as she moved toward the anvil sign. She took a deep breath and slowly let it out. The sensation didn't worry her. She was exactly where she needed to be.

Lyssa pulled out her phone. She had messaged ahead before leaving that morning, and Serafina Dale, the Sorceress owner of the gallery, had sent one not-so-simple message in response.

Your custom order is ready!!!

Heart and anvil emojis had followed the message, and for some reason Lyssa couldn't fathom, a string of squids and Scottish flag emojis came next. Serafina had never mentioned having Scottish ancestry.

Trying to understand Serafina was harder than understanding Jofi. Sometimes Lyssa thought she might be a spirit of creation in human form.

Lyssa walked toward the large bronze doors, taking a moment to appreciate the careful scrollwork and the intricate, almost hypnotic patterns. They were different every time she came, but surprisingly, based on what she'd read online, no one had caught on.

As she pushed into the gallery, a bell overhead tinkled and signaled her arrival. A curved dark hardwood desk stood in the corner with a slender black sales terminal on top, but the rest of the wide space was filled with stands featuring Serafina's work.

Exquisitely lifelike figurines and statues of animals made of different metals filled one section. During Lyssa's last visit, it'd been mostly farm animals, but the current menagerie appeared to be a mix of chimerical beasts combining the traits of deadly predators of the land and sea, including a shark-bear and a squid-tiger. The latter might explain the squid emoji.

Another section displayed intricate metal models of major cities. Some were easy to identify, with the Space Needle marking Seattle and Big Ben indicating London. Lyssa peered at one model for a half-minute before realizing it was Chicago.

Twisting lines of metal woven into tapestry-like creations decorated an entire wall. Unlike the chimeras and the cities, these pieces were more abstract, playful riots of color and shape. She didn't spot anything that resembled sorcery glyphs, at least not in the style Serafina preferred.

The next section featured objects suspended in the air with no obvious support. She stepped closer but didn't feel any strong sorcery. Once she was closer to the objects, she understood.

The trick involved portions of the art being connected by all-but-invisible metal wires that were remarkably strong. They were products of sorcery that only a woman with a metal essence could pull off, but otherwise, they were not subject to active enchantment. That meant they were something that, in theory, Shadows could create with the appropriate technology.

Serafina always had something new on every visit. She was always testing different techniques, unlike Lyssa.

Sometimes Lyssa wondered if she'd become overly reliant on the same spells, but combat was different than art. Success wasn't in the eye of the beholder, and art critics didn't murder a woman for failure.

Serafina didn't publicly identify as a Sorceress, nor did

she maintain a true secret identity. She bore the Imperfect Smith regalia and had lived in Las Vegas as a metalworker for years without encountering any trouble.

Someday, someone might realize her art was a product of sorcery, but her tendency to eschew media attention helped keep her shop available for people to enjoy without many questions, both for lovers of metalwork-based art and people who needed something a little more specialized, such as Lyssa.

After a few more minutes of looking around, Lyssa glanced at the staff door leading to the back and Serafina's workshop. Busting in there would be rude, especially if the other woman was working, but she was surprised Serafina hadn't come out. The pressure from the passive spells all over the gallery remained constant, so she hadn't reacted using sorcery.

There were other possibilities. This wouldn't be the first time Lyssa had had to track Serafina down.

Lyssa frowned. "She better not have fallen asleep again."

"To be fair," Jofi replied, "that was a visit after her normal business hours."

"She told me to come right away, so I did. Then I found her snoring in the back." Lyssa shrugged. She ran her fingers underneath her jacket. The current transformation of her regalia did not do anything to change the texture of the enchanted mesh.

That little helpful item was another of Serafina's creations. It was arguable which had saved Lyssa's life more often, the armor or the enchanted bullets Serafina supplied her. All Illuminated had their strengths and weaknesses, and Lyssa had done her best to make up for hers by cultivating good contacts.

"Maybe she didn't expect me to come right away." Lyssa chuckled. "Half the time, she barely knows what's going on around her when she's working on something."

"Might she be playing some sort of joke on you?" Jofi asked.

Lyssa shook her head. "That's not how her sense of humor works."

She continued her stroll, yawning, her arms behind her head, wandering closer and closer to the staff door. There was a sign that said it was for staff only, but there were no other employees and hadn't been since Lyssa had first visited. The shop effectively doubled as Serafina's home, but she maintained a barebones apartment elsewhere.

Lyssa walked over to the door and knocked. "Serafina, it's Lyssa."

A loud thump sounded from beyond the door. Lyssa frowned and stepped back, unzipping her jacket.

"Whoever you're hunting might have followed you here," Jofi said.

Lyssa shook her head. "If they know Hecate is Lyssa Corti, I doubt they'd bother going after Serafina. I doubt they'd be that proactive, too."

"But you're preparing to draw. You're worried about trouble."

"Trouble comes in a lot of forms. It doesn't hurt to be cautious. Let's hope it's nothing more than a sleepy woman." Lyssa pounded on the door. "Hey, Serafina, you in there? I don't have all day. Drink a cup of coffee if you're so tired."

Pressure built in Lyssa's chest. Active sorcery. The intensity rose and fell in a rhythmic pulse, almost like a slow heartbeat.

Lyssa hissed and narrowed her eyes. The sensation was far stronger than the passive spells she'd felt since arrival.

"Serafina?" she shouted. "I'm not playing. If you don't want something broken, you better answer me."

Lyssa gritted her teeth. Life was simpler when people didn't give her a reason to be suspicious.

With a deep breath, she pulled her folded-up mask out of her pocket. After slipping it over her face, she willed the regalia to revert to its natural form.

Lyssa kicked open the door. She'd been in the gallery enough times to know the layout. Another door at the end of the short hallway led to the main workshop. There were storage closets and bathrooms behind the other doors.

The sensation of sorcery intensified. More loud thumping and crashing noises followed. The workshop wall rattled.

Lyssa inched forward, lifting her guns as she headed toward the workshop. The door was cracked open a couple of inches. A loud bang rattled it.

She stopped in front of the door. Holding her breath, she tilted her head and peered inside. Power and hand tools were scattered all over the room, fallen from destroyed metal shelves. A massive anvil had been knocked on its side. One of Serafina's large worktables was broken in half and had huge holes spread over one side. Buckets filled with metallic slivers and small bars had been knocked off the wall, their contents spilled over the area.

Something had smashed holes the same size as the

tables' holes high in a wall near an exhaust vent. The damage had left a pile of wood and ceiling tile mixed with metal and insulation in the far corner of the room. The pile reached the ceiling.

Half-smashed bricks along with bent metal were the remains of the forge. Large dents marred the metal walls, all roughly the same size as the holes.

"What the hell?" Lyssa muttered.

Something huge had been in the room, and it had caused a lot of damage. There was one problem. Lyssa didn't see it, but she'd heard it. No one liked an invisible angry giant.

There were many possibilities: camouflage, invisibility, thinning. Without knowing the essence and regalia of her opponent, she couldn't begin to guess what tricks he might be pulling.

The bastard needed to come out. She wanted to get it over with. Anyone who hurt Serafina wouldn't be leaving the building alive.

Lyssa sucked in a breath, her stomach knotting. Serafina might not be a Torch, but the woman could defend herself, especially in her gallery. Whoever had done this was a dangerous and powerful foe. That suggested Torch or Eclipse training.

"It's a trap," Jofi said.

"Maybe," Lyssa whispered. "Probably."

"Then shouldn't you avoid it? Miss Dale is not answering. Given the situation, there's a good chance she's dead."

"Aren't you sunshine on a cloudy day?" Lyssa muttered. She pushed the door open. "I'm not leaving to save my ass while my friend is missing. She could be here somewhere and hurt."

"Where?" Jofi asked. "If she's in one of the other rooms, that's all the more reason for you to leave."

"I need to take down the threat first."

Lyssa looked around, unsure if the rhythmic sorcerous pulse was from the room or her unseen enemy. Her brief sweep stopped as she narrowed her eyes on the corner pile.

"Why don't you come out of there and we'll talk?" Lyssa frowned. "If you haven't hurt my friend, this doesn't have to go badly for you. I'm never eager to take down Illuminated."

A huge four-fingered silver fist punched out and the pile shook, causing pieces to fall. A leg emerged.

Seconds later, the entire body emerged, a massive silver humanoid statue radiating enchantment and covered with glyph work. There were no obvious eyes, though the head was covered with denser glyph work than the rest of the body. The silver figure took a step and smashed debris under its enormous foot.

Lyssa pointed her guns at the new arrival. "Okay, didn't see that coming. You have a lot of balls, sending a construct after a Sorceress."

The silver construct lumbered forward. Other than the crunch of trash beneath its feet, it didn't make any noise.

"Tell me where my friend is. I bet you can talk through that thing."

The silver construct smashed a fist into the wall, adding a new dent. Wood snapped and trash rustled as it lumbered toward her.

"You're threatening me?" Lyssa scoffed. "You might have gotten lucky surprising Serafina, but she's got a much kinder heart than I do." She narrowed her eyes on the construct. "Wherever you are, Serafina, I hope you sound-proofed this place because things are about to get loud."

CHAPTER FIFTEEN

Lyssa's first couple of shots bounced off the silver construct. Bright glowing azure cracks snaked out from the impact points. A matching aura surrounded the entire body.

"Okay," Lyssa growled, "this is damned annoying."

The construct stopped moving. It couldn't have been that easy. Serafina would have discarded a construct who couldn't take a bullet with ease.

"Is it dead?" Lyssa murmured.

"I think you'll have to hit him a lot harder," Jofi said. "Total annihilation will ensure pacification of the enemy."

"Gee, you think?" Lyssa rolled her eyes. "Wow. You must secretly be the Spirit of Tactics. I'll save the big stuff for when I need it."

She took another shot. More cracks and a brighter glow appeared. The enemy remained immobile.

Lyssa took a step back. "Okay, big guy, sounds like you don't have a microphone for anyone to talk through you.

What's the plan, then? Smash everything that moves? But you stopped. Why?"

She kept her distance. The ravaged condition of the room made for uneven footing and not many places to hide.

"I might be overthinking this. It might be out of power."

"It hasn't fallen," Jofi reminded her.

"Good point." Lyssa kept her guns trained on the glowing but unmoving construct. "It's not standing in a weird way. It wouldn't necessarily have to fall."

Lyssa had seen similar creations before and had fought some, too. Her limited experience didn't translate into analytical confidence.

There was no single easy way to defeat a construct. Some constructs possessed a weak point. Others would keep operating until they were blown to pieces. Others only had limited operating times. A construct could have one or all those weaknesses.

Without being able to inspect the construct more closely and leisurely, Lyssa had no chance of figuring it out. She might not need to worry if it didn't start moving again soon.

Lyssa's guns dipped. "It looks like our boy doesn't want to fight anymore." She looked around. "But that doesn't answer the question of where Serafina is."

She furrowed her brow. A body could fit under the pile leftover in the corner, but there was no blood anywhere.

"Serafina might have weakened it." Lyssa sidestepped to peer at the pile. "That might be why it stopp—"

The construct took a step forward. So much for it being out of power. She didn't want to take a hit from something that strong, but it was so slow that there was no way it could land a blow.

"Recharging, huh?" Lyssa lifted her guns. "I've got a lot more than a couple of bullets for you."

A final flash surrounded the construct. It dissipated, along with the glow, both from the cracks and aura.

The construct barreled through the room, the lumbering giant replaced by a fleet Olympian. Each step knocked trash and debris out of the way or crushed it underfoot. Lyssa hissed in surprise and silently thanked Jofi for not choosing that moment to offer an "I told you so."

It closed the distance and flung a silver fist at her. Lyssa ducked the blow and jumped to the side. With quick trigger pulls, she walked bullets up and down its body, hoping to find its weak spot or forcing it into another recharge cycle. Her shots bounced off with bright sparks.

The construct charged her again, and she twirled out of the way like a matador taking on an angry bull. Its heavy silver fist smashed into the wall. Chunks shot out, leaving another deep dent.

Lyssa emptied her pistols into the construct before leaning back to avoid its latest blow. Unlike the enemy, she'd not left a dent. She had not accomplished anything but scratches.

Her enemy got lucky in its next attack, and its fist clipped her in the side. The hit sent her to the floor with a loud crack.

She had never been sideswiped by a truck, but she imagined it felt similar. Hissing in pain, she rolled out of the way of a heavy stomp. Testing her defenses could wait for another day.

Lyssa ignored her pain and sprang to her feet. "All you do is punch. Up your game."

The construct charged again, but this time she was ready. She jumped onto an overturned piece of table and backflipped off, leaving nothing but air for the construct.

"Taunting an unintelligent creation is a waste of concentration and time," Jofi said.

Lyssa holstered one of her pistols while dodging another blow. "But it's fun, and it makes me feel better about myself."

"Destroying the enemy would do more to raise your self-esteem."

"True enough. I'm getting to that."

The construct tried a kick. Lyssa's dodge helped her escape its foot by inches.

"Great, now it's learning."

"Recommend you increase your level of engagement," Jofi said.

Lyssa's body and head jerked side to side, keeping any more hits from landing. Her opponent struck fast and hard, but at least he hadn't mastered combos yet.

Jofi was right. The enemy was fast, dangerous, strong, and it didn't appear to be running out of power. She didn't know its weak point. That left one option. She needed to obliterate enough of its body so nothing was left to threaten her. It was time for enchanted ablative rounds.

"You're going to regret messing with me." Lyssa vaulted off another piece of table with her free hand.

A punch missed her, close enough to muss her hair. The

heavy blow crashed into the sad remains of a shelf, collapsing it and sending the containers of tiny steel nuts it held to the floor. Pieces of the shelf bounced off her mask.

Lyssa reached into a specific pocket to grab a magazine. She didn't have time to reload before there was another attack, another kick. Her quick sprint took her to the other side of the room.

She slapped the magazine into her pistol while the construct turned to face her. It charged again, bringing back a fist. She aimed at the center of its chest and loosed three rounds in rapid succession, taking a step back with each.

Yellow-tinged purple flames exploded from the points of contact. The blasts vaporized huge chunks of the construct and surrounded it with dark smoke. Lyssa's opponent stumbled back with each strike and molten metal splattered, hissing as it hit the floor.

The attack left a nasty uneven gouge in the enemy's chest. Dozens of cracks shot from the wounds, glowing like they had earlier. A bright aura surrounded the construct.

Lyssa frowned. "Oh, come on! That's not fair."

The construct became a blur of speed. Its next blow nailed Lyssa square in the chest with such force that it launched her across the room. Something crunched in her torso. Fiery pain spread everywhere, and it was hard to breathe.

Lyssa managed to get off more shots before smacking into the wall at high speed for another date with Mr. Pain. She groaned and tumbled forward. Doing her best to ignore the pain suffusing her body, she kept her gun aimed at the construct's chest and rapidly pulled the trigger before landing on her knee. She emptied the rest of her magazine into her opponent, screaming in defiance.

"Take that, you stupid piece of crap!"

Each shot exploded and obliterated more of the construct. Despite her unsteady state, the enemy couldn't get closer to finish her. The force of the attacks knocked it back. By the time her gun went dry, she'd forced the construct against a wall. Thick dark smoke billowed from its chest, hiding its upper body. An acrid stench filled the air.

"That was expensive," she muttered. "And painful."

Her vision swimming, Lyssa hopped to her feet and loaded a penetrator magazine on pure muscle memory. She steadied her pistol with both hands, trying to spot her target, her eyes tearing up from the smoke. Being able to see in the dark with the help of her regalia wasn't the same thing as being able to see through and be immune to every challenge to her vision.

"Don't make this more expensive," she spat.

She wiped her teary eyes, trying to pick out movement through the smoke before gripping her pistol with both hands again. Another couple hits like the ones she'd already endured, and she wouldn't be able to dodge.

Something creaked within the smoke. Lyssa put her finger over the trigger.

The construct emerged from the cloud. Lyssa's attack had vaporized most of its chest. The damage exposed a pulsating sphere connected by gossamer strands of light.

She had not been expecting to see that, but she didn't have to be an expert on construct sorcery to recognize an artificial heart. Twitching and jerking, the construct advanced toward Lyssa, its earlier speed a distant memory.

"Whoever built you cost me a lot of money," Lyssa muttered. "They should feel good about that, but I like to tell myself you cost more."

The construct advanced, each uneven step accompanied by tremors. It looked like it could fall over any second.

"Goodbye."

Lyssa pointed at the heart and fired. Her bullet ripped through the organ, which shattered in an earsplitting, room-shaking boom. Dozens of inert pieces of dull metal shot everywhere. The strands connecting the heart to the rest of the body vanished.

The construct was still. There were no glowing cracks or aura and no heart, nothing but a huge hole in the chest.

Lyssa made a circle in the air with her gun. "You can die already, please."

The body toppled over, landing with a loud crash and adding dust into the polluted air. Lyssa nodded, satisfied.

"Thank you."

She holstered her gun. Gritting her teeth, she rubbed her chest, hating to think about what would have happened if she'd been hit without her regalia or the vest. She reached for one of her herb packets.

"Have you suffered any serious injury?" Jofi asked.

"I think it cracked some ribs." Lyssa took a deep breath and winced. "But I don't think it punctured a lung. I don't know if that counts as serious injury."

"I would humbly suggest it does."

Upon second thought, there was no way she'd be able to avoid using healing herbs to supplement her regalia's healing. She couldn't sit around healing for weeks and not follow up on whatever lead Reed planned to give her.

"This was supposed to be nothing more than a supply run." Lyssa waved smoke out of her face. "I'm still not seeing blood anywhere, but maybe you're right. This could have been a trap. They might have snagged Serafina and left that here as a surprise for me. I can't imagine they'd want a random customer or a cop running into it."

The wall rumbled. Lyssa whipped out her guns and spun toward it, ready to continue the fight despite the ache in her chest and her labored breathing. A slab of metal moved forward and slid to the side, revealing a familiar Sorceress tucked into a coffin-sized alcove.

Lyssa gasped. "Serafina!"

CHAPTER SIXTEEN

"That's a tight fit." Serafina stepped out of the alcove, stretching. "Much tighter than I thought it would be. I didn't measure it well." She tilted her head and put a finger to her bottom lip. "Oh! Measuring height without accounting for comfort. It all makes sense now. Silly me."

For a moment, Lyssa didn't trust what she was seeing and thought the woman in front of her was another trick. She soon accepted it was her friend, or at least a perfect facsimile.

Serafina was a beautiful short, dark-skinned woman. Her long hair was elaborately braided and adorned with different-colored bright metal hairpins. Her muscular arms spoke of her years working with a hammer and anvil. She wore jeans and a white tank top under her thick gray apron, which was covered with blackened marks and scratches. Golden jeweler's glasses covered her eyes, but she flipped them up and offered a bright smile to Lyssa.

The Torch holstered her gun before reaching into a pocket for a small baggie containing painkiller herbs. She couldn't keep up with Serafina even when her mind wasn't clouded by pain. After taking a deep breath, she munched on one of the bitter golden-blue flower petals.

Fighting while under the effects of herbs wasn't a smart idea since a woman needed to know when she was hurt, but the battle was over. Lyssa didn't bother saying anything else, waiting as the intense pain quieted to a minor ache.

Serafina turned from the alcove to survey the destroyed workshop, an amused smile on her face. "Wow. That thing went to town, didn't it?"

Lyssa shook her head. "Serafina, are you okay?"

"Oh, and good timing!" Serafina clapped her hands together. "Yes, I'm okay." She dusted her hands on her apron and stepped out of her alcove. "Why wouldn't I be?" She lifted her hands and spread out her fingers. "No cuts, no bruises." She patted the back of her neck. "You see something?"

A gaggle of tiny constructs shaped like the monster Lyssa had fought fell from a vent into the alcove. She doubted they packed the same punch, being only six inches tall, but she drew a gun anyway, ready to send them to join their big brother. They ignored her and spread out along the wall.

"What the hell is going on?" Lyssa continued tracking the tiny creations. "Why were you in the wall? What are those things? Why is your place trashed, and why did a huge construct try to kill me?"

"Oh, the wall is part of a new safety system I've been testing in case something unplanned happened. And something unplanned happened!" Serafina glanced at the destroyed construct. She scratched her cheek. "The intention was to use the alcove to survive an explosion, but it worked out nicely in this scenario." She threw up her arms. "Hooray for more than one use. That's good design."

Lyssa gestured with her gun at the marching constructs. "You were attacked by their big brother sent by an assassin, so you hid in there? It trashed the place looking for you?"

"Big brother? Oh, no. Not at all. Uh. Actually, yes. That's perfectly correct." Serafina gave a firm nod.

"Huh?" Lyssa grimaced. "You're not making any sense. Or you're making less sense than usual, which isn't a lot."

"Aren't I? I was attacked and used the security system, but it's mine. The construct, that is. Oh. And the security system. That's mine too. And I'm not an assassin. There was that one time Elder Samuel said I was an Assassin of Dignity, but you're talking about the killing people kind of assassin." Serafina shrugged.

"Yes, I'm talking about the killing people kind of assassin." Lyssa groaned. "And you don't care that there are a dozen of those things around you now? I get that they're smaller, but it doesn't mean they can't break your ankle or your nose."

Serafina waved her hands in front of her. "Don't worry about my dolls, Lys. They're going to help me clean up. They were doing that before the incident. These aren't designed with any sort of battle abilities. They couldn't fight you even if they wanted to."

"Don't worry?" Lyssa inclined her head at their destroyed large brother. "That thing just tried to kill me. It trashed your workshop. It's a miracle you weren't killed." She took a couple of deep breaths and found that the ache was better than before but not gone. "You don't have your regalia on." She gestured at the alcove. "If you didn't have your panic room, it would have smacked you through a wall and killed you. Trust me, I know. It hit me more than once."

"It hit you and tried to kill you?" Serafina looked confused. "That makes sense. It's not unexpected, but I wasn't sure things would work out that way." She bobbed her head. "Hmm. Excellent test against someone I couldn't have ever asked to do it. It has battle abilities, but the generalized attack response wasn't what I'd intended at all. What went wrong?"

"To be clear on this, you're saying you made that thing into a killer on purpose?" Lyssa tucked away her gun but took her time. She stared at her friend, dumbfounded, her irritation and surprise distracting her from the residual pain not handled by the herb.

"Yes! It's a new experiment. A guardian doll." Serafina gestured with both hands toward the destroyed construct like a model on a game show introducing the grand prize.

Lyssa tried to fold her arms and grimaced at the resulting pain. She reached into another pocket to grab a healing herb bag. "I didn't ask to be part of an experiment."

"Of course. I'd never do that without your explicit permission." Serafina shook a finger. "This was all an accident, but you can't spell serendipity without Serafina."

"Yes, you can. They're only the same at the b…" Lyssa rubbed her temples. "I'm so *glad* me getting punched into a wall helps you."

"Oh, thank you." Serafina smiled brightly.

"I'm not…forget it."

"I've been interested in constructs for a while, and it's a

good way to apply some of the newer techniques I've been developing." Serafina pushed her cheeks together with her hands. "I need to be more flexible." The words came out muffled. She released her cheeks. "I thought I told you about this. I remember having a whole conversation about it. We discussed the pros and cons."

"You never mentioned it! I think I'd remember if you said you were building huge killer constructs." Lyssa jabbed a finger toward the destroyed construct. "Especially one that dangerous."

"Oh. I didn't mention it?" Serafina looked to the side for the moment and laughed. "That's right. That conversation was with someone else entirely. She didn't look like you, and for that matter, she was a man, not a woman." She nodded firmly. "Yes. Not you at all. Sorry for the confusion."

Lyssa scrubbed a hand down her face. "This isn't a game, Serafina."

"Of course not. It was a test and a successful one. It wasn't intentional, but you have to roll with the punches in life, right?"

"This woman always presents interesting reactions," Jofi said. "She defies the normal human behavior patterns I've come to expect."

"You've got that right," Lyssa muttered.

Serafina rushed over to Lyssa. The Torch's hand twitched toward a gun by reflex but stopped when her friend skidded to a halt in front of her, her face only inches away.

"You're talking to him, aren't you?" Serafina whispered.

"What's he saying? Is he interested in a construct body? Maybe we could do a project together."

"I would prefer not to risk my existence in one of her creations," Jofi said.

Lyssa shrugged. "He thinks you're interesting."

"Good." Serafina spun on her heel and hurried to snatch a scratched ball-peen hammer off the floor. She lowered her glasses and eyed the tool. "Thanks for stopping by. I know I said things were ready, but you still came at a great time. I would have been stuck in there for a while if you hadn't come in. The threat spell needed to dissipate before I could get out, and the doll might have killed me when I did."

The mini-dolls picked up debris and hauled it to the corner pile. It might have been adorable if Lyssa hadn't just fought something dangerous. All they needed now was high-pitched nonsensical singing. On another day, she might have been tempted to ask for a tiny doll in Kawatsu-chan form.

"Did you not hear me earlier?" Lyssa asked. "Your toy tried to kill me. I don't mean it accidentally bumped me. It came at me and punched me into a wall. If I hadn't been in my regalia, it could have gotten nasty."

"Don't take it personally, Lys." Serafina giggled and walked over to the downed doll. "It tried to kill me, too. The poor creation didn't recognize its goddess." She crouched and poked the hole in the doll's center. "Hmm, blew right through it, didn't you? That's so Hecate of you. Run into a roadblock and blow it away with overwhelming force. Who needs flexibility when you've got force?"

Lyssa frowned, insulted, but she stowed the feelings.

She couldn't complain about Serafina being right. She was more concerned about getting the woman back to the real world and understanding the seriousness of what had happened before she made more killer constructs that ambushed people.

"What if that thing had gotten out of your place?" Lyssa asked. "You want it rampaging down Fremont Street? That mime I saw doesn't deserve to be punched into a wall, invisible or not."

"Of course not." Serafina waved a hand. "Without the power being fed from the gallery, it would have collapsed the second it stepped outside. Then it would be nothing but a boring-shaped statue with some interesting detail work." She traced glyphs on its arm with her finger. "By the way, it's only boring-looking because it's a prototype. I wanted to get the fundamental design down before I worked on the appearance. It's hard to balance everything when they are this big."

"You're planning to make another one?" Lyssa pulled off her mask. She wanted Serafina to see the exasperation on her face. "You're kidding, right?"

Serafina shook her head. "Not right away. I need to figure out what went wrong with this one first. I kind of know, but I don't completely know." Serafina shrugged and gave her a frustratingly doe-eyed look of innocence. "You know how it is."

"I would recommend not being here when it's completed," Jofi said. "Or if you must, bring extra magazines and explosives."

Lyssa frowned. "Agreed," she murmured. "I used up a whole magazine of ablative rounds and a penetrator to take that thing down." She walked over to the construct and kicked it in the head. "You better replace those for me, along with a bonus since I'm having to use herbs."

"Doesn't Tricia give you those for free?" Serafina looked confused.

"It's the principle of the thing."

"Sure." Serafina smiled. "Don't worry about the other stuff. It's the least I can do. I also owe you for the surprise field testing. And since it was against a Torch, even better. I'll give you everything you came for today for free and get started on some new bullets for you." She hopped up and stuck her tongue out of the corner of her mouth like a happy puppy that didn't know what to do with herself. "Did it speed up when you attacked it? I forgot to ask that, or maybe you said it, and I didn't listen."

"Yes." Lyssa took a deep breath, trying to calm herself. "Why did your doll attack me? Was it designed to attack anyone who came in here? I get that, but it also went after you."

"That's my fault. I screwed up some of the glyphs, not having considered the size differential." Serafina tittered. "Sorry! I should have used a nested northern crane when I used an eastern snapping turtle, and that's before we get into the formation density. Scaling it to the size I did requires different techniques than I used on the prototype dolls. I didn't realize it until it started going crazy and trying to kill me. By then, I was, like, 'Oops, I'm probably going to die if I don't get out of the way. Silly me.'"

Lyssa frowned. "Where's your regalia? Shouldn't you be wearing it when you're testing something so dangerous?"

Serafina pointed at the corner pile. "It's in a box under

that. I didn't need it for the activation. I didn't expect my doll to go nuts. But I see your point." She rubbed her chin. "I'll have to set up a better testing system for larger constructs, something that traps berserk creations rather than me. That makes sense, right?"

"Yes, it makes a lot of sense to me."

Serafina leaned closer to Lyssa, a hungry look in her eye. "You know how hard it is to make a good doll without using spirit sorcery?"

Lyssa shrugged. "I've never been interested in that kind of thing."

Serafina raised a finger slowly before jabbing it toward one of Lyssa's holsters. "I'm complete garbage when it comes to spirits. They might as well not exist as far as I'm concerned, but you've got one bound to those two guns."

"I would prefer not to be examined by that woman," Jofi said.

This wasn't the first time Serafina had expressed interest in Jofi, and it was difficult to deflect her attention without offering the whole truth, something Lyssa wasn't at liberty to share without pissing off Lee.

"I had help when I bound Jofi," Lyssa replied. "And some of that came with me having the Night Goddess." She shook her head. "Now that you're okay, I need to pick up the ammo I came for and get out of here. I'm working a job, and I don't have time to stick around and chat about your latest killer projects."

Lyssa accepted she would need at least one day at home for recovery. She couldn't risk getting into a major fight before her ribs were in a better state. Getting home wouldn't be much of a hassle thanks to the herbs, assuming no one ambushed her along the way. Reed had said he would have something for her by evening, so the timing worked.

"Oh, sure." Serafina looked around the room, then all but dived into a pile of trash. She threw pieces of wood and metal out of the way until she found two narrow boxes. "Here we go." She stacked and offered them to Lyssa. "I'll let you know when your reward pay is ready. Sorry about the almost-killing-you thing. Mondays, am I right?"

Lyssa took the boxes and gave them a light shake, enjoying the quiet rattle of the enchanted bullets inside. A couple of bungee cords would secure them on the way home.

"And a new job, huh?" Serafina cocked her head to the side. "Anything interesting?"

"I'm investigating shard smuggling. Some Shadow criminals in Phoenix had a bunch of combat shards."

"Oh." Serafina looked disappointed. "That's boring." Her eyes widened, and the interest returned to her face. "Hey, you interested in having a doll when I get these worked out? You can have a partner. Ride around with him. Hecate and the Silver Man! Well, I have no idea how to get one with decent long-lasting autonomous power, but I'll figure it out eventually."

The idea of Kawatsu-chan puttering around at her home returned. An image of the mascot bashing Lyssa's face against the wall and chasing her with a kitchen knife killed the desire.

Lyssa grimaced. "I think I'm okay." She lifted the boxes. "And I really should get going."

"Okay." Serafina waved. "Let me know if you change your mind."

Lyssa backed away slowly, half-convinced the tiny dolls would malfunction and swarm her. Picking up supplies wasn't supposed to involve fights. It wasn't an auspicious beginning to this job.

CHAPTER SEVENTEEN

Lyssa lay on her bed in her regalia. Her mask was on her nightstand. She had spent most of the day in bed, trying to heal her ribs. Between the Night Goddess and healing herbs, they were now in one piece, though she still needed painkillers to do anything useful.

She would be fine by tomorrow. Any thoughts she had about luck giving her more time to recover died when her burner phone rang with the expected call.

Lyssa grabbed her mask and put it on since the vocal filter wouldn't activate without it. "Reed, I've had a crap day, so I hope you have something useful for me about Alvarez and the shards. I don't want another 'Hey, I totally led you on' deal like last month."

"Yes, ma'am," Reed replied. "I'm here to help you out. You have to trust me."

Lyssa snorted. "I trust you to give me information in exchange for money. Nothing more, nothing less."

"Then we're on the same page." Reed laughed. "I ain't

gonna piss off a Sorceress, especially one with a temper like yours."

"Until you can make enough money doing it."

"That would be an interesting day." Reed clucked his tongue. "But I get you, and I've got you, so let's get down to business."

"That would be nice." Lyssa sat up. There was something ridiculous about being in her full regalia, including mask, in bed, but it wasn't like Reed could see her.

"You know about the Lone Five Stars?" Reed asked.

"A little." Lyssa frowned. "They're a big organized crime group out of Texas. I don't know much about them other than that."

"All you Sorcs have tunnel vision," Reed whined. "It's always about the magic for you. It's going to bite you in the ass."

His observation applied more to her than to the Society in general. The Society had had its hand in many aspects of the Shadow community in the past, including using influence on certain criminal groups. She'd found it repugnant, but through the centuries, the argument had always been that no one could eliminate all corruption, so it was better to have a hand in guiding it to minimize its excesses. The Society had allegedly pulled away from such groups by the twentieth century, but most people doubted that.

"Get to the point before I eat your soul," Lyssa said.

"You're joking, right?" Reed asked.

"Maybe," Lyssa growled. "Do you want to find out?"

"You ain't gonna do that over the phone. You can't."

"Says who? You? You're a sorcery expert now?"

"Okay, okay. Calm down." Reed let out a mirthless

laugh. "The Lone Five Stars ain't just about Texas anymore. Yeah, they're from Texas, but their reach stretches all over the Southwest. Some of the guys at the top are as smart as they are ruthless, and the word is they're trying to grab the best of the best from other gangs. They don't care about where you're from or who you are, just that you can take orders and keep your mouth shut and do your job."

"They're the UN of organized crime. Got it." Lyssa shifted her phone. "How is that relevant to Alvarez? He's not a member of the Lone Five Stars. He's a cartel boy connected to worse people down south."

"Now you're thinking like me and not a Sorc. Good for you, Hecate." Reed coughed. "Yeah, you're right. Alvarez was loyal to his cartel, but his cartel uses connections with the Five Stars to move all sorts of crap. You got it all wrong."

Lyssa hated not being face to face to intimidate Reed. Things always worked out better that way.

"You just said I was right," she replied. "Before saying I'm wrong."

"Not about it all. Just about some things. You see, the Five Stars ain't the UN. They're the UPS of big crime in the Southwest. Ain't that always the way? The smartest way to get rich is as a middleman."

"Am I supposed to be impressed?" Lyssa asked. "I don't care about where criminal scum are located on the ladder of depravity."

Reed snorted. "Just saying. You ain't got to work harder, you got to work smarter. Criminal business-to-business services, you know? The Five Stars have been hooking up with everyone to expand. You a large street gang? They want to deliver to you. Cartels in Mexico? They want to help. They've even been trying to get some stuff established with Russians in Texas lately, but that ain't the most interesting part."

Lyssa scoffed. "I hope 'interesting' is the same as useful. These people aren't delivering pizzas and PlayStations. They're helping facilitate misery."

"Oh, Hecate, you'll love this then because it's what you self-righteous types want: a reason to feel good when you're beating a man up." Reed chuckled. "The thing is, the word went out that you don't just use the Lone Five Stars for smuggling anymore."

"Dealing?" Lyssa asked.

"Got it in one, but this is where it gets weird."

"Weirder than me?"

Reed snickered. "The word is also they're going into the direct supply business for people interested in being less than legal, but they're playing it close to the chest as to what they're selling."

Lyssa chuckled. "Maybe *you* don't know, but that doesn't mean no one does. This might just be their way of feeling out the cartels about competing in the drug trade."

"Nah. There's no point in them trying to make their own drugs with all the cuts they get along the way from everybody else. Most people are thinking they're talking about guns, but a couple of weeks ago, a rumor about them surfaced among us people who like to live on the edge of the law. Something very, very interesting."

Lyssa narrowed her eyes, her heart rate kicking up. "And what did this rumor say?"

"There was some fool who got in an accident in New

Mexico. The Five Stars were supposed to be involved. Nobody knows what they were hauling, but when the cops showed up, they found an empty overturned truck. It was cold in the back, nothing left but some melting ice." Reed shrugged. "You can look that part up. It was on the news."

"So, they had a refrigerated trailer." Lyssa's shoulders slumped. She had thought he had something. "Who cares? They could have taken up smuggling stolen high-end beef for all we know."

"Nah, that's the thing." Reed's tone bordered on smug. "Ain't no cold machines in the trailer. The news said that too, but no one put two and two together, at least not that they're saying publicly. You had to have your ear to the ground to get it." He lowered his voice and whispered conspiratorially for effect, "And that's where I heard real interesting stuff."

Lyssa hissed. "Get to it, then."

"There's an underworld doc near where the accident happened who said a guy got dropped off at his place, all but frozen solid like a freaking human popsicle."

"Okay," Lyssa replied. "I'll give you that. It's different."

"The doc couldn't do much for him, so the guys who brought him took him and said they'd take care of the rest. I don't know about you, but if I found a popsicle man and a mysterious half-frozen truck with no refrigeration gear, I'm thinking abracadabra. That's what's going on."

"Interesting." Lyssa nodded slowly. "Okay. You might be onto something."

"It gets better. Because I happened to have heard something the other day you'll like. You might think I'm a lying piece of crap, but you pay me well, and you've done me enough solids in the past that I owe you."

"Then spill."

"The Lone Five Stars got themselves a base in Midland." Reed sounded impressed with himself. "It's their big hub. All the important product goes through there before it heads out farther west."

"Do you have the address?" Lyssa asked gruffly. "I can't kick in every door in Midland, and I don't want them smelling me coming and scurrying away."

"Uh..." Reed swallowed audibly over the line. "Yeah, actually, I do, but..."

"Don't ask for more money. I'm not in the mood. You're already going to get a big bonus as it is."

"That ain't what I'm saying, Hecate. What are you planning to do? Just walk in there and say, 'Any of you bitches smuggling magic artifacts?'" Reed laughed. "You're scary, but even you can be killed."

"You worry about you. I'll worry about me."

"You pay the best of anyone I sell to, and I know you ain't gonna help anyone trafficking girls or crap." Reed snickered. "Just trying to make sure a good employer doesn't bite it."

Lyssa scoffed. "I wonder about that, but for now, all I need to know is where they are."

"Your funeral," Reed replied. "If they have enough abracadabra stuff to sell to other people, there ain't no way they ain't keeping some around for them. And if they're connected to Alvarez having fancy stuff, that means they're gonna know you might come sniffing around. They're gonna be ready for you in a way he wasn't. It's not like you need to be a guy in the know to hear on the news about how you went and beat all those guys down."

Lyssa let out a slow-building chuckle that turned into a mocking laugh. "I'm Hecate the Night Goddess, a Torch of the Illuminated Society. I am the darkness that comes for evil men. I am a Torch that will burn the impure from the world. I'm not afraid of some Shadows with shards."

"Okay. You do you."

She grimaced. The speech had sounded a lot better in her head.

"Give me the address, and you don't have to see or hear from me for a while," Lyssa rumbled.

"But I love your money," Reed replied. "But sure, I've got that address for you. Take care. I'll be watching the news and checking the obituaries."

CHAPTER EIGHTEEN

"Damn it." Lyssa eyed the empty pint she'd pulled out of her freezer. "Why did I put this back if it was empty? My vice is ice cream, not booze. Why can't I remember?"

"You said yesterday it would serve as a reminder to go buy more ice cream," Jofi said. "That was right after you said you needed a long shower. You looked exhausted."

"That's the problem with using healing herbs," Lyssa complained. "It always leaves me tired when it's heavy healing. Another problem is this rip-off empty pint." She tossed it in the trash. "I need to learn how to make ice cream out of darkness sorcery."

"I think your endeavor is unlikely to succeed."

"Quiet. You can't even taste."

All sorts of things made sense in the middle of the night when a woman was so sleepy she might as well have been drunk. She could have used another of Tricia's herbs to wake up, but wasting one when she planned to go to sleep soon anyway was pointless.

"I did need a long shower, which was why I took one

when I got up." Lyssa rubbed her arms. "Every time I deal with someone like Reed, I feel like I need to shower. He might not be hurting innocent people directly, but he's a parasite sucking the blood of society. What I need for my job as a Torch and what I'd prefer to do are two separate things."

"You could always take care of him, violently or otherwise," Jofi said.

Lyssa blinked. "You want me to kill Reed?"

"I'm simply noting the possibilities. If he is a threat to your vision of a just society, it might be warranted."

A cold shiver passed through her. Jofi spoke with the same calm tone he always did, but she couldn't help but wonder if his true nature was seeping through. He'd made similar suggestions before. Even in his sealed form, his morality was alien on the best days, but he understood her political limitations and generally guided her accordingly.

Lyssa blew out a breath. "If he crosses the line, I'll pass something along to the cops. For now, he's useful."

"I see," Jofi said. "Useful and necessary?"

"I'm always going to need to have some fingers in the underworld." Lyssa opened her freezer again and peered into it. She shoved a package of ground beef aside to make sure there were no hidden pints. "It's nice when every job is as clean and straightforward as 'Go into this house and beat the bad people down,' but long before I met you, I learned the hard way what it's like to do an investigation as an Illuminated without decent Shadow leads or contacts. Elders don't focus on that kind of thing. It makes jobs a lot harder."

"I have no memory of our first meeting," Jofi said. "I can

only speculate from what I've heard you say when you speak of it to others."

Lyssa pulled her hand out of the freezer and slammed it shut, unease heavy in her mind. Not all spirits were sapient, and the ones who were varied wildly in personalities and basic psychology, if applying such concepts made sense with their kind.

There was no such thing as an average spirit. People, even Illuminated, seldom dealt directly with them, making them the closest thing to aliens humans could encounter.

Worrying too much made no sense. Jofi had no reason to be suspicious of her. Besides, he was better off sealed. In that form, he was helping fight darkness in the world, not adding to it. The procedure had also saved him from being destroyed.

The excuses didn't comfort her. Jofi wouldn't be easy to destroy. Lee had admitted as much. Sealing him was a plan birthed of desperation, not mercy.

The whole situation was strange. Lyssa was like a spirit parole officer, and that made it hard to process, even after all these years together. What would it be like to be a person stripped of their past and fundamental essence?

It wasn't impossible. Lee could do something like that if he wanted to. She shuddered at the thought.

"Are you okay?" Jofi asked.

"Don't worry. I'm just overthinking some things." Lyssa frowned at the freezer door. "I should probably have something other than ice cream for breakfast before I head to Texas. Dealing with criminals is exhausting enough without being hungry."

A chill shot through Lyssa. Shadows clawed at the edge

of her vision. She was about to blow it off as another visit from overeager HOA reps when pressure built in her chest.

"Were you expecting another visitor?" Jofi asked.

"No."

Lyssa sprinted toward her bedroom to open her safe. Her doorbell rang as she yanked out an enchanted pistol. She grabbed a magazine containing penetrator rounds and loaded the gun. The doorbell rang again.

She ground her teeth. Without her full regalia, she might not be a match for a Sorcerer in theirs, but she also didn't want to wait and risk someone launching a public attack outdoors. The penetrator rounds drew as much on Jofi's power as her own.

"Just a minute," she called as the doorbell rang again. She walked toward the door holding her gun behind her back. When she checked her peephole, she saw a frowning man she didn't recognize in glasses and a gray suit. "Can I help you?"

The man leaned in closer toward the door. "In your last message to me, you suggested we speak face-to-face, Miss Corti. It was right after yet another unnecessary comment about herbs and spices."

Lyssa opened the door and gestured to the living room. "You could have told me you were coming, Samuel."

The man entered. Once Lyssa closed the door, his form warped and blurred, revealing an older-looking man with white hair, along with a matching mustache and Van Dyke beard. The Sorcerer's white suit was accessorized by a long, skinny white tie. He was Elder Samuel, the bearer of the Distinguished Aristocrat regalia and master of light sorcery.

She'd not been expecting him, but his arrival didn't surprise her. No EAA jobs passed to the contract stage without an Elder's approval. That didn't mean she welcomed his arrival, but she did her best to keep her expression calm and neutral.

Samuel inclined his head toward the couch. Lyssa got the point. If he wasn't behind a desk, he liked to talk down to her rather than the other way around. She set her gun on her end table and folded her arms before taking a seat.

He stared at the gun, distaste visible on his face. It wasn't about disliking firearms. He knew the truth about Jofi but rarely mentioned it, despite his penchant for criticizing her.

The spirit didn't seem to care for Samuel, even though he consistently urged Lyssa to respect the man's orders. The spirit never spoke to Lyssa when the Elder was around, but when she'd asked him about it, he'd repeatedly denied ill-feelings. She wasn't sure if a sealed spirit of his nature could lie.

"Sell any chicken lately?" Lyssa asked, losing the battle between professionalism and petty entertainment.

"That doesn't become more amusing with repetition." Samuel narrowed his eyes.

"It does to me." Lyssa grinned. "And you didn't even laugh the first time. It's because you have no sense of humor."

"As you grow older, I find myself less tolerant of your disrespect. Talent isn't a license to behave without restrictions or common courtesy."

"It's called a joke, Samuel." Lyssa shrugged. "Lighten up."

"I don't have to lighten up over disrespect, Miss Corti." He glared at her, disapproval coming off him in waves.

Dialing it back might not be as fun, but it would save her pain. There was no reason to prolong the meeting.

Lyssa wasn't sure why they had such trouble getting along. She'd dealt with other Elders without this much trouble, and regalia aside, she wasn't a BBD—bitch by default. Given that his essence was light and hers was darkness, there could be some fundamental repulsion between their souls.

She waved a hand. "Okay. I apologize. You caught me off-guard, and I'm hungry."

"I'll accept your apology for now." Samuel lifted his chin, going into full-on haughty mode. "I thought it best if we talked directly concerning the shard incident, given this is a matter of importance beyond your new city or even your general region of primary responsibility."

"The investigation is proceeding," Lyssa said. "I've got some solid leads. The EAA hasn't come up with anything since I last talked to Agent Riley, but they're not getting in my way. I can't guarantee anything yet, but this isn't anywhere near going cold. It's heating up. I'll be checking out a place tonight."

"I see. I'm glad to hear that." Samuel stroked his beard. "Setting aside your questionable personality, I have confidence in your ability to rapidly see this incident through. That was why I decided to come here directly—to place it in the proper context and reinforce my expectations. I wanted us to both understand your position in this."

Lyssa tensed. "Expectations?

"There's extreme concern in the Society over this incident," Samuel said.

"The Alvarez Shard incident?" Lyssa asked, wanting to be sure.

Samuel nodded. "Of course. You've not been involved in anything else of note in recent months."

"I was well within my rights to take Alvarez and his men out." Lyssa shrugged. "Those were powerful shards they had. I could have been seriously injured."

"Yes, I agree with that evaluation. Please note I have other people tracking down the provenance of the artifacts. The robe goes back centuries, so it's unlikely its creation will be traced to a living Sorcerer, but the crossbows present a better possibility." Samuel held up his palm, and tiny three-dimensional images of the crossbows appeared and circled it. "It's because of our concern that we aggressively encouraged the EAA to ask for a formal contract in this incident."

"Huh?" Lyssa stared at the fire crossbow. "Why go through middlemen? If this is something the Society needs to handle, we don't have to beg their permission. That's not like you."

Samuel waved his hand, and the images vanished. "Miss Corti, I hope you learn to consider the future. I'm disappointed but not surprised you aren't doing that in this case."

So much for controlling herself. What was the point? It was like Samuel couldn't go a minute without being insulting.

"Enlighten me, O Great Elder." Lyssa rolled her eyes.

"We need to strengthen our political image and power

with the rest of the world," Samuel replied. "M-Day weakened it in many ways, although it was necessary. One method to increase our power and influence is to ensure that when incidents exposing potential rogue activity occur, the relevant Shadow governments are kept well-informed about what's happening and our efforts at mitigation. Having them hire you does that while reinforcing the appearance of control on their part, but it also leaves you free to do what is needed and filter information as necessary."

Lyssa ignored the rest of the political considerations to focus on one word. "'Rogue?' You've confirmed there's a rogue Sorcerer? Not saying I'd be surprised, but we need to consider the possibility that someone might have gotten lucky and found a cache of shards somewhere. I'm looking into an organized crime group that might be supplying people, but it's unclear how many they have."

"We haven't confirmed anything on our end." Samuel returned his hands to his back. "It's the most likely explanation, but we're more concerned about the damage this might do to the Society's relationship with the United States government."

"What about it?"

"There was an unfortunate spate of similar shard smuggling incidents in Japan last year. The Society was better able to control the news with the help of the Japanese government, which was why it didn't penetrate much into the media."

Lyssa nodded. "I heard about that, but I didn't realize it was a big deal and that they'd had a lot."

"The incident created extreme friction between the

Japanese government and the local Elders." Samuel's expression darkened. "What's worse, they were never able to determine the ultimate source of the shards. The Torches assigned to the matter solved it by helping the government crush the Shadow smugglers involved. The Japanese accepted that outcome, but the belief that the Society was covering something up lingers."

"That's too bad since that's probably where we'll end up with this job, too." Lyssa shrugged. "If it is a rogue, they might be good at covering their tracks. They'd have to be if they didn't want to end up on the bad side of a Torch or an Eclipse."

Samuel stood silently, looking at her for a long while, concern etched on his features. "I tell you all this to encourage you to please keep in mind the political considerations of this job. It's a delicate time for the stability of the relationship between the Illuminated Society and the Shadows. Every time an incident such as Phoenix occurs, groups like the ACSS take their chance to denigrate us. At least they've stopped bringing up the Sicilian Inferno at every opportunity, but that doesn't mean it's not in the back of many people's minds."

The incident was one of the highest-profile public massacres involving sorcery, where a rogue Sorcerer had participated in a Mafia war and killed not only criminals but scores of innocent people. The Society had declared it a heinous abuse of power, and in an unprecedented move, they had assigned an entire team of dedicated Eclipses in the hunt for justice.

Lyssa protested, "That was four years ago, and Eclipses took out the Sorcerer responsible, and it was criminals—"

Samuel lifted his hand to quiet her. "We won't be able to convince the Shadows not to be suspicious if we use their criminals as excuses. They already view us as dangerous puppeteers, and I can't say that's completely unfounded. For now, we need to remember it'll take many more years, if not decades or longer, to achieve some sort of equilibrium in our coexistence, given the general public's knowledge of us."

"I don't know how you can have equilibrium with a handful of Sorcerers and billions of Shadows." Lyssa shrugged and gave him a defiant look when he frowned at her. "I get what you're saying, but you're talking about the distant future."

"Our true numbers are increasing again for the first time in a long time. Our revelation to the world has worked out better than we planned and fits well with our other increases in fortune. The Society is growing stronger." Samuel's expression turned stern. "We need a probable path toward equilibrium, not a guarantee based on any one timetable."

Lyssa didn't bother to press Samuel on that. With the sinking of Lemuria, the last of the pure-blooded Sorcerers had passed into the dustbin of history. The Cataclysm had also taken most of the knowledge and records concerning their relatives. The event and the spread of Illuminated into the cracks of Shadow society had resulted in a steady decline in their numbers, along with a loss of overall power.

It was hard to separate the propaganda from the truth about greater power in the past and success in the future, but the Society had trumpeted steadily increasing numbers of Sorcerers since the 1960s. Before, a family might produce a true Illuminated once every few generations, and now some families spit out more than one, such as the case of the Cortis. Some rumors attributed this to the moon landing, but no one was able to explain how a Shadow technological achievement would contribute to Illuminated sorcery.

"What good is the equilibrium of the Society to people like me?" Lyssa mumbled. She hadn't realized she'd said it. aloud until she noticed the angry look from Samuel.

"Without the Society," he replied, enunciating each word, "the Shadows would sweep over the Illuminated like a tsunami. They'd scour us from the Earth. They'd find a way to get to Last Remnant and destroy it with their nuclear and chemical bombs." He sniffed in disdain. "Is this latest fit of pique about your brother?" He frowned. "Ah, yes, the anniversary of his *death*. And let's be clear about that. Just because his regalia—"

"I know," Lyssa snapped. "Somebody already shoved that in my face recently." She scrubbed a hand over her face. "And I know she was trying to help me when she said it. But that doesn't matter, I'm not here to talk about him, and I honestly don't care much about politics. I've got a contract to track down the source of the shards and clean up the mess. I'll do that, and I'll leave the rest to you. If there's a rogue at the end of this, I'm not going to call you to ask for permission. I'll clean that up the second I find it, whether or not it's politically convenient."

The mention of her brother rekindled a pathetic hope that this incident was targeted at her and related to him somehow, but the rational part of her had given up on that.

Finding and taking down the smugglers would help her get past the emotions piling up from the anniversary.

A subtle look of discomfort flickered across Samuel's face. "I might have misspoken when I suggested the possibility of a rogue. You were right before. Many shards have slipped through the Society's fingers throughout the millennia. The Shadows now fully appreciate their value and know better how to use them."

Lyssa gave him a skeptical look. It sounded like he was trying to convince himself more than her.

"Do you honestly believe that?" she asked.

"I choose to believe until presented with less annoying evidence, but I encourage you to be prepared for all possibilities."

"Understood." Lyssa grabbed her gun and waved it. "I should probably spend less time talking to you and more time investigating."

Samuel's form blurred into the boring disguise from before. "Keep me apprised of your progress."

Lyssa offered a mocking salute. "Don't worry, Great Elder. I'll get this mess cleaned up."

"I sincerely hope so."

CHAPTER NINETEEN

Pulling into a gas station in east Scottsdale, Lyssa yawned, already mentally exhausted even though it wasn't noon yet. A man filling his black Silverado watched her out of the corner of his eye. The Ducati drew plenty of attention in its normal form.

Everyone liked a sexy bike. Getting attention as Lyssa rather than Hecate wasn't unwelcome, but she'd bought the Ducati for her and her love of the road, not to get a man.

Sometimes when she stopped at a gas station, she wanted to laugh. For all her clever rituals and help from a spirit, in the end, she couldn't avoid having to pump 93-octane into her motorcycle.

The Silverado owner, a broad-shouldered man with a cute boy-next-door look, continued to do his best to pretend he wasn't looking at her while watching her every move. What would he think if he knew the great Hecate the Night Goddess needed to hit a Shell now and again?

Five years after M-Day, the average Shadow still didn't

understand sorcery. The Society encouraged that. A lack of information wasn't misinformation, the Elders claimed.

Lyssa furrowed her brow. She didn't agree. Stratagems and politics should come after the truth, not before, but she'd follow the fossils' rules until they convinced her it would make things worse, not better.

There wasn't much she could do as an individual. The future didn't care about individuals, even Illuminated. Power wasn't the same thing as omnipotence, even though the Tribunal camping out on Last Remnant liked to pretend otherwise.

Her nozzle clicked, and the gas flow stopped. She replaced the nozzle on the pump.

"That man is paying excess attention to you," Jofi said.

"I know," she whispered. "He's just hoping for a hookup. Don't worry about it."

Lyssa grabbed her receipt from the pump and tucked it into a pocket. Checking on a suspicious warehouse that might be related to organized crime in broad daylight was dumb even for a Sorceress, but she didn't want to spend all day sitting on her ass in a diner in Midland, making up excuses for why she was nursing her coffee.

That was one problem with having a motorcycle. It made stakeouts more difficult. Wraith form and other types of darkness sorcery cloaking took energy to maintain, and that wasn't infinite. Draining herself before a potential big fight was idiotic.

Lyssa frowned. She'd need a better plan. Waiting until night, then making her move made more sense. It also gave her regalia and herbs more time to heal her. Just because she wasn't in pain anymore, it didn't mean she was healed.

She'd rushed out of her place because of Samuel's visit, but it wouldn't hurt to go back.

Her hand jerked into her coat when Silverado Boy-Next-Door started toward her. Torch reflexes could be annoying. He slowed, offering her a smile.

"Hey." He kept his hands in his pockets.

Lyssa dropped her hand away from her hidden gun. "Hello. Can I help you?"

"Not exactly." The man inclined his head toward her Ducati. "Nice bike. I'm more of a truck guy, but it's hard to ignore a hot girl on a hot bike."

She grinned. "I like to be close to the road, feel that wind around me. It's hard to do that in a truck."

"I get that. In another life, I'd be a Harley dude, but it's hard to haul things with a bike." Boy-Next-Door's gaze flicked to the side.

Lyssa tensed and almost reached for her gun again. She told herself it was because of the ambush at Serafina's place. It was close to the truth, but she hated to think she was always that paranoid.

Two other guys around the man's age emerged from the gas station, holding plastic bags filled with snacks and sodas. They stepped away from the door and stopped, watching their friend with eager attention, stupid grins all over their faces.

"Are you sure this man isn't an enemy?" Jofi asked.

Lyssa let a laugh escape before she could stop herself. Boy-Next-Door looked confused, then insulted. She felt bad for the guy, but she couldn't risk explaining the situation to Jofi. Spirits could always make an awkward situation worse.

On some other day, when she wasn't getting ready to gun down gangsters wielding powerful sorcery-based artifacts, she might have been willing to give Boy-Next-Door a try, at least a single date. He wasn't her type, and her life was more complicated than most, but Tricia was right. Lyssa needed to try to live life.

Juggling the many balls of her day-to-day life would continue until she died or quit. Given her lifestyle, it might not even be when she expected it. Finding some temporary fun and floating along with the river of normal existence on occasion didn't seem so terrible.

"So," Boy-Next-Door began, "I'm Bill."

"Lyssa." She smiled. "I hate to do this, but let me save us both some time. You're cute and all, Bill, but I'm not looking at this exact moment, and I'm kind of on the way to something. I know that sounds like a line, but if you'd met me some other time, things might have been different."

Bill's mouth twitched, but he kept his smile. "That's cool. Thanks for your honesty." He waved and headed toward his truck. "See you around, Lyssa."

"See you around, Bill."

Lyssa headed toward the building. She'd stabbed the man in the heart, but he'd live. His friends hurried past her, one smirking, the other looking pained. She'd reached the door when they arrived at his truck.

"Yo, Bill, what the hell, bro!" the smirking man said, clapping his friend on the shoulder. "Did you think you were gonna get a hot biker chick to go out with you? And look at that bike. It's crazy-expensive. Out of your league, bro. Out of your league. That was like a high school running back getting smashed by an NFL linebacker. It was painful to watch."

Lyssa grimaced and entered the building. Bill was all right. She wouldn't say she was out of his league. She wasn't even sure what her league was.

The obvious choice would be to limit her dating pool to men who knew her identity and weren't freaked out by a woman who routinely dressed like a scary force of nature and gunned down dangerous criminals and terrorists. That was a damned small pool. She sighed as she made her way to the cold section.

"Do you desire companionship?" Jofi asked.

"I've got you," Lyssa whispered.

"Human companionship."

Lyssa found the ice cream section. Her eyes darted back and forth as she surveyed the available brands and flavors. Not enough strawberry varieties.

"I don't know what I want," she murmured. "If Samuel keeps me this busy, it won't matter for a while."

"You could combine your desires," Jofi said.

None of the pints was calling to her. That was rare. She shifted a couple of yards to grab a water bottle.

"Combine my desires?" Lyssa snickered. "That sounds kinky."

"It would be useful to seek companionship from someone you're in close contact with," Jofi said, conveniently ignoring her joke.

"Someone I'm close to?" Lyssa pulled a water bottle from the shelf. "I already thought of that. I don't have a lot of choices."

She lingered near the drinks, wanting to finish her

conversation with Jofi before going to pay. Sticking in an earbud was a nice cover in some situations, but she hadn't brought one and often didn't bother. It didn't help when they needed to discuss Society matters.

Damien's face flashed into her mind. He could be frustrating, but he was handsome and intelligent. It wouldn't hurt to get to know him on a more personal level. Unless she was crazy, there was something there.

Sparks? Maybe. Enough to start a fire? Maybe that, too.

"I've been thinking about your situation," Jofi said.

"You're worse than a middle-aged mother pressing her daughter to start popping out grandchildren."

"I assure you, it's hardly the same situation," Jofi said. "I have no investment in your potential offspring."

"Fine." Lyssa chuckled. "What do you want to tell me?"

"My strategy would allow you to better ingratiate yourself with the Shadow authorities. I'm not saying you need to maintain a relationship beyond the point of physical and emotional satisfaction, but it could aid your work."

"Wait, what?" Lyssa strained to keep her voice quiet. "You're saying I should seduce someone for the job?"

She should have known better than to take advice from a spirit residing in two guns, who had been stripped of his true nature—not that she wanted to hear what the original grand emptiness spirit had to say about her love life. For now, she'd wait for him to spit out the answer she already knew, Damien, but she wasn't fond of Jofi suggesting him.

"I'm stating that there can be a convergence of opportunities," Jofi continued. "It's the most logical choice."

Normally, Lyssa didn't mind his calm and measured tone. It provided a nice anchor in her chaotic life. This was one time, though, when she would have preferred the spirit inject a little emotion into his voice.

"I'm not dating someone for the job." Lyssa frowned. "That's not how I work."

That wouldn't do. It couldn't be so simple. As she thought about it, she wasn't even sure if Damien was allowed to date a Sorceress, let alone one he was monitoring. It wasn't something she'd thought to check, but the feds were all about avoiding conflicts of interest.

Having Jofi push her made her want to find out. It couldn't hurt to ask. Eventually.

"I think convincing Lieutenant Lopez of your worth as a woman would go a long way toward solidifying your relationship with the largest local police force," Jofi said. "If the Phoenix PD backs you, the others will."

"Huh?" Lyssa stood there with her mouth open, processing what she'd heard. "You think I should date *Lieutenant Lopez*? The guy who went on and on about how he didn't like me?"

"Yes," Jofi replied. "I'm not a good judge of human appearance, but he seems to match the general parameters of what you'd find acceptable. Taking advantage of that should reduce his antipathy toward you. I'm confused. Who did you think I was talking about?"

"This isn't fifth grade, where I'm supposed to pretend the boy who sticks gum in my hair likes me. I can't believe this." Lyssa burst out laughing, earning a curious look from the attendant at the counter. She shook her head. "It's a good thing you're not a love spirit. Forget it. Let's go back home and bleed off some daylight before heading to Texas."

CHAPTER TWENTY

An owl hooted in the distance. Lyssa enjoyed the avian commentary as she lay on her stomach atop a four-story building a couple of blocks from the suspects' warehouse. She'd found a comfortably deep shadow and wrapped herself in wraith form. The moon was barely visible through the clouds, making the night darker than it otherwise would have been.

She'd eaten a good chicken fried steak meal and downed a strawberry shake at a diner on the edge of town earlier, lying about how she was passing through on her way to Washington, DC. It'd been a while since she'd last been in Texas, and she'd enjoyed the casual friendliness of the small family-owned place.

A cool, refreshing breeze passed over her. It was perfect weather for a stakeout. She didn't need sorcery to keep herself comfortable. The light chirp and click of cicadas filled the air, joining the occasional owl noises—surprising at this time of year. Even though she was in town to investigate smuggling, everything about the evening relaxed her until a stray thought popped up.

Lyssa snickered. "How messed up is it that I'm calmest on top of a random roof? Oh, well. I might as well enjoy it until I have to shoot someone or threaten to eat their soul."

"You haven't had much chance to relax since the move," Jofi replied. "As you pointed out."

"Stakeouts are relaxing?"

"The lack of activity does provide a meditative atmosphere."

Lyssa laughed. "I'll start doing videos about the new meditation craze, *Be Zen Like a Narc.*"

She peered through her compact binoculars at the warehouse, focusing on the loading entrance in the back. There weren't a lot of streetlights near the building, and none of the surrounding buildings had any lights on.

That was perfect. She'd been able to get close to the building without trouble. She had been watching for a little over an hour and hadn't seen anything to worry her, though she also hadn't seen anything that made her think they had shards in there. At this distance, she wouldn't be able to feel the sorcery.

The Lone Five Stars might have gotten their hands on some shards, but that didn't make them Sorcerers. She could draw on her powers with little risk of alerting them. Avoiding a fight might not be possible, but she wanted to delay one until she confirmed they had the contraband.

Lyssa didn't mind gangs being afraid of her, but she also didn't want them believing she was going out of her way to hunt them. It would complicate things in the future.

"This isn't sad, is it?" Lyssa asked. "Not relaxing. Not Zen."

"What do you mean?" Jofi asked.

"I'm spending my night on a Midland rooftop, spying on gangsters instead of going out with guys in Silverados."

"It's necessary for the job. Would you feel better if you were on a rooftop in a different city? Or with Bill? He is the only Silverado owner of note you've encountered recently."

"He wouldn't enjoy this." Lyssa snickered. "I don't know if I feel *bad*. I've been thinking, but no, now that I think of it, it's not the city. I think it's more the roof. I do like the animal noises. I liked them in San Diego, too. I'm not sold on what I can hear in Scottsdale."

"The roof is necessary," Jofi said. "An elevated position makes for better reconnaissance. An excess of animal sounds would only raise the chance of you being ambushed. All tactical considerations must be remembered."

"Here lies Lyssa Corti, aka Hecate. She died because of too much nature appreciation." She chuckled. "You think someone's going to jump me because I'm too busy listening to cicadas?"

"Not in particular, only pointing out the possibility."

"Why do I have a feeling that in five years, you're going to burst out of my guns, cackling about how you've been putting me on all this time?" Lyssa shook her head. "You are probably the Grand Spirit of All Humor."

"I assure you, I'm not a spirit of humor," Jofi said. "I don't understand your jokes, Lyssa."

"That much is obvious. I've been working with you for years, and you don't learn."

"It's not in my nature. I'm a gun spirit."

"Sure." Lyssa frowned. "That's what you are."

Her breath caught. She didn't see anything new through her binoculars, but a question begged to be asked. It wouldn't be the first time she'd asked, but it'd been a long time. Lee would have been outraged to know she wasn't asking it weekly. The answer could be an early warning of Jofi's seal weakening.

"Hey," she asked quietly. "How does it feel to be a gun spirit?"

"I feel satisfied when you use me," Jofi replied. "I don't take pleasure in the destruction of your enemies, only in your use of me, but I do wish rapid defeat for all your enemies because of the risk they represent to your life."

That was a solid enough reply. There was no hint he doubted he was a gun spirit.

"We could hit the range more."

"I'd like that."

Lyssa yawned and pulled out her phone. Wearing a watch while she was in her regalia presented complications. "It's been forty-five minutes since we saw any movement in the back, and those guys were leaving. The first security guard and the guy who relieved him haven't been near the back that I can see, either. I doubt they're going to do another shift change after only an hour."

"We can't see everything," Jofi said. "There could be hostiles inside who haven't passed a window. Or they could be invisible."

"That's true, but I'm thinking this is as good a time as

any to check out the back." Lyssa shifted to her knees and twisted her body in a stretch. That was enough recon yoga. "What it comes down to is that we haven't seen anyone other than the guy in the front in a while. I'm a little surprised. Reed might be wrong about this, but it won't hurt to check it out."

"And if it doesn't belong to the Lone Five Stars?" Jofi asked.

"We poke around for a while and then leave." Lyssa shrugged.

"If it is them, they could be prepared for inspection by hostile Torches."

"I'm sure they can get reinforcements there quickly, but it's not like they're going to call the cops if something's off at their gangland warehouse. That guard in the front looks an awful lot like a gangster to me, down to the resting bitch face with a messed-up nose, ill-fitting suit, and the not-so-hidden gun. I think if this were a legit place, there would be a rent-a-cop there in an obvious uniform, not a reject from a Martin Scorsese flick."

"Do you intend to clear the warehouse out if you confirm it belongs to the criminals?"

Lyssa stood and dusted off her knees. Her long coat fluttered in the wind. "No. We could burn down that entire place, but we'd risk this ending up like it did in Japan. If we cut off the middlemen, we'll never find the source. This is going to require more finesse. We look first, then we shoot."

"You don't enjoy finesse."

Lyssa chuckled. "I enjoy solving problems in a straight-forward way, but that's not always possible. I prefer to win efficiently. Sometimes that means going in guns blazing, and sometimes that means convincing a guy not to fight. That's a type of finesse."

She walked over to the edge of the building, folding the binoculars and tucking them into a pocket. Stepping off, she filled her mind with interlocking glyphs and pictures of flowing smoke. She gently floated down to the ground, where she released the spell and jogged toward the back of the warehouse.

A six-foot chain-link fence protected it from would-be robbers. She didn't need sorcery to vault over it. After landing in a crouch on the other side, she scanned for trouble. She spotted cameras, but any review of the footage would have a hard time proving she was there. That was one advantage her abilities presented over the mind sorcery of someone like Lee.

The ample rear parking lot could easily accommodate a semi, but there was only a handful of nondescript vans. That supported Lyssa's suspicion that the place belonged to criminals. Companies liked to advertise. Criminals didn't.

Lyssa took careful steps as she worked her way toward a window. She made a point of staying away from doors, especially the loading door. She approached a barred window and peeked inside.

She saw a darkened warehouse loading floor with a single parked forklift and empty pallets piled up and stored along the wall. There were crates scattered around the room, and open crates circled a concrete support column in the center.

There was no truck inside, nor any men. It didn't

impress her as a major distribution hub. There was no busy hive of men packing drugs and weapons.

Reed might have given her bad intel. She needed to make sure it wasn't on purpose before she dished out too many threats.

Her chest tightened. Sorcery. She ducked reflexively and held her breath. Could they feel her?

Lyssa slowly lifted her head. She might have jumped to conclusions. It was time to go back to basics. She'd hoped to find shards there, and sensing their power could feel like normal sorcery. That didn't mean there was a full-fledged rogue here, and even if there was, knowing her general direction wasn't the same thing as being able to blow her away from a distance with a surprise attack.

The sorcery pressure remained constant. What that implied about potential shards couldn't be discovered without more information, but it did mean she could track the source with the help of triangulation.

Lyssa crept sideways, moving yards away from the window and paying close attention to the feeling in her chest. A return trip sent her past the original window and into the back. She now had a decent bearing on her target.

Whatever the power source, it lay inside the warehouse, most likely in one of the crates or behind the column. Her viewing angle from the windows produced a blind spot.

Someone could be waiting there, or it could be big, powerful stuff waiting to be sold. There was only one way to find out.

The chances of the location being an innocent warehouse had dropped nearly to zero in her mind. Owning a shard wasn't technically illegal, but there was no way a random warehouse in Midland would have one sitting in a crate when said building had come up in a conversation discussing an organized crime group specializing in smuggling. The universe didn't have that sick a sense of humor.

Lyssa spread her arms and took a breath as she tried to decide her next move. Bashing through a door would be easy, but it was guaranteed to trip an alarm. Slicing the bars and going through the windows was another possibility, but that also could signal a nearby Sorcerer. She remained unconvinced she was only sensing shards, but the steady level of power pointed to that possibility.

A moment of consideration turned into a plan and a chant. Thinning would scream power to anyone who could sense it, but she was willing to gamble that this was another Alvarez situation. There might be a rogue Sorcerer, but he wasn't hiding behind a column in this Midland warehouse.

Lyssa flowed through the window and released the spell, then took a moment to catch her breath. Passing through tight passages always strained her. Her spells and the deep shadows of the unlit warehouse floor guaranteed her invisibility.

She reached into a pocket and pulled out her batons. The wraith form swallowed the click when she expanded them. She didn't enchant them with her strength or knockout spells, figuring kneecapping a gangster would be enough to take him out. It was a mostly empty building, not a house filled with men who were ready to fight.

The soft overlapping ticks of large clocks echoed through the room. She continued forward, paying close attention to the increasing pressure she felt. The source was close.

About a quarter of the way into the room, Lyssa stopped, her heart pounding. She walked to the left and then to the right. Something didn't feel right. She craned her neck upward, hoping to find a shard hanging above her.

"This was easier than I thought, friend." The mocking voice came from above her. "And here I believed this was going to be a wasted night."

Lyssa sucked in a breath. The voice was sultry, young, female, and spoke elegant English with a touch of a Hindi accent. It wasn't an innate talent for linguistics that let her pick out the detail, just simple recognition.

Perfect. Just damned perfect. Of all the people she could have run into that night, why did it have to be that woman?

Blinding balls of white-hot fire shot out from behind the column and spread throughout the room. They hovered a yard off the floor, bathing the room in an eerie, flickering light.

"You can hide," the woman shouted. "But I know you're here. I'll burn you out if necessary." A sinister laugh followed. "And thank you. You've saved me the trouble of having to track you down before I kill you, Hecate."

CHAPTER TWENTY-ONE

After the ball lanterns flew out, the pressure intensified again. Lyssa jumped backward instinctively. A flash preceded two fireballs blasting from near the roof behind the column. The fireballs curved mid-flight to head straight toward her. A leap to the side saved her from a direct hit, and the spells exploded in bright flashes. The shockwave knocked her off her feet and disrupted her wraith form. She jumped up, growling.

Whatever doubts she'd had about her conversation partner being a rogue vanished. Honest Torches didn't attempt to murder other Torches with surprise attacks.

Flickering light spilled from the top of the column. The Sorceress responsible for the attack floated away from the back of the column and revealed herself. A bright aura surrounded her.

Four flaming wings extended from her back, and white-hot jets of fire flowed down from the tips, supporting her in the air. Her regalia consisted of a loose high-slit dress dominated by red with patches of saffron and yellow throughout, marking out glyphs. A golden mask covered the top of her face, leaving patches of her smooth brown skin exposed. Her glowing yellow- and red-streaked hair fluttered as if it were in a wind, resembling the flames behind her. Gold bangles adorned her ankles, and gold bracelets ran up half her arms.

There was no mistaking her. It was Aisha Khatri the Fire Deva, bearer of the Flame Goddess regalia. Of all the people Lyssa had expected to run into when hunting a rogue, Aisha was at the absolute bottom of the list.

This couldn't be happening. Even Lyssa's luck couldn't be that bad. She'd had issues with Aisha in the past, but she couldn't believe the woman had turned a family feud into a betrayal of the Society.

She didn't want to believe it, but Aisha had tossed fireballs at her. The evidence was in.

Aisha's earlier spells had killed most of the ground-floor darkness in the warehouse. Wraith form or thinning would be risky anyway because of her guided fireballs and the concentration required. The woman knew Lyssa's capabilities far too well. This would be a hard fight.

"I recommend maximum force," Jofi said. "Miss Khatri has already demonstrated an extreme willingness to kill you. Given your previous encounters, you should take her threat seriously."

"Yeah. Not planning to blow her off." Lyssa threw her batons to the ground and drew her guns, then backed up slowly, keeping them trained on the Sorceress hovering above her. "We don't have to do this, Fire Deva," she called. "You haven't done anything you can't take back. Don't be an idiot."

Avoiding real names might encourage Aisha to do the same. Lyssa didn't know who was listening. This could end with her convincing Aisha to see the folly of her actions or a brutal fight, but thinking ahead wouldn't hurt.

"Do you know what it is like to be lucky, Hecate?" Aisha laughed. "To find you of all people, you daughter of thieving cats, here. I'm truly blessed. It's like you've been delivered to me, complete with an excuse to kill you."

"Don't you think tossing fireballs and lanterns around is going to attract interest from the Shadow cops? Whatever twisted excuses you have, you start hurting them, and you're going to get an Eclipse on your ass."

Aisha shook her head. "There's a sound-swallowing shard outside this room. It's on the back of the column. How could you of all people not know? Pathetic."

Lyssa frowned. She hadn't noticed it, but she hadn't tested for sound and hadn't been alert for a different type of shard. She also wasn't the rogue helping the scum. Why would Aisha expect her to know about that?

Damn it. Aisha had set things up too well. Lyssa wasn't surprised. The woman might have a temper, and she was letting revenge guide her down a dangerous path, but she wasn't an idiot.

"We all have things that slip by us." Lyssa chuckled. "But I don't like the part where you tried to kill me. This doesn't have to happen. I don't want to kill a Sorceress, but you're really pushing my buttons."

Aisha rapidly chanted something in Sanskrit. Her wings vanished and she dropped to the ground, smoke rising from the concrete floor beneath her feet. A pulse of sorcery preceded the appearance of a hazy, wavering field around

209

her, flecked with bright sparks of red and white. A ball of flame hovered in her palm.

"I see you're still using guns." Aisha scoffed. Her voice dripped contempt. "Are you Illuminated, or are you a Shadow who has to rely on such tools?" She chuckled, but there was no mirth in the sound. "It fits your essence perfectly."

"Yeah, nothing says Shadow like enchanted guns with a bound spirit. You got me. I'm so sorry, O So Great Flame Deva."

"Excuses." Aisha scoffed. "Typical for someone like you. Typical for a Corti."

Lyssa kept her distance, slowly walking in a circle while Aisha did the same. This wasn't some idiot gangster playing with her first shard. Aisha was a trained Torch with an essence that lent itself to combat.

But she'd also given up Lyssa's family name. Time to return the favor.

"There have been darkness essences in the Khatri family, too," Lyssa said.

"Not like you," Aisha shouted. "Your soul is as dark as your essence. You have no standards. No true pride."

"By the way, you're not the only one surprised to see someone," Lyssa said. "I suspected I'd run into someone eventually, but you? Whoa, boy. I didn't see that one coming."

Aisha tossed her fireball from one hand to the other. "A thief from a family of thieves. Of course you'd end up here. In that sense, this was inevitable."

"Screw you," Lyssa growled. "You can call me what you want, but you don't disrespect my family. I don't talk trash about the Khatris, even though you've ridden my ass for years."

"Your thieving mother took the Night Goddess!" Aisha shouted. "When it had been in my family for generations!"

"Really? We're going to do this now?" Lyssa scoffed. "This is what you want to talk about, with everything else that's going on?"

"Why shouldn't we discuss it?" Aisha asked. "Don't you understand what this is? What's going on?"

"I see someone who can't let go of an unfounded decades-old grudge, who I'm trying to stop from making an even worse mistake."

"No." Aisha shook her head. "It's fate guiding us together. Fate granting me a gift. I can't punish your dead mother for my family, but I *can* punish her daughter with the knowledge of my virtue."

Virtue? How could she talk about virtue when she was helping shard-smugglers? Lyssa was done with the self-indulgence, especially since Aisha had insulted her mother.

Her jaw tightened, and her heart thundered in her chest. She wouldn't be able to hold back much longer, Sorceress or not.

"She didn't steal crap!" she yelled. "The Night Goddess didn't reject her. It didn't reject me. Your family doesn't own this regalia. No one gets to declare dibs on a regalia. Stop being an idiot."

Aisha sneered. One advantage of her half-mask was that she could get her facial expressions across a lot easier than Lyssa.

"Is that your excuse for how far you've fallen?" Aisha

asked. "It won't matter. Once I kill you here, my family will reclaim it in the next generation."

"What makes you think I'm going to be so easy to kill?" Lyssa closed on the crates and the column. Cover could make a big difference in combat. "Don't get cocky, bitch. You're not the only Torch in this room."

"A Sorceress who has to use the tools of the non-Illuminated is one who is not confident about her abilities," Aisha replied. "I will destroy you."

Lyssa hoped to talk Aisha into surrendering by appealing to her pride and honor. At the least, she hoped she could get the woman to leave.

A Khatri, let alone Aisha, being a rogue didn't make sense. They were a proud line that had produced great Sorcerers and Sorceresses for centuries. Working with criminal scum to smuggle shards when she already had wealth, status, and influence was insane. Aisha had always been competitive, but it was hard to believe it would come to this.

"Don't diss the guns." Lyssa waved one. "The best Sorceresses work smarter, not harder. This is your last chance not to do something stupid. You didn't hit me, so I'll let it go. I can't speak for anyone else." She stopped behind an empty crate near the column. "But that's the limit of my tolerance."

"Others? You dare speak of others? They won't matter if you're dead." Aisha brought her arm back, the fireball floating above it. "You honestly think you can beat me?"

"I've got more experience, and I've beat you before."

"In sparring, not a real battle."

"Your current ammo load is insufficient to defeat her," Jofi said. "I recommend higher-powered rounds."

"I'm trying to convince her to give this up, not put her more on edge," Lyssa whispered. "She can still plead for mercy. I don't know why she'd involve herself in this, but she *is* a Khatri. Samuel might think I don't give a crap, but I do understand a little bit about Society politics."

Aisha snorted. "Appealing to your spirit for help won't save you, Hecate. Time to burn the trash."

CHAPTER TWENTY-TWO

With a shout, Aisha threw the fireball. The dangerous spell screamed toward Lyssa, but she spun behind the column, avoiding the attack. The fireball crashed to the floor, scorching the concrete and producing a fountain of fiery sparks.

It was a beautiful sight, like a firework. Too bad Aisha was trying to kill Lyssa.

Aisha threw up her hands and chanted rapidly under her breath. Burning blasts ripped from her hands in streams, pelting and blackening the column. "I've always thought you were a degenerate, but I held out some hope for you. Killing you is a mercy. You should thank me."

"And I always thought you were a crazy bitch," Lyssa replied. "You're only proving me right."

Aisha couldn't maintain the stream for long. Lyssa just needed to wait for her chance.

When the stream of fiery death stopped, Lyssa burst from behind the column and opened fire with both pistols. The bullets struck the shield surrounding Aisha, vaporizing in a sizzling, sputtering mass that left molten lead burning the floor. Not unexpected, but still annoying.

Lyssa retreated behind the column as Aisha tossed another fireball her way. It exploded against the column and blasted out a small chunk. A blanket of heat wrapped around Lyssa. Aisha wasn't playing around.

"You won't be able to hold back," Jofi calmly noted. "She will kill you if this continues."

"Gee, thanks for the update, Great Spirit Lord of the Obvious," Lyssa snapped. "But I have to play this smart. Her damned shield will take out my rounds before their spells can go off."

"Come now, Hecate," Aisha shouted. "Are you going to let me roast you there without showing your face?"

Two more fireballs chipped away at the column. By staying there, Lyssa risked Aisha blowing out the entire column and bringing down part of the roof. She was hoping the woman would be exhausted before she destroyed the building.

A loud boom shook the room. Aisha jetted to the side, propelled by flames shooting out of her feet and gaining line-of-sight on her opponent. Lyssa sprinted toward the wall, trying to keep pace with Aisha's rocket-girl act.

One advantage of Lyssa not being obliged to use only sorcery in a fight was not having to worry about exhausting her power. The flashier the spell without a careful ritual, the more tiring it was. It didn't take a lot of strength to pull a trigger.

Lyssa fired a couple of times at Aisha but didn't stop moving. The bullets didn't make it through, but all they needed to do was throw off the aim of the other Sorceress.

Fireballs sputtered toward Lyssa in an erratic line. Her quick movements kept them from hitting her. Even a second's pause would end with her taking a direct blast. The attacks might be missing her, but their intense heat passed over her, a reminder of what waited if Aisha hit her.

Lyssa continued her run, seeking out decent cover that could survive more than a single fireball. Aisha continued walking explosions across a concrete wall, leaving a trail of scorch marks.

Aisha's aim became less precise when Lyssa shifted to serpentine movement. Pallets near her exploded in showers of burning wood.

Lyssa offered a silent prayer of thanks that the walls were concrete. She didn't want to fight Aisha while they were trapped in a conflagration. There were already enough burning pieces of wood to give the flame Sorceress the advantage.

This strategy couldn't continue. Jofi was right; Aisha was going all out. Lyssa needed to repay her in kind. She also needed a couple of seconds to prepare.

"Stop delaying the inevitable," Aisha yelled. "There is dignity in accepting your death at my hands. I will listen to your end formally if you wish."

"How about a big no?" Lyssa called.

She vaulted over a large yellow forklift. The machine took the brunt of the next few attacks before she landed in a roll and popped back up. She ducked, shoving one of her guns into her holster before reaching into a pocket.

Quick ammo changes required good muscle memory, something Lyssa had taken advantage of in Las Vegas and was now taking advantage of in Midland. She brought along the same types of ammo on jobs, and each had its designated pocket.

A magazine wrapped in red tape came out with her hand. She ejected the current magazine and reloaded her pistol in one smooth motion, caught the half-empty mag filled with normal bullets, and shoved it into another pocket. She never wanted a fight to be lost because she was out of ammo.

Aisha stopped her Saturn V impression and dropped to the floor before launching another wide fire blast that spread over the side of the forklift. Her breathing had become ragged. "You can't run forever, Hecate. It's your poor luck. Darkness is nothing before light and fire. I'm a true Torch. I will burn the impurities from this world, starting with you."

Lyssa grimaced. Aisha sure liked to talk. Was that what she sounded like to the men she took down?

"You're insane," Lyssa shouted. "This doesn't have to happen."

"It has been inevitable since the days of our birth."

Lyssa popped up. Aisha was ready for her. A fireball ripped from her palm. A round from Lyssa went wide and struck the ground. The enchanted round exploded, staggering Aisha, but her fireball did its part by hitting Lyssa's side.

The blast knocked Lyssa to the floor and left a blackened hole in her shirt and her mesh vest red-hot. She grabbed the forklift and pulled herself off the ground, ignoring the pain in her side. She was glad she'd taken the time to mostly heal before heading to Midland.

Aisha shook her head and raised her hands. Lyssa had

already steadied her gun on the back of the forklift. Four lightning-fast trigger pulls placed explosive rounds in a square around the fire Sorceress.

The explosions knocked Aisha about like a petal in a hurricane. She grunted, her mouth twisting in pain before she fell to one knee. With a shout of defiance, she shot off the ground, flames trailing from her feet and palms.

"That's annoying," Lyssa shouted.

Her follow-up shots missed. They struck high on a wall, raining concrete on the hard floor.

Lyssa gritted her teeth. She'd known Aisha for years, and the flame Sorceress got better each time they fought. Before, it had always stopped at overenthusiastic sparring. Aisha might leave Lyssa no choice but to use her ultimate bullet, the showstopper.

Fire rained from above. Explosions burst around Lyssa as she jerked, sprinted, and danced to avoid the attacks. Cement dust puffed up in clouds. Dark smoke drifted upward. She kept waiting for an alarm or a sprinkler.

Lyssa replied with another four shots, making sure to count them. Her attacks missed the flying Sorceress and blew pieces out of the roof. Falling debris forced Aisha to dive toward the floor. Aisha's fire shields could burn away all threats, but only so many and only so quickly. It was time to remind Aisha that bullets weren't the only trick in Lyssa's arsenal.

She pointed a finger on her free hand and concentrated. A small inky cloud grew on the tip and shot toward Aisha. The spell struck the floor and expanded for several yards, swallowing both the Sorceress and one of her nearby lantern spells in a juddering mass of darkness.

Lyssa allowed herself a triumphant grin. She'd hadn't won, but she was forcing Aisha to meet her tempo.

Repeats of the same spell cloaked that portion of the warehouse floor in impenetrable darkness but tired Lyssa. The blinded Sorceress' eyes widened in concern as she jerked her head back and forth. Flaming jets blasted from her hands and feet and launched her into the air.

Lyssa could see through the spell, thanks to her regalia. She followed Aisha's flight arc with her gun and aimed for her landing spot, firing another exploding round.

Aisha landed in a crouch, but Lyssa's explosion sent her careening through the air. She landed hard on her back, her head cracking against the concrete. She cried out in pain.

Lyssa boxed Aisha in again by shooting all around her. The combined blasts propelled Aisha into the air. She crashed to the floor again, bloodied, burned, and her regalia filled with tears and holes. The attacks had cleared out most of the darkness.

After loading her last magazine of explosive bullets, Lyssa pointed her gun at Aisha. The other Sorceress stood, swaying, and wiped blood off her split lip. She extended her arm, and a blazing sword of bright white flame appeared.

"I'll die before I surrender to a degenerate like you, Hecate." Aisha spat blood and gestured for Lyssa to attack. "You disgrace our kind by selling shards to criminal scum. You're the opposite of what a Torch should stand for, friend. I'll exchange my life for yours, so at least this travesty ends with you."

"Wait." Lyssa kept her gun pointed at Aisha even as her

mind swirled in confusion. "I'm not the one helping some gangster shipping service spew out shards to the entire Southwest. That's *you*."

The anger on Aisha's face remained, but she didn't release her spells. "You're claiming you don't work for the scum?"

"No!" Lyssa snorted. "Of course not. I came here on a tip from an informant to find the smugglers. Next thing I know, you show up and try and kill me."

"Why should I believe you?" Some of the arrogance had drained from Aisha's voice.

Lyssa grimaced. "Because it's the damned truth, you crazy zealot. Now this is all making sense. I couldn't figure out how you of all people would end up working for these bastards. I might have issues with you and your family, but I couldn't buy that you'd smuggle shards with the help of Shadows."

"Why did you attack me then?" Aisha asked.

"Because you were tossing fireballs at me," Lyssa shouted. She groaned. "It's called self-defense."

Aisha wrinkled her nose. The light of her flaming sword gave her a face a sinister cast. "A likely story."

"Think about it. Do you think I'd work for criminals? Or can you accept, for at least a few minutes, that you let your hatred run wild, and you made a bad call?"

"Don't trust her," Jofi said. "That was lethal intent."

"I'm not happy about what went down," Lyssa whispered, "but I'm not going to kill a Torch if she made an honest mistake. Well, a mistake, anyway."

Aisha was an annoying pest and had been from their first meeting ten years ago. The then-twelve-year-old

Aisha had kicked the twenty-year-old Lyssa in the shin and called her a thieving cat. At the time, Lyssa had been as impressed as she was annoyed.

That shin-kicking little girl had grown into a skilled young woman and a powerful Torch. When she wasn't attempting to murder Lyssa, she was good at her job. They might never be friends, but they could at least be colleagues.

Lyssa took a deep breath. Time to gamble with her life. She lowered her gun but kept her attention focused on Aisha, ready to dodge.

Aisha watched Lyssa with suspicion before chuckling and waving her arm. The sword disappeared.

"No's one dead." Aisha sniffed. "My mistake."

CHAPTER TWENTY-THREE

Lyssa holstered her weapon and stared, dumbfounded, at the other Sorceress. Relief warred with irritation and pain. "A mistake? You almost turned me into fried Hecate!"

"Yes, and I stopped. You don't have to be so petty about it. And I believe it would have been baked or roasted in this case. There was no oil involved." Aisha smirked and wiped more blood off her mouth. "When I saw you here, I assumed you'd come with shards for the scum. You can't blame me for how suspicious you looked."

"A mistake is drinking the last pop in the refrigerator without asking me. It's not trying to kill me. You can at least say, 'Hey, Hecate, I'm sorry I jumped to conclusions and almost killed you. Sorry I almost made you use a powerful obliteration spell.'"

Aisha scoffed. "You wounded me. I wounded you. It's your fault for interfering in my investigation and showing up at the exact place the criminals are using as a base. I'll admit to jumping to conclusions, but given your family history, you can hardly blame me."

"Interfering with *your* investigation?" Lyssa glared at Aisha. "Has your heat finally fried your brain? I was assigned to investigate how the criminals in Phoenix got their shards, with an official EAA contract sanctioned by Elder Samuel. What, you think I have so little to do that I just decided to take a trip to Midland and roust criminals?"

Aisha narrowed her eyes. She placed her hands on her hips and glared back at Lyssa. "I was assigned by Elder Theodora to investigate rumors of shard-smuggling out of Texas."

Lyssa ground her teeth. Torches technically didn't have territories, though the Elders encouraged them to move around to ensure there was at least one within theoretical striking distance of most places of significant population and not too many in any one area. That had been one of the main motivations for Samuel's suggestion that Lyssa move to Phoenix from San Diego.

The Elders, however, did have distinct areas of responsibility, including the eight Elders assigned to North America. Samuel's area included the southwestern United States and northwestern Mexico.

The problem was where those territories met and overlapped. The Society only marginally cared about Shadow geopolitical lines, and it wasn't as if Elders ruled their territories like medieval nobles. They were focused on the safety of the Illuminated in their territories and making sure that nothing was happening that might threaten the Society.

An Illuminated who wasn't a Torch or an Eclipse rarely had to deal with Elders. Theory implied Elders should be able to coordinate to handle problems.

Lyssa had never been sure if that idea was aspirational or a way for ambitious Elders to excuse certain actions in border areas. From what she'd heard and read, this had been a problem back to the Post-Cataclysm years. A problem that wasn't fixed after thousands of years was never getting fixed.

Before M-Day, it'd been less of an issue. Torches were rarely deployed for needs outside of direct Society business, and there was more careful coordination. No one wanted to risk exposing the world of sorcery. Now, with Torches taking on Shadow threats, things had become murkier.

Midland lay on the border of Samuel's and Theodora's territory. Lyssa could see where the mistake might happen, but there was one thing that bothered her about the whole situation—something that felt wrong on a deeper level.

"And Theodora didn't bother to mention it to Samuel?" Lyssa asked. "Or the EAA?"

Had Samuel not bothered to mention it to her? It would make sense to have more than one Torch working a big, politically sensitive case, but Lyssa and Aisha had gotten in each other's way because their Elders hadn't told them everything. They had been lucky the night didn't end with one less Sorceress in the world.

Aisha shrugged, looking unconcerned. "This isn't an EAA contract. This was an order directly from Elder Theodora. She preferred that the Shadows be kept ignorant about this, but I suppose you and Elder Samuel have made that difficult by involving the American government."

Lyssa hissed. Flagging adrenaline allowed the pain of

her injuries to pierce her consciousness. Getting blasted by flame sorcery at close range was never enjoyable, even with her defenses. Smug demeanor aside, the cuts and burns on Aisha proved she wasn't in much better shape, and they might need to be ready for more action soon.

"You know what?" Lyssa threw a hand in the air. "Who cares? Now we know. We're both working this case, and I know you like me about as much as a thieving cat likes water, but we both have the same goal in the end: stopping those shards from getting into the wrong hands."

Aisha tried to fold her arms but grimaced as she rubbed her wounds. "You have a point. It's rare for you to have one, but I won't deny anything you've said."

Lyssa reached into a pocket and pulled out her small baggie filled with painkiller petals. She put one in her mouth and swallowed before offering one to Aisha. "It's not healing. It's for pain. I'm saving the healing ones until I have a better idea of what comes next."

The other Sorceress eyed the petal with a faint frown before snatching it out of Lyssa's palm and downing it with a delicate swallow. "It's from your foster mother, I presume?"

"Yeah." Lyssa let out a sigh of relief as her aches faded. "I know you hate me, but at least you respect Tricia."

She realized the reason Aisha had dared to use her family name before. There was no reason to hide names if they were inside a sound shield. That reminded Lyssa of another open question.

"Did you put the shard up there?" she asked, gesturing above.

"No," Aisha replied.

Lyssa waved smoke out of her face and coughed. The fight had been short enough and there was enough concrete around to stop the area from burning out of control, but there were still crates and pallets on fire.

"You going to do something about that?" Lyssa gestured at them. "They probably disabled the sprinkler so they can test shards that blow things up, but I'd rather not choke to death, and you're not immune to smoke either."

Aisha raised her hands. She walked toward a burning crate. The flames flowed away from the crate toward her palms, leaving a charred, smoking mess. They formed a burning fireball in her hand before disappearing in a flash of light.

She repeated the process until every fire was out, apart from a single lantern spell. With a flick of her wrist, she set it to orbiting her.

"Wait." Lyssa frowned. "I'm not trying to accuse you of anything, but how did you know about the sound-eating shard?"

"I paid attention when I walked into this room from the front instead of sneaking in like you and not taking in my environment." Aisha scoffed, this time successfully folding her arms. "This is the worst part about you, Corti. You always act as if I'm a fool. I'm a trained Torch. I passed the Trials too, you know."

"You're hot-headed, not a fool." Lyssa shrugged. "But sometimes those categories blur."

"Don't make me burn you again, Corti."

"Wait a sec. You walked in the front?" Lyssa's gaze flicked to double doors leading to a hallway and the front of the building.

"Yes." Aisha offered a condescending smile. "I borrowed some potions. One hypnotized the guard. It made the whole thing rather easy."

Lyssa barked a laugh. "You hypnotized him? I thought you always said that kind of spell was for weaklings. I'd kill to have something that useful."

"Of course you would. You like to skulk about like a black cat."

"What about cameras?" Lyssa asked. "You figure out a way to make cameras drink potions?"

Aisha shrugged. "I had him shut them off and erase the portion where I came in."

"That could have alerted someone off-site," Lyssa said.

"Do you see anyone other than me?" Aisha gestured around.

Lyssa rolled her eyes. "You still need to learn to ask questions before you blast away, but progress is progress. Aisha Khatri not burning down everything in sight. What a miracle! You're learning self-control. What about the cameras after you left the front?"

"There are blind spots. I made sure he explained them to me in detail."

"Good job." Lyssa rubbed her chin in thought. "Then we haven't lost the element of surprise against the Lone Five Stars."

"I don't need your praise. I'm a competent Torch."

There was a hint of satisfaction in the younger woman's voice. At thirty years old and with twelve years' experience as a Torch, Lyssa had eight years of both chronological age and job time over Aisha. On some level, she wanted Lyssa's approval.

The Khatri-Corti feud had mostly been a one-way affair, and Lyssa had never been sure of the best way to handle it. Her mother had largely ignored it, and it hadn't boiled over to more than occasional verbal abuse and the shin kick until Aisha had come of age and taken the Flame Goddess regalia.

Lyssa had already cycled through different potential solutions. Beating Aisha down in the past during sparring sessions hadn't helped. Trying to reach out directly hadn't helped since Aisha had insisted Lyssa first admit her mother was a thief. At least now, Aisha was only trying to kill Lyssa when she thought she had a legitimate Torch excuse. That wasn't progress, but it wasn't backsliding.

Aisha might think of Lyssa as a thief from a family of thieves, but it was hard for Lyssa not to think of the other Sorceress as a bratty, ultra-violent pyromaniac younger sister. In some other life, where the Khatris had kept the Night Goddess, maybe they could have been closer.

Lyssa blew out a breath. "Now that we're done with the Khatri-Corti Violence Hour and we know there's at least one shard in here, why don't we look for more?"

"I've already done that." Aisha pointed to the column. "I searched this area for two hours before your arrival."

"Of course, you did. That makes sense. Otherwise, I would have spotted you going inside." Lyssa nodded slowly. "That means you were here during the shift change."

"I had *two* potions." Aisha smiled.

Lyssa furrowed her brow. "I was only able to spot one guard on duty from the outside. Are there more?"

"There's only the one now." Aisha's tone dripped smugness. "I think they're overconfident about their security or reputation."

"There's another possibility," Jofi offered.

"I know," she whispered.

Aisha wrinkled her nose. "Relying on a spirit is a type of weakness too. I won't ask what it's saying. I honestly don't care."

Lyssa gave Aisha a tight smile. There was petulance in the woman's tone that made Lyssa think she cared far more than she let on. They didn't have time to get lost in petty bickering or more sorcery duels.

"You've been searching the place for a while," Lyssa replied. "You might be an annoying pain in the ass, but you're thorough."

"Get to the point, Corti."

"Even inactive, you'd sense something from the shards if you were close enough. That means they're probably not here, other than the sound-swallowing bad boy. That would be part of their standard defenses."

Lyssa walked toward the column. A tiny straw doll hung from a string looped around a small stub. She concentrated and raised an arm, and a long, shadowy tentacle extended up. Her new shadow limb grasped the doll and yanked it down. She caught it in her palm and shoved it into a pocket. After a moment of consideration, she pulled the doll out and tossed it on the floor.

Aisha glared at her. "Have you lost your mind? You're going to leave it here for the criminals?"

"I'm under an EAA contract. It'll help things along if they process all the shards before they hand them back. We can have them pick it up."

"It's a waste of time to involve Shadows when we don't need to, and we might not be able to contact them until this is all over. There's no guarantee the Lone Five Stars will continue to use this facility. I might have put out the fires, but the damage is obvious."

Lyssa considered that before concluding, much to her annoyance, that Aisha was right. She knelt and stuffed the doll back into her pocket, then tapped her forehead with a smile, channeling her inner Samuel as a weapon. "I'll be handing this over eventually so they can process it. You need to think about the future. We have to establish an equilibrium of coexistence with the Shadows. Little things like this might help."

Aisha scoffed. Her gaze moved to a scorched wall clock. "Do what you want. I'll go get the guard. I haven't interrogated him yet, and his rounds will bring him by this place soon. I had him ignore this area, thinking he'd already checked it. The effects of the potion won't last forever."

"This doesn't have to be a big deal. He might not know anything. Let's keep this short and to the point.

"How do we do that?" Aisha asked, sounding doubtful.

"All we need to ask him for is the name and address of whoever is most likely to know where the shards are coming in. If he claims he doesn't know about them, we ask about special cargo." Lyssa shrugged. "Easy." She lifted a hand and cloaked it in darkness. "After that, I'll handle it if necessary."

"You're going to kill him?" Aisha asked, raising an eyebrow.

"Of course not." Lyssa lowered her hand. "I might not

have a handy hypnosis potion, but I can put them to sleep just fine."

Aisha snickered. "I can do that."

"Using the spell will last longer, and it hurts them less. We're supposed to avoid unnecessary pain and death unless our lives are directly in danger, remember?"

Aisha snorted. "These are criminal scum."

"Maybe." Lyssa shrugged. "But we shouldn't make too many assumptions."

"Do what you want with your otherwise inferior power," Aisha said and looked away.

"Let me get my batons, and let's go have a chat."

CHAPTER TWENTY-FOUR

After convincing the guard to leave the cameras disabled and putting him to sleep, the two Sorceresses strolled out the front door and walked away from the warehouse, still clad in full regalia. Even with their damage, it would have been an impressive sight if it weren't a deserted industrial area in the middle of the night with no one to see.

"Where are we going?" Jofi asked.

Lyssa blinked. She'd followed Aisha without thinking. The other woman had been confident while walking out of the building, but it wasn't like their new target, a man named Chad Sellers, lived across the street.

The guard had given them the name, address, and directions, along with a cheerful confirmation that Chad would know where everything was. He was *important*, the guard insisted, far more important than anyone responsible for watching the warehouse at night.

Aisha strolled into an alley and headed toward a dumpster. Lyssa followed, unsure of what was going on until Aisha ducked behind the large metal box.

Flames enveloped her body. A short black skirt, a blue top, and calf-high boots replaced her dramatic regalia. She pulled her mask off and folded it into a tiny square before palming it.

Lyssa transformed her regalia into jeans, a t-shirt, and a black leather jacket. Her cuts and burns remained. Someone stumbling across them might think they'd gotten into a nasty fight in the alley, and that wasn't far from the truth.

Lyssa cleared her throat. "Uh, Jofi pointed something out to me."

"What?"

"Where are we going, exactly?"

"I have a car I rented under a false identity." Aisha nodded at the other end of the alley. "It's around the corner. I'll have to drive to the location to interrogate Sellers. I'd rather not wait for him to arrive at the warehouse."

"That's okay. I'll revert to being the full Night Goddess and get my bike." Lyssa peered at her. "I don't know why or how the Elders got their wires crossed on this, but neither of us is the kind of person who's going to back off, and I think we both want this over with as quickly as possible. Two Torches can clear out a bunch of shard-users a lot faster than one. Whatever happens with Sellers, I doubt this situation will end with the gangsters apologizing and promising nicely never to do it again."

"I don't need your…" Aisha sighed in exasperation. "You're right. The good of the Society must be placed above my desires. You can help me. You're good for a few things, Corti, even if you're a thief."

"Will you shut up about that already?" Lyssa glared at

Aisha, not wanting to repeat the old, tired fight. "Even if my mom hadn't chosen the Night Goddess and even if the regalia had rejected her, it wouldn't have mattered to you. There was no one in your family at that time or in your generation with a compatible essence. No one stole anything."

"That's not the point." Aisha sounded more sullen than angry. "It should have waited for a Khatri. The tradition should have been maintained."

"Well, it didn't happen. Get over it before you make another mistake like tonight." Lyssa waved a hand dismissively. "Park up the street from the address since you can't hide your car like I can my bike."

"I'm not an idiot, Corti."

"No, but you do impulsive crap that raises my blood pressure. The sooner we get this job over with, the sooner we can go back to hating each other."

CHAPTER TWENTY-FIVE

Fifteen minutes later, Lyssa and Aisha were hidden in the shadow of an empty house a couple of blocks down the street from Chad Seller's place. They had confirmation of the man's appearance from a local news article on Lyssa's phone. They had no way of confirming the guard's story, but the details rang true, especially the way the guard kept referring to Chad as "important" and "one of the boss's favorites."

Illuminated Society Torches weren't cops. They were trained in combat to execute the lethal will of the Society when diplomacy wasn't an option. Giving governments the ability to hire them was a way of keeping the Illuminated independent while letting Shadows feel like they had some control over sorcery.

Neither woman was there to take down the Lone Five Stars, and they didn't care about the organization outside of the shard-smuggling. Once they solved that problem, the criminals could go back to being the concern of the FBI and the police. However, Lyssa would enjoy weakening them along the way.

Aisha and Lyssa downed some healing herbs before setting out. The effects were far from instantaneous, but between the painkiller and the healing herbs, they were both ready for another battle. Operating at reduced capability wouldn't hurt them as much when there were two of them working together.

Lyssa had never thought she'd end up with Aisha as a partner on a job. She had to applaud the universe's sense of humor.

An earlier sweep by Chad's place in wraith form had netted intel at the cost of irritation. Unlike the sprawling Alvarez estate, Sellers lived in a wide, modest ranch house that didn't look like it could hold an entire army. The man hadn't bothered putting a fence in the front yard.

The lack of exterior security would have played to Lyssa's strengths on most nights, but the lights were on and men were gathered at the house, drinking beer and chatting. They were visible through the half-raised curtains. She didn't spot any weapons, but she had no doubt they were there.

Lyssa related all this to Aisha. "We're on the clock on this, so we might have to be more aggressive than I'd like."

"They could have shards," Jofi said. "Exercise caution."

Aisha eyed Lyssa with more than her usual distrust. "I don't dislike a direct approach, but what brought on this sudden courage?"

"You put out the fires, but we left obvious signs of a fight in the warehouse," Lyssa said. "You were right about why we couldn't leave the shard, and the guard's going to wake up eventually, too. Even if he decides there was a good reason he fell asleep when he goes into the back, he won't need to be Sherlock Holmes to figure out something happened, and it involves sorcery. And that's assuming the next shift doesn't show up and find him." She gestured at the house. "We have a narrow window to accomplish what we need to do."

"You do have a small point." Aisha sounded disappointed, but a cruel smile followed. "Then we don't bother with tricks. We make them surrender." She conjured a dancing flame in her palm. "We cow them with force."

"Yeah, that's the idea. If not, we beat them down until Sellers is the only one left conscious." Lyssa patted one of her holsters. "This is a time when subtlety is for suckers. I think if we strike hard and fast, we can find Sellers and get him to spill what he knows. The only problem is, I don't want to get tangled up with the local cops." She grinned. "But I've got an idea about that."

"Is it a decent one?" Aisha raised an eyebrow in question.

"It's an idea." Lyssa pulled the doll out of her pocket. "Didn't you notice along the way, Little Miss Great Ears?"

Aisha stared at the door, then looked around, her eyes darting in all directions. "Ah. It's still working."

"Exactly." Lyssa grinned. "Let me sneak up to the front door and slip our little buddy in. Then, we'll go around the back and make ourselves heard. If it can cover that entire warehouse floor, it can cover this house."

"What if they run?" Aisha asked.

"They won't. We're going to trick them." Lyssa grinned. "We're going to yell that we're bounty hunters, and they'll get cocky and come for us. By the time they realize what's going on, it'll be too late."

"I like this plan." Aisha rubbed her hands together.

"Good. Let's talk about signals and get into position."

Cloaked, Lyssa hurried up the cement steps to the porch. She cast an occasional glance at the front windows. Sellers downed the rest of a bottle of beer before gesturing around with the empty bottle. His men laughed at an unheard joke, no one noticing anything going on outside.

There had to be a border to the doll's silencing effect, but Lyssa had gotten lucky, and it wasn't revealed to the men inside. She approached the front door and set the doll in a corner.

Between the obvious internet-enabled doorbell and camera, she was being recorded, but she doubted if anyone was watching the live feed. Taking on criminals was part of the contract. Any complaining police could be redirected to take it up with the EAA and explain why they were allowing a major criminal gang to operate in their jurisdiction.

Lyssa took a deep breath and moved her hand away from the doll. She waited and counted to five in her head for any reaction.

Nothing happened. Step one was complete.

She wasn't used to working with anyone other than

Jofi. Aisha's willingness to go along with her plan without trying to take over had surprised Lyssa a little.

Lyssa stood and jogged off the porch and around the corner, dropping her cloak as she approached the backyard. There might be no fence in front, but Sellers had a high stucco-covered cinder block privacy fence protecting his backyard and pool from attention.

She couldn't have gotten away with that at her house. Maybe his HOA was afraid of him. She chuckled and realized she was getting used to life in Scottsdale.

Such thoughts could wait. She was in position for stage two.

Lyssa gave her best owl hoot impression, then winced. The noise came out more like a vuvuzela than the bird. After all the hoots she'd heard that night, it was an embarrassing effort.

Accuracy aside, the call did its work. A flash came from behind the fence before Aisha flew over it and landed in the soft grass. She hurried toward Lyssa, and the women took up positions on either side of the door. Aisha moved well, considering the only light in the yard was spilling out from under the closed kitchen blinds.

"You can go first," Aisha whispered.

"Oh?" Lyssa asked. "Giving me the glory?"

Aisha smiled. "I'm using you as bait."

"Whatever gets you through the night." Lyssa inclined her head toward the door. "In that case, you blow the handle, and I'll go in first."

"That's acceptable to me." Aisha lifted her palm and stepped a couple of yards away from the door. "Get ready, Hecate."

Lyssa expanded her batons before adding the strength and knockout spells. "By the way, it takes special training to reach the levels of pure bitch you do. You should be proud."

"From you, that's a compliment. And I know you're not so incompetent as to let a handful of Shadows with toys seriously injure you."

Lyssa grumbled under her breath, unsure of how to take the compliment. "Be careful with your heat shield here. We don't want to burn this place down."

Aisha smiled. "Then we need to make sure we use over-whelming force to subdue them."

"Let's try to keep this from being a massacre. These guys might be scum, but think of the paperwork for the EAA."

Lyssa moved behind Aisha's shoulder and examined the door. It was wood, not metal, and not all that thick from what she could tell. Chad Sellers was relying on his reputation and location to protect him from serious threats.

Her breath caught. "You know what I don't sense?"

"A future life of honor and respect?" Aisha asked.

"Very funny." Lyssa patted her chest. "Nothing other than your spells, and unless I'm wrong, the doll."

Aisha stared into the distance. "You're right. If they have any shards here, they're well-hidden or inactive. That's convenient."

"This is one time they should have kept more of their product. This is going to be easy." Lyssa chuckled. "On three. Ready?"

Aisha gave a curt nod. "Just so you know, if they

attempt to fight seriously with shards, I won't hold back. I don't care about EAA paperwork."

"Try not to kill everyone until we get more leads." Lyssa tapped her batons together once before pulling them apart. "One, two, three!"

A blinding white fireball burst from Aisha's hand and blew the lock and handle apart. Burning wood and red-hot metal shrapnel blasted in all directions. Lyssa didn't wait before kicking in the damaged door.

"Bounty hunters, everyone on their knees with their hands behind their head!" she shouted and charged into the kitchen.

Open chip and pretzel bags covered the table. Empty beer bottles filled the trashcan in front. Although the living room was blocked by a wall, the dining room was visible from the kitchen, as was a man on the phone. He dropped the phone and reached to a table that Lyssa couldn't see, bringing up a gun.

Aisha launched a marble-sized fireball over Lyssa's shoulder. The spell missed Lyssa by inches but was close enough that she could feel the heat before it traveled through the kitchen and struck the man's arm. It burned through his sleeve and scorched the flesh underneath. He screamed and dropped his gun.

Another man ran around the corner from the living room, gun in hand. He raised it but hesitated, his eyes widening in panicked recognition. "They aren't boun—"

Lyssa cracked him across the head. He smacked into the wall and fell to the floor. Two other men rushed around the corner, also armed. She was already near the end of the hallway when they made their appearance.

Her sweeping strikes knocked their guns out of their hands. A follow-up kick sent one man flying before her batons propelled his friend through the drywall in the hall.

"What the hell is going on?" shouted someone from the living room. "Waste those assholes!"

Heavy footfalls sounded from the opposite end of the house. Sellers wasn't among the men she'd taken down. That might be a problem.

Glass crashed. More footfalls followed

"Runners," Lyssa shouted. "It might be him."

"You've got this," Aisha called. "I'll handle the cowards."

"Works for me." Lyssa waited near the front of the hall.

A turn to the left would take her into the living room, and a turn to the right would send her to the other side of the house and the bedrooms. She didn't have time to consider her choices when more men boiled around the corner, not having learned the lessons of their silent friends.

She jabbed a man in the throat with a baton before knocking him back with a kick. He crashed into another man, and they both tumbled to the floor. There weren't many left, given those she'd counted earlier through the window.

Lyssa crouched and took a couple of steps back. She tossed a baton into the air and pointed her hand at the main hallway light above her while imagining crashing inky waves. Shadows spread out like a time-lapse image of fast-growing slime, coating the light and darkening the hallway. She caught the baton.

Low whispers came from the living room, then

gunshots shattered the quiet. Bullets ripped through the wall but missed her.

Lyssa continued backing away before tossing her baton into the air again and smothering another light with darkness. Light from the kitchen and living room spilled in from either end and from the holes in the wall, producing an unnaturally gloomy tunnel in the middle of the house. The remaining survivors continued firing and blasting new holes.

"So much for cowing them with force," she muttered.

"Excessive beatings were also mentioned," Jofi replied.

"True."

Lyssa tucked her batons into her pockets, their extended forms protruding, before coating her hands with an impenetrable dark cloud. She jumped onto the far wall and scuttled along like an angry, vengeful ghost from a Japanese horror movie. At the corner, she jumped off the wall toward another wall in the living room and pulled out her batons mid-flight.

Three men remained in the living room, including Chad Sellers, all cowering on their knees behind an overturned card table. They shot at the leaping Night Goddess, but they didn't land a hit. She kicked off another wall to hurl herself over and past the table, her batons crossed in front of her.

Two powerful backswings knocked out the two men flanking Sellers. He shouted and fired another shot, and the bullet whizzed past her head.

Lyssa crushed his gun hand with a solid blow. Sellers yelped. She kicked the gun toward the wall before it hit the floor. The man winced and clutched his bent fingers.

"Chad Sellers," Lyssa rumbled. "Do you know who I am?"

He nodded quickly. "Hecate. B-but why are you here? Phoenix is damned far away from Midland."

Lyssa pointed a baton at this head. "Too bad your stench reached Arizona. I've got some questions for you."

CHAPTER TWENTY-SIX

A groaning man crashed through the remains of the front door, his upper chest scorched. Aisha strolled in behind him like she was fashionably late for a dinner party. It was over the top, but Lyssa couldn't complain after her horror movie performance earlier.

"Hecate *and* Flame Deva?" Sellers slumped forward. "I've got crap luck. Y'all both came here?"

"When one causes enough trouble," Aisha replied with a sneer, "one attracts appropriate levels of punishment. And you're a big troublemaker, friend."

"How would you like to die, Sellers?" Lyssa asked. "In the dark or in fire? In both? We can accommodate your last wish."

Remaining slumped over and staring at the floor, he shook his head. "This isn't fair, and y'all are blaming the wrong man. I'm not a criminal. I don't deserve to be treated like this in my own home."

"You could have fooled me." Lyssa pointed a baton at an unconscious man. "You have a lot of men with guns here."

"This is Texas." Sellers shrugged. "We have a right to those guns. Y'all have your magic powers. We have guns. Fair is fair."

Aisha scoffed, "smuggling is a crime, even in Texas."

"This is America, and I'm a businessman," Sellers argued, "I move products people want, nothing more. Does that make me a bad guy?"

"Moving products?" Lyssa grew waving tentacles around her head for effect. "Like people?"

"People?" Sellers shook his head. "Go ask the FBI. We don't do that."

Aisha scoffed. "Because you're such honorable men with limits?"

"Because it's more trouble than it's worth." Sellers sat up. "But moving drugs, guns, and that kind of thing? Small, easy, good profits. We help get products to customers. What's so bad about that? If people want them, who am I hurting? Some of the Founding Fathers were smugglers. John Hancock was a smuggler. John Hancock!"

"And you're John Hancock in this situation?" Lyssa snickered. "I think I liked Alvarez's straightforward arrogance better than this self-serving garbage."

Sellers' gaze shifted between Aisha and Lyssa. The panic in his eyes seemed genuine. "We ship products people want. That's all. We haven't stolen from anyone. We're not even making the stuff."

"Well, now, that's an interesting choice of words." Lyssa crouched next to him. She collapsed her batons and tucked them away before reaching out to squeeze his cheeks with her cold, gloved hand. "That means you think we're here because we believe you stole something?"

Seller swallowed. "I can pay you. Whatever you want. I have a lot of money."

A flaming knife burst into existence in Aisha's hand. "Killing you would make the world a better place."

Lyssa squeezed Seller's jaw and pitched her voice lower than the demon bronchitis imitation delivered by her regalia. Interrogations were a lot like negotiations. She needed to give the man a win by letting him think he was improving his situation with each answer. She already knew the most likely answers to her questions, but she wanted him to confirm them by stumbling into them himself.

"You killed a Sorcerer, didn't you?" Lyssa let out a sinister chuckle to cover her doubt. "You got lucky some-how, killed him, and found a bag full of shards. That's not technically stealing. Is that what you're thinking?"

Sellers laughed hysterically and yanked out of her grip. "If I could take one of y'all out so easily, why am I the one on the floor with a bunch of knocked-out guys?" He grimaced and nodded at the unconscious man at the front door. "Is he still alive?"

Aisha pointed the knife at the man. "For now. We'll see what happens over the next few minutes, smuggler."

Lyssa pulled Sellers's head back roughly. "What then? Oh, did you find the Sorcerer dead already? That's it, isn't it? Found a dead Sorc and figured you'd take his things? You figured, what's the harm? Give some Shadows an edge the next time a Torch shows up? Huh? Is that it?"

"I don't ask people what they're going to do with the products." Sellers trembled. "It's not our job to ask. We move product, and we're paid for that. People can do bad things with anything. I read about a guy who stabbed another guy through the eye with a pencil. Y'all going to raid a pencil factory now?"

Lyssa let go, and he fell forward. "Just a middleman, huh?"

"Yeah."

"That's not what I heard."

Sellers swallowed. "Meaning what?"

Lyssa half-closed her eyes and murmured in Phrygian. Sometimes the show could sell the illusion. Shadowy lines crawled up her arm, growing in number over several seconds before covering the whole thing. Oversized dark fingers twitched and contorted at the end, their unnatural angles changing with each passing second. Sellers' eyes became saucers.

Stripped of everything else, fear was about the unknown. A violent criminal who associated with other violent criminals lived a life steeped in death. The loss of life wasn't an unknown, and most in his line of work had inflicted or witnessed it. That experience made it a familiar thing, regrettable but expected on some level.

To terrify such a man, Lyssa needed to expose him to something he didn't know and had no experience with. Chad Sellers might have believed he would die at the end of a gun or knife someday or even imagined he'd die specifically at the end of Hecate's gun, but she doubted he'd ever imagined facing long, contorted shadow fingers that looked like something from a nightmare.

Lyssa moved next to his ear to whisper, "I'll be honest. We don't care about you. We care about the shards, and we know you've been selling them. The word is you're a supplier, not a middleman, but we both know you aren't making them, and I'm willing to bet you didn't find them. You know what I want, Chaddie Boy? What will keep you from getting eaten?"

"What?" he whimpered.

"I need to know where they're coming from. The FBI and EAA may come for you, but you can live through the night with your soul intact. You're not that important to us."

She tried not to laugh. She deserved an Oscar for her performance. She wasn't going to execute a helpless, defeated enemy, but he didn't need to know that.

Aisha watched impassively. The flames of her dagger licked the air.

"W-what happens if I tell you?" Sellers asked. "If I give up my source to y'all, I'm dead anyway."

"How can your source hurt you if we stop them first?" Lyssa stood and tilted her head, the depth of shadow making the angle look more severe. "Tell us the truth and maybe die later, or die now in an awful way. Your choice, but if it were me, I'd choose later."

"I-I don't know where he's getting them." Sellers licked his lips. "He approached me last month, showed me some things, made me an offer. Said he had a good source. I don't know if he's one of you Sorcs. He had a mask on, but he didn't do any magic. I didn't care when I saw what he could get me, but it wasn't a fancy mask like yours. It was just a ski mask."

Aisha lifted the flaming dagger in front of her face. "Interesting story. I almost want to believe you. *Almost.*"

"I'm telling the truth. You have to believe me."

Lyssa frowned. The mask screamed Illuminated, and not every Shadow appreciated how easily they could be disguised. It was time to press harder.

"Where is he?" Lyssa shouted. "Tell us where he is if you want to live."

"I don't know that!" Sellers doubled over again, shaking, cradling his mangled hand, which was starting to turn purple and black. "B-but I know where he's going to be. There's a cargo transfer in Houston tomorrow morning." He glanced at the clock. "I mean this morning. The shards are going to be in a shipping container that's getting offloaded there. I have guys down there to drive a truck and pick it up, but Nelson's guys are the ones who are going to make the transfer."

"Nelson's the masked man?" Lyssa asked.

Sellers gave a shallow nod. "I can give you the exact time of the drop-off. Nelson supervises them all. He's always there, and we've already done a half-dozen drops. He'll be there."

"How do we know you won't call Nelson the second we leave?" Lyssa asked.

"Because you'll kill me."

"True." Lyssa shrugged. "I'm glad you understand your situation."

Admitting she wouldn't do that in cold blood wouldn't help the interrogation, so she let the implication hang in the air. But another idea came that would ensure surprise against the mysterious Nelson.

Lyssa returned her hands to normal and removed the more intimidating aspects of her current appearance. "When is this handoff?"

"It's at 7:00," Sellers said. "And I've got the terminal and cargo container ID." He rattled off the info. "I don't know if he's pulling strings, but there's never a lot of other people there during the handoffs."

Lyssa chuckled and pulled out her phone to tap in the ID. Not exactly the stuff nightmares were made of. "You memorized a container ID?"

Sellers shrugged. "Yeah, so people like you couldn't find it if they were sniffing around. Phones weren't secure even before you Sorcs showed up. And now I'm going to have to sit here and think I'm going to be dead soon."

"Don't worry about any of this." Lyssa reached toward him with her hand outstretched. "By the time you wake up, this will all be over."

Ten minutes later, Lyssa and Aisha stood next to a smoldering pile of phones. Deep-sleep spells had been cast on all the men and their phones incinerated.

The finishing touch was far less impressive, a handwritten sign saying, DO NOT DISTURB UNDER ORDERS OF MR. SELLERS. It was embarrassing.

Lyssa had her doubts it would work, but she wanted to fend off any potential housekeepers who might show up. Random smugglers who had all-night parties must have all sorts of odd quirks their staff was used to. She hoped so, anyway.

"You sure we shouldn't burn down the house?" Aisha cocked her head.

"And guarantee the fire department comes? Not to

mention, these guys might be scum, but we didn't identify ourselves as Torches when we came in, nor do we have an extermination contract for them. Killing them would make things complicated not just for the EAA but for the Society." Lyssa shrugged.

"We could move them all somewhere else and then burn down the house." Aisha smiled. "It would be a nice punishment for this scum."

"Not everything needs to be solved with fire." Lyssa snorted. "Sometimes you have all the subtlety of a nuclear weapon."

"And you walk around in a skull mask, friend." Aisha shook her head. "We only have four hours until the handoff."

"We can both get places fast when we need to, but I can do it without letting every Shadow in five states know. I don't think you can maintain your speed as long as I can on my bike." Lyssa groaned. She didn't like what needed to come next. "You said your car was registered under a fake identity, right?"

"Of course. I don't leave easy trails."

"You leave trails of destruction," Lyssa replied. "The point is, you can leave it here, and it'll eventually end up back where it needs to be. You can't push that whole car with your sorcery for that long."

"But we have some time before the handoff." Aisha's face twisted into a frown.

Lyssa shook her head. "It's better to get there with time to spare so we can get set up."

"We're going to use your non-elegant toy?" Aisha wrinkled her nose in disgust.

Lyssa reached into her pocket to fish out more healing herbs and some stimulant herbs to offset her building fatigue. She would have preferred more time for their regalia and bodies to repair themselves, but it looked as though they were getting a perfect opportunity to end everything.

"Yeah." Lyssa nodded. "We're taking my bike. Get ready to hold on tight."

CHAPTER TWENTY-SEVEN

Lyssa maintained wraith form as she put down her kick-stand. She and Aisha had parked in a pitch-black empty parking lot near a long-closed department store, judging by the sorry state of the sign and the extensive graffiti. Adding Aisha to the ritual hadn't strained Lyssa as much as she'd expected, which made sense upon reflection. The bike weighed a lot more than the lithe flame Sorceress, and it wasn't a thinning spell. The port was twenty minutes away at a reasonable non-enhanced speed.

"Why are we stopping here?" Aisha asked. "Why not go all the way?"

"Because we need to make sure we're both on the same page," Lyssa replied. "And I want to do that before either of us needs to blast or shoot anyone. There's no way this doesn't end in someone getting hurt, but that doesn't mean we shouldn't set some limits."

"I'm working with you and I rode your motorcycle, even though you're from a family of thieves." Aisha snorted. "Isn't that enough to establish that we're on the same page, *friend?*"

"We have time left," Lyssa said. "And it doesn't hurt to dial it down. Plus, it gives our regalia and the herbs that many more minutes to put us back together. Because of our previous little mistake, neither of us is at our best."

Between Serafina's construct and confronting Aisha, it'd been a painful couple of days. Most of Lyssa's pain was gone, and some of her smaller cuts and burns had healed, but she was far from recovered. The same could be said of Aisha.

This wasn't the first time Lyssa'd had to finish a job while injured. Tricia was right to be scared. Torches had lower life expectancies than most Illuminated for a reason.

Aisha peered into the distance at the twinkle of the skyscrapers that marked the heart of the city. Wistfulness haunted her voice as she spoke. "Hunting shards in a Shadow city. Pathetic. How far our noble kind has fallen from Lemuria."

"Lemuria sank ten thousand years ago." Lyssa shrugged. "Kind of too late to give a damn, and it's not like we know they were good people."

"They were powerful Sorcerers." Aisha frowned at Lyssa. "Any degeneration of the Society is because we were forced into the greater world."

"Illuminated are just people with tricks, which is why Shadows rule the world. Whining about what happened ten thousand years ago is pointless."

Aisha gave her a cold glare. "This is why I find you so disappointing, Corti. You have no respect for your heritage or tradition with your attitude and your guns. You might as well be a Shadow."

"That's where you're wrong." Lyssa peered at the rising sun. "I'm proud to have been born a Sorceress, but I also accept there are limits to everything in this world, even sorcery. We barely know what life was like on Lemuria. Don't you get it? For all we know, the Cataclysm was the fault of the Illuminated. And I don't buy all those stories about how much more powerful we were. Shadows do that same thing, you know—tell themselves pretty stories about their history to pretend they don't have to do the hard work of making a better future. It's an excuse, nothing more."

Aisha snorted. "You can't possibly be comparing us to them. Their ten thousand years of much-vaunted civilization has brought them to nothing."

"It brought them to control the entire planet, trips to outer space, and the conquest of much of the disease and famine." Lyssa leaned over her handlebars. "It brought a lot of nastiness, too, but we're not so different."

"You believe that nonsense about harmony, don't you?" Aisha rolled her eyes. "We'll never be equals. They'll never trust us, and we'll never trust them. The best thing we can do for the Illuminated is grow our power and numbers so we don't have to fear them."

"You're missing the point. We're Illuminated, but we're still human. That means we're not perfect, and there was no great Golden Age of the past where everything was better. Until someone is born with a time essence, we won't be able to do anything about the past. I don't know about harmony, but all we can do now is try and make a better future."

"We had our land and power that didn't need to be hidden." Aisha leaned back on the seat. "Our continent. Things would be different with the Shadows if that remained the same. The future is what I'm talking about. Last Remnant isn't enough. It's too..." Pain filled her voice. "It's too vulnerable."

Lyssa blinked in surprise. She couldn't remember ever hearing Aisha sound like that.

"I get it," Lyssa murmured. "I do. But it's not about having our place. That wouldn't change anything."

"Why wouldn't it?"

"We don't have enough of our kind, and it's going to take a hell of a long time to catch up with the Shadows." Lyssa gestured at the store. "There's only one real path left for us: true coexistence."

Aisha jumped off the bike, her wraith form dissipating. "It doesn't bother you at all, does it? M-Day, having all of them know about us, living among them. I thought it would bother you more because you're older. You were a Torch when M-Day happened."

"No, it doesn't matter to me that much. And living among the Shadows?" Lyssa snickered. "We've always lived among the Shadows. Are you telling me every single relative in your family is Illuminated?"

"Of course not." Aisha turned her head, embarrassment coloring her cheeks. "That's not the same thing. They grew up with the knowledge of their potential and the potential of their descendants, but the rest of humanity..." She shook her head. "They think their toys mean they have power when they don't know true power. They are self-destructive and short-sighted."

"I don't know. The internet, jets, and strawberry ice cream are impressive. Both sides have power, just different kinds. And we wouldn't have Torches or Eclipses if we were perfect." Lyssa patted her bike. "Balanced coexistence is a pipe dream with so few Sorcerers, but I don't see how things work out without it. Right now, there's not much I can do about it other than my job, and I figure if I'm doing my job right, that helps both sides."

"If you say so. I'm not so sure."

A strange expression played across Aisha's face. If Lyssa hadn't been looking straight at her, she would have missed it. All the pride, confidence, and arrogance she'd come to associate with Aisha Khatri disappeared and was replaced by the discomfort and pain she'd expect of a young woman unsure of her place in the world.

They weren't so different in a lot of ways. It was no wonder they didn't get along. But it was time to change the subject and focus on the job.

"Something's been bothering me since I ran into you." Lyssa looked away as she spoke.

"Are you attempting to impugn my honor again, Corti?" Aisha frowned.

"I'm wondering if we should contact our Elders and await further orders. And trust me, I don't say that lightly. I made a speech to Samuel about how I was not going to do that."

Lyssa kept her wraith form up. Someone spotting them and somehow tying their presence to the port delivery would only be able to pick out Aisha and not realize two Sorceresses were working the case.

"Elder Theodora doesn't want to be bothered with petty details." Aisha narrowed her eyes, obviously trying to pick out Lyssa's location in the darkness. "It annoys her to be bothered with such things. I'm surprised Elder Samuel wants them."

"He doesn't normally, either." Lyssa sighed. "And I don't know about Theodora, but it's not like he always responds quickly when I contact him. That's not the only thing. Something's still bothering me about both of us being assigned to the same job. I've tried to ignore it, but I can't anymore."

Lyssa also couldn't ignore that her thought process might be clouded because of the recent anniversary. The farther the case progressed, the less she believed it had anything to do with her brother. Mentioning that to Aisha now wouldn't help.

None of that changed her conclusions. Something smelled off, something far more than territory overlaps.

"It's obvious that you—" Aisha began.

"I know you hate me, but that doesn't extend to Samuel," Lyssa interrupted. "You don't think he'd ask around? You don't think Theodora wouldn't mention it to the other Elders in North America? I feel like we're both missing something obvious."

Aisha's angry look didn't soften, but when she spoke, her words were quiet. "There are some irregularities about this assignment, given its nature. I'll admit that. It would have made more sense for the Elders to coordinate with each other, given the smuggling started in one region and is influencing another."

Lyssa laughed. "This might be about you and me."

"What do you mean?"

"Our relationship isn't exactly secret." Lyssa shook her head. "They might have worried we couldn't work together, but that doesn't change what we should do."

Aisha folded her arms. "And what is that?"

"I think we should clean it up as much as possible before reporting to our mutual Elders," Lyssa replied. "I don't know if this is a big deal, maybe only some political crap, or they were worried about us, but I don't like the idea of them yanking us back home when we've put in all this work."

"Agreed." Aisha tapped her foot impatiently. "Now we should go to the port and get set up."

"Dial it down, Nuclear Deva," Lyssa teased. "We've got to save our appearance for right after the drop."

"Why is that?"

"Think about it. You heard what Sellers said about his supplier."

Aisha's fingers clutched into a fist. "A mask and no mention of where he was getting the shards."

Lyssa nodded. "Then we both agree we'll find a Sorcerer at the other end."

"That changes nothing. Our orders are the same, to end the smuggling. I assume we both suspected the same thing, considering we each assumed the other was the rogue."

Lyssa was unsure. "Just to be clear, you don't think we should ID the guy and leave it up to an Eclipse?"

Aisha looked insulted. "I would have thought you of all

people wouldn't buy into the myth of their superiority. They'd get all the credit for the work we've done. Setting that aside, even if we're dealing with an experienced Sorcerer, he might present a challenge to only one of us, but two of us will make short work of the scum."

Lyssa almost dropped her cloak and mask to smirk at Aisha but fought the urge. "No, I wanted to make sure we agreed on what to do. But it's almost like you're admitting I'm not half-bad at what I do."

Aisha snorted. "You're not half-bad at what you do, which makes you only half-good, friend."

"I'll take the half-compliment," Lyssa replied. "The point is, we have to assume we're dealing with a paranoid rogue who's aware the people using his supplied shards have been caught. If we just charge over there, he might sense us coming. We need to show up at the last minute, after the container is on the ground and right before they load it on a truck. We don't know his essence. If we spook him, we end up trying to chase a water walker across the Gulf."

"We go to the lot almost exactly at that time, hoping to catch them in the act?" Aisha nodded firmly. "If he's paranoid, he might have spells set up."

"It's like you said; there are two of us. It sounds like we have a plan. We hit the guy, and we clean up before we call anyone."

"Very well." Aisha smiled. "Our little scuffle earlier is proving to have been a nice warm-up."

"You mean, between you and me?"

"Yes."

"We're not fully recovered from that. It was a waste of resources."

"How often does either of us get to fight another Illuminated full-out?" Aisha's eyes brimmed with excitement. Even the regalia-influenced flutter of her fiery hair appeared to speed up. "I prefer being a Torch to being an Eclipse, but facing another of our kind is the ultimate challenge."

Lyssa sighed. "We're here to do a job, not prove anything. Remember that. If he surrenders, we take him alive."

"And if he doesn't?" Aisha shot her a thin smile.

"Then we fight him. Maybe he survives. Maybe he doesn't." Lyssa shrugged.

"You sound reluctant. Are you afraid, Corti?"

Lyssa prepared a taunt before tossing it aside. Aisha could be annoying, especially when she was trying to kill Lyssa, but it wasn't like she couldn't understand where the other woman was coming from. Being a young person trying to prove herself in the stultifying morass of the Illuminated Society would mess anyone up, but someone needed to be the bigger woman.

Whoever they were going after wasn't some greedy criminal dazzled by the idea of cash. It was most likely a Sorcerer who had turned his back on his people to help destabilize the Shadow world. When Samuel spoke of coexistence, he didn't mean giving arcane weapons to criminals.

"You're right." Lyssa smiled. "Two Sorceresses? This will be easy. You ready?"

Aisha offered a hungry grin. "Always."

"Jofi, you've been quiet. You ready?"

"As she said," Jofi replied. "Always."

265

CHAPTER TWENTY-EIGHT

Lyssa waited astride her bike. Cloaked, she watched the array of long metal shipping containers spread out on the asphalt before them. With the help of Lyssa's spells, the Sorceresses had established a hidden recon perch on a flattened pile of stone and dirt in an adjacent field filled with large piles of various types of rocks.

A massive yellow crane on the dock whirred and rumbled as it unloaded containers from a cargo ship waiting in the channel. Lyssa hoped the mysterious Nelson didn't flee to the ship when they caught him. She relied heavily on experience, and she'd never had to fight aboard a ship before. She could already imagine Samuel asking her to explain why she had sunk a huge cargo ship and how he was supposed to justify it to the government.

She snickered quietly. What was she thinking? Aisha would be the one to sink the ship. All Lyssa might do was put some holes in it.

Uncloaked, Aisha lay flat next to the bike, peering through Lyssa's binoculars. Her low profile would make her hard to spot from land, but anyone or anything flying overhead would notice her easily. Lyssa hoped they wouldn't regret that.

The plastic was warped and the lenses were scratched from the flame Sorceress' attack in Midland, but the binoculars still worked. Lyssa wasn't going to bother asking Aisha to pay her for the damage. It was enough that they could work together without killing each other.

The recon position looked uncomfortable, given the nature of Aisha's regalia and lack of defensive spells, but she claimed she didn't mind. Whether that was true or part of her continued quest to one-up Lyssa wasn't clear. Lyssa was more than happy to let Aisha feel like she was proving something.

Twenty minutes remained until the handoff. They hoped to tag the container as it was unloaded rather than running around the lot looking for it with minutes to spare. A survey of the unloaded containers closest to the docks hadn't located it.

They also came up with a more specific battle plan. Not a complicated plan, but a plan nevertheless. Lyssa wasn't used to working with other Torches on jobs, but she couldn't deny how useful it was to have a brave partner with combat training.

"Do you trust Aisha?" Jofi asked.

Lyssa jumped, startled by Jofi seemingly reading her thoughts. She realized she'd been staring at Aisha and probably had a confused look on her face. Being observant wasn't the same thing as being telepathic. At least, she hoped it wasn't.

"No." Lyssa didn't bother to whisper. "But I trust her to

get the job done, and I know she can deliver the pain when necessary."

Aisha snorted. "It's rude to talk about someone when they're right there, and twice as rude to do it when said person can only hear one side of the conversation."

"Sorry, I honestly don't know a way to invite anyone else to a conversation with him. It would be handy a lot of times."

Lyssa had asked Lee about it once, and the Sorcerer had spent five minutes screaming at her about the seals and the risk. He didn't even want anyone else knowing she had any sort of spirit in the guns, but she'd made it clear a half-lie was easier to swallow than a full one.

"See our container yet?" Lyssa squinted and surveyed the lot. "As much as sitting on rocks outside a Houston port is how I love spending my days, the sooner we take Nelson down, the sooner I go back home and enjoy my bed and a couple pints of premium strawberry."

"No, I haven't spotted it, but there are five left on the ship." Aisha furrowed her brow. "This scenario does make me question our earlier conclusions."

Lyssa resisted a rude reply. Aisha might be stubborn and obsessed with their families' shared past, but she wasn't a novice Torch. She'd been operating for four years, three years without a mentor. She'd completed plenty of contracts.

Aisha wasn't Lyssa's bratty younger semi-sister. She was a colleague, and Lyssa needed to keep that in mind.

"What did we get wrong?" Lyssa continued sweeping the containers with her gaze. "I don't think Sellers was lying. I'm good at telling that sort of thing. With both of us there, I don't think he could bring himself to lie. We have extreme reputations."

Aisha smirked. "True, but that's not what I'm talking about. Sellers didn't know if Nelson was Illuminated." She gestured at the ship with the binoculars. "Would one of us use such a cumbersome way of transporting shards? One prone to interception by the Shadow authorities?"

"It depends on how and what they're using to conceal their trail." Lyssa shrugged. "Taking advantage of cumbersome Shadow methods makes it far less likely that an Illuminated sniffing around is going to figure out what you're doing. I'm half-surprised they're not boxing them up and shipping them through the mail. How often do Sorcerers expect UPS to drop off that kind of package?"

"That would be amusing, but my point stands. I suspect this Nelson is nothing more than another middleman." Aisha sounded disappointed. "He might be using the mask to deceive fools into thinking he's a Sorcerer, so they'll give him more favorable treatment. The trail might take us farther. There is a rogue at the end of this. I'm certain of that, but they might not come to the port today."

"Then we'll have to hand it off to another Torch or Eclipse." Lyssa frowned. "I don't think our Elders want us going overseas and making a mess. We're not the only Torches in the world."

"'Making a mess?'" Aisha chuckled. "Making a mess in pursuit of justice is most commonly called virtue, Corti. To stand idle while the wicked infect the world with their diseased souls is the rankest sort of cowardice. The Society might have problems, but we also have power we can use to help clean up the darkness."

"You know what? I can't find anything to disagree with there, Aisha, but that doesn't mean our Elders are going to want us to follow up if this is too far outside our regions. Let's not worry about it for now. Let's concentrate on grabbing whoever shows up. If they're a Sorcerer, then it's our lucky day."

Aisha wrinkled her nose. "There is no luck in one of our kind betraying the Society."

"I guess you're right there, too."

Lyssa leaned over the handlebars of her bike, watching the orange and red of the dawn sun push back her natural ally, darkness. From this distance, the ship in the channel looked both massive and small, depending on what she focused on. The sailors on it were specks without the binoculars, but the water under and around it reminded her that humans always bowed before nature in the end.

"I assume you'll show less restraint when we encounter the rogue than you did with me," Aisha said. "Although I'll again admit my mistake, this will not be a situation we can solve by talking."

"I don't like killing people." Lyssa kept her voice steady. "Contrary to what you might think, I only kill when necessary, but as a Torch, not killing isn't always an option. If he leaves me no choice, I'll do what I need to."

Aisha fell silent with a thoughtful look on her face. She continued to scan with the binoculars before speaking again. "Were you holding back with me?"

She sounded disappointed. Lyssa took a deep breath and slowly let it out. Running from the truth wouldn't help.

"A little, but only a little," Lyssa said. "I thought about

using a showstopper for a second if it makes you feel better.

Aisha looked up at Lyssa, her brows lifted. "That would have been rather extreme."

"Were you holding back with me?" Lyssa asked. "You know I have that capability. It could have easily gotten that bad."

"On some level, perhaps I *was* holding back." Aisha returned to looking through the binoculars. "It's not just that I wanted to kill you. I wanted to humiliate you and then kill you. That required more artistry and less efficiency."

"And now?"

"We need to work together on this job. Our duty comes before our personal feelings. I only regret that I was not clear-headed in my hatred. I don't want my actions to weaken the Society, even indirectly."

Lyssa smiled. "I know you hate me, but I don't hate you. I... You know what? Forget it. We both screwed up back there, and we're a little singed from it, but it's nothing bad."

"It's frustrating." Aisha narrowed her eyes. "I thought I had been handed a perfect opportunity for revenge." Her voice softened. "But it didn't feel right. I ignored my instincts because it was perfect. I don't like making mistakes."

"We all make mistakes." Lyssa smiled.

Aisha scoffed. "Some more than others."

Lyssa chuckled. "Sure, but next time, maybe ask a couple more questions before you attack someone. Just a crazy idea I came up with."

"If you were a rogue, I could have died." Aisha scowled.

"I realized that on the way here. I made a mistake by exposing myself and talking instead of immediately following up my attack."

"That little delay might have stopped both of us from killing one another." Lyssa shrugged. "Maybe that was you listening to your gut. Instinct's a good thing to develop as a Torch."

"Just so you know, if you ever do go rogue, I'll kill you without a second thought, friend." Aisha delivered the line in a low, pained tone. "Don't let yourself be killed by anyone else before that time. The only one allowed to kill you is me."

Lyssa chuckled. "I'll keep that in mind. I'll even go so far as to say I'm honored."

"Humans are bizarre," Jofi said. "I don't think I'll ever fully understand your kind."

Lyssa ignored him to smile at Aisha. Her way of saying "I'm sorry, I didn't mean to try to kill you" and "Be careful and take care of yourself" might be twisted, but Lyssa would accept her intentions for what they were.

"Ah." Aisha smiled wickedly. "They're unloading it now. The blue one. The ID matches."

"Get ready to get back on the bike, and remember the plan. We try to take them on the road after they leave the port." Lyssa nodded. "Less chance of collateral damage that way."

"And if that doesn't work?"

"Then we improvise." Lyssa shook a finger. "But we keep it under control. If we find a rogue at the end, I will try to get him to surrender. If he doesn't, we take him out, but that doesn't mean we can heavily damage this port or fling spells wherever we want. You start throwing fire everywhere, and the next thing we know, we'll have an oil tanker burning, and both Elders pissed, along with the entire state. We might be Torches, but I don't want to take on the entire state of Texas."

Aisha shifted to her knees, an eager look on her face. "You know I *can* be precise when necessary." She rotated her wrists and stretched out her arms. "We'll be fine. The criminals and the rogues will suffer."

"Knowing you *can* do something is not the same as knowing you *will* do something."

Lyssa stared at the giant crane moving the container. Serafina's killer doll had been a product of dangerous experimental sorcery, but the Shadows had golems, dolls, and constructs with just as much power. A fusion of the best of both might be centuries off, but that would be a true Golden Age. Humanity just needed to get there first without one side killing the other.

Lyssa and Aisha waited for a couple of minutes as the crane lowered the container to the edge of the loading zone. Aisha turned, feeling her way along the edge of the bike until she found the back and hopped on, allowing Lyssa to extend the wraith form over her.

"I think my original suggestion of death from above would have had more impact." Aisha sniffed. "Shadow thugs don't like being attacked from the air."

Lyssa chuckled. "I think we'll stick to surprising them using my wraith form."

"It lacks style and elegance, but so be it."

Lyssa started the bike and drove down the rock pile toward a road. The bike revved under her skillful touch, accelerating and heading toward a sharp corner. She turned and cut across, which was easy without traffic. Her bike shook as they left the road and entered a grass strip before crossing it to another road.

The disguised Ducati zoomed down the new road before sharply turning again and heading toward the maze of stacked cargo containers covering the area. Lyssa sped up as a semi with a large empty bed pulled through an open gate. She slid to the side and drove past it. The driver glanced her way, frowning at the strange shadows moving into the field of cargo containers, but he didn't stop driving.

Lyssa continued forward before making a hard right and heading toward three stacks of containers at the far edge of the maze. The crane had swung away from the ship minutes before and gone quiet. Beyond the man running the crane, she noticed dockworkers in the area inspecting containers, but none were close to the Torches' target. That simplified matters and lowered the chance of collateral damage.

She maneuvered her bike between containers, following a narrow passage between two rows until she was around the corner from their target. She stopped, and Lyssa visually confirmed the cargo ID.

"That's it, right?" she whispered.

"Yes," Aisha replied. "But we didn't need to know that number, did we?"

Lyssa took slow, even breaths. Aisha was right. There was no doubting the familiar pressure of sorcery in her chest. It had built far past anything she'd recently felt.

The container must have been jammed full of semi-active and active shards. Lyssa had clung to the hope that Sellers had represented the pinnacle of the smuggling, but now she worried Aisha was right, and he was just the beginning of a long, painful trail.

"I don't see anyone yet." Lyssa frowned. "It's almost time for the pick-up."

"Sellers could have woken up and warned them." Aisha looked around.

"And have them drop a container full of shards that reek of sorcery and let us grab it? That's a lot of money to throw away." Lyssa sucked a breath through her teeth. "I doubt it. They'll be here. We don't know how punctual these guys are. Sellers is afraid of Nelson. Maybe he doesn't care if his guys wait all day for him."

The truck she'd passed earlier pulled past the target container and stopped one container-length ahead. Their target lay on the top of another container.

Two men in yellow reflective vests, hard hats, and heavy boots jumped out of the truck. One pulled out a phone and tapped something into it before looking around.

"No masks." Lyssa peered at the men. "Nelson isn't here?"

"Then he's running," Aisha growled. "He's been warned. Sellers is living up to his name."

"We don't know that yet. Calm down." Lyssa drew and expanded her batons, prepping them with her spells. "And we can still secure the shards. As long as we don't kill everyone, we'll be able to follow up on this."

"Should you be doing that?" Aisha nodded at the batons. "If the rogue is here, he could sense it."

"It'd be hard to sense that kind of low-level sorcery when he's got that crate of shards interfering with everything. Let's wait and see what happens."

Lyssa and Aisha waited in tense silence as the minutes ticked past. Jofi remained silent as well. The two men from the truck readied chains and hooks for the load.

"It's past 7:00." Aisha hissed in frustration. "He's not coming."

Lyssa had to face the possibility that Sellers somehow tipped Nelson off. Grabbing the container and warning the Society about a smuggling port would put an end to the shard business for a while, but as in Japan, the people behind it would wiggle away and try again in a different country. A half-victory would taste like ashes.

"If we follow up on the ship and the manifest, we might figure something out." Lyssa frowned. "We can at least pass that on to the Elders. For now, we stick to the plan. We're Torches. We're supposed to burn away the trouble of the world, not make more."

A lift truck arrived at the container, pushing its tines underneath the heavy metal box. With a rumble, the truck lifted the long blue container and backed up until it was on top of the bed of the semi. Another minute passed as the truck operator finished positioning the cargo. He lowered his tines, turned in a wide arc, and departed. The two men who'd exited the truck scrambled over it to finish securing the load.

Lyssa didn't bother to check the time. It was obvious Nelson wasn't going to show. She put her batons away and waited with grim determination until the men got back into the cab and pulled away. They could figure out the why later. The job wasn't over, and they'd planned to hit them on the road anyway.

Accelerating, she stayed close to the rows of containers. The early dawn challenged her wraith form, but towers of containers and machinery cast enough shadows to introduce doubt to anyone looking. Thinning, even for a short period, wasn't practical with another person. Lyssa wasn't even sure she could put the spell on any living thing other than herself.

The truck took a wide turn and headed toward an exit gate. Lyssa kept close to the load so she wouldn't be visible in the mirrors. Anyone knowingly hauling shards might be suspicious of a strange shadow in their mirror, especially after having seen one earlier.

"We should hit them a hundred feet after we're on the main road," Lyssa murmured.

"Just tell me when," Aisha replied, her voice tight.

The truck's brake lights turned on. The wheels screeched, and the trailer swung wide. Lyssa hit her brakes and turned.

Aisha released her grip and leaped backward, her wraith cloak disappearing. She avoided a nasty spill with a last-second jet from her hands and landed on one knee, her eyes narrowed. Lyssa's bike continued sliding on its side, throwing up sparks. Her spell failed.

She hissed and rolled off her bike before jumping up and pulling her guns. The container door shot off with a loud, echoing pop. Steam billowed as the door flew toward her head.

CHAPTER TWENTY-NINE

Lyssa ducked. The heavy metal passed over her head, failing in its decapitation attempt. Aisha jetted to the side and landed on her arms before righting herself with a cartwheel, chanting the entire time. Her heat shield appeared around her as the container door slammed into the ground with a resounding thud.

Instinct propelled Lyssa. She darted for the nearby container stacks while firing into the obscured container. Loud, heavy gunfire rattled from inside in reply. A river of bullets flowed out.

Lyssa hissed as rounds struck her before she made it behind her cover. The bullets vaporized against Aisha's heat shield.

She couldn't see through the steam. Was the source a shard? Could the men inside see through it?

"Don't get cocky, Flame Deva," Lyssa shouted. "Remember the shards."

Something hissed inside the container, and the hiss became a roar as a rocket sped out. Aisha jumped and spun in the air with the help of a flame jet. The projectile missed and exploded against a container stack, knocking one container askew and leaving a ragged, blackened hole.

That wasn't fair. They weren't the ones blowing things up, but they were the ones who would get yelled at. It would be Sacramento all over again.

"Restraint seems foolish at this point," Aisha shouted.

"Okay, we've got no choice," Lyssa called back over her gunshots. "Let's do this the loud way, but try not to blow up the port, Flame Deva."

Lyssa's rounds flashed when they entered the truck, but she couldn't tell if anything was stopping them. The thick steam hid her enemies.

"You keep talking about me blowing up things," Aisha yelled. "But what about that incident in Tucson? You might have kept your name out of it in the media, but don't think I didn't hear about it, Hecate."

"That building was scheduled for demolition anyway. I was doing them a favor."

Lyssa's question about her attacks' penetration was answered when Aisha tossed a fireball at the open container. The spell struck the same invisible barrier before dissipating in a brighter flash than the ones earned by the bullets. Another rocket ripped out of the container.

Aisha jumped into the air and shot forward on jets from both hands and feet. She flew toward a container stack. This time the explosive meant for her continued at a descending angle until it struck the road. The blast left a small crater and chunks of asphalt spread all over.

"One-way forcefield," Lyssa muttered. "Annoying."

Men in dark helmets and black coveralls emerged from

the obscuring steam in the container and advanced toward the opening, submachine guns in hand.

They opened fire and showered the area with bullets. Whatever hope Lyssa had for an easy victory vanished with the bullet's first hits. Each bullet exploded on contact with anything solid, blasting up dirt, asphalt, and rock.

The pressure continued to build in her chest, confirming sorcery. The explosions lacked the power of one of Lyssa's Serafina-supplied rounds, but the shooters were spraying them around with little care and at a much higher rate.

Lyssa fired a couple of shots before leaping back to avoid three blasts. The shooters were starting to get on her nerves.

A large fireball screamed from Aisha's hiding place. The red-orange globe changed direction, curving hard and heading toward the back of the container. The shooters backed away before it struck.

The massive blast consumed the back of the container and lifted the rear of the truck into the air. When the explosion and smoke cleared, the back wheels lay yards away, and the container was hanging halfway off the truck bed. The thick steam remained.

Lyssa stopped firing after a couple more rounds didn't go through. "Take out the other wheels. We need to keep the shards here."

She waited until another curving fireball struck the center of the truck, then spun around the corner and coated the front cab in a black cloud.

Exploding bullets struck all around Lyssa, showering her with chunks of metal and asphalt. One round hit her stomach and knocked her back. Fiery pain spread in her abdomen, but the attacks ceased once another of Aisha's powerful spells struck the truck. The latest blast gave Lyssa the opening she needed to finish covering the entire truck in a black blob that was impenetrable to everyone's sight but hers.

"You should consider the destruction of the container," Jofi said.

"If you didn't notice, Aisha's draining herself to try to do that."

Lyssa ejected one of her magazines and pulled out one wrapped in black tape from her pocket. It was her show-stopper. The magazine only contained three rounds, but that'd be more than enough to win a fight. She didn't want to use it, but her options were dwindling. The enemy would win by attrition if the Torches couldn't get through their defenses.

The ammo was not rare because of the cost. While expense was one consideration, time was another. The creation of the rounds required a lot of preparation and ritual work by Lyssa before Serafina could finalize them.

The gunmen should be proud of themselves. They'd pushed Lyssa to a point she hadn't reached in a year.

Lyssa shoved the magazine into her gun before loading penetrator rounds in her other gun. She winced and checked her body. There was a blackened hole in her regalia, and some of the links in her mesh were missing, but she wasn't doing too badly for someone who had been directly hit by an exploding round.

She eyed her guns. This was turning into a mess.

There was a fundamental threat associated with the

showstopper rounds that was specific to her: the powerful combination of enchanted ammo, ritual, and active sorcery risked Jofi's seal. She'd seen no indication that using a showstopper had done that in the past, but she couldn't ignore the possibility.

It would be all right. It had been before. Why wouldn't it be again?

Some of the shooters had made it to the open front of the darkness-choked container. They felt along the sides, guns in hand. They weren't spraying wildly, but their continued shots kept Lyssa pinned. After a moment, the top of the container shot into the sky with another loud pop.

"Now what?" Lyssa muttered.

The top turned end over end before crashing and embedding itself in a nearby field. The sides of the container fell with a loud clang. There was no reaction from the men.

Lyssa could now make out the entire group of shooters, all in helmets and dark overalls. They stood in front of a group of crates. Half of them held guns. A discarded rocket launcher sat next to one man. They weren't the biggest worry.

A small group of men held a bizarre collection of objects, undoubtedly shards. One man held a skull with glowing rubies in the eyes. Another held a lit candle. A third man wore a bandolier filled with small darts.

The men were all surprisingly calm considering not one of them could see, thanks to Lyssa's spell. The shard-wielding men crouched near the ground, looking back and forth. They might have been awaiting orders or reinforcements or were trying to outwait Lyssa's spell.

Their shooter friends dropped lower. The constant fire ceased, replaced by sporadic shots in the general direction of the Sorceresses.

Aisha hadn't fired off a big attack in a while. Her ragged, heavy breathing proved how far she'd pushed herself, but she'd left the semi an immobile, smoking mess. Whatever else happened in the battle, the men wouldn't be escaping with the shards.

"Give up, idiots," Lyssa muttered. "You lost."

Lyssa carefully aimed the gun with the penetrator rounds and lined up a shot. She fired once, clearing some of the darkness, but her bullets still didn't reach her target, again striking an invisible field. The men returned to spraying explosive bullets her way, forcing her back behind a container. She took some small pleasure in realizing she was costing the gang far more money than they were making her spend.

The gunfire subsided after another half-minute. The men seemed far less eager to fire when they couldn't see. Blackness quickly filled the hole she'd created with her attack.

Keeping a grip on her guns but moving her fingers, she concentrated on producing an image in her mind. She controlled her breathing while chanting her spell.

A dark circle appeared in the air a yard away from her, then another slightly higher and a third lower than the second circle and farther out. Within seconds, an uneven path of flat black circles reached from the ground and circled the now-open container and nearby area.

The good thing about pushing her sorcery to the limit without rituals was that natural exhaustion made the pain from her wounds seem distant. She sucked a breath through her gritted teeth. The Dark Steps wouldn't last all that long in the direct sunlight, but she planned for the fight to be over before they evaporated.

Lyssa pulled shadows from the ground over her legs, leaving them obscured but recognizable, and lifted her guns. She stood with her back against the damaged container she was using for cover. "Ready to end this, Flame Deva?"

"Are you finally getting serious, Hecate?" Aisha called back, her voice strained.

"Something like that. I'm going to take down the shield."

"I see. That would be helpful."

Lyssa expected a volley of deadly bullets or shard sorcery from the men after their shouting, but none came. The men could hear her, judging by their shifting positions, but they weren't shooting her way.

Sirens screamed in the distance. This whole raid had gone sideways, but she didn't have time to chat with the cops and get it figured out. The Torches needed to end the battle before any innocents got hurt.

The man holding the candle stood up. He waved it, and the dark shroud surrounding the container disappeared in a bright flash, along with the candle.

His form wavered for a couple of seconds, then his helmet and uniform changed, shifting color to become gray and white, the pattern vaguely reminiscent of concrete. His helmet turned the same color and pattern, and opaque dark-blue-tinted goggles extended across his face. He lifted his hand, and a piece of metal tore from the fallen sides of the container and formed into a long, sharp blade—a sword without a hilt.

"Our primary target arrived after all," Jofi said.

"I noticed," Lyssa murmured.

She frowned, not recognizing the regalia. That wasn't unheard of since there wasn't any Society law forcing a Sorcerer to tell the entire Society his regalia's current appearance. In theory, the Elders who attended his Initiation and binding ceremony would be aware of it, but it wasn't like she could ask them in the middle of a fight.

"Hecate and Flame Deva," the Sorcerer called. His voice carried a faint French accent.

Lyssa tried to place the voice but failed. She ran into far too many people who ended up wanting to kill her later.

She allowed herself to chuckle. The rogue knew who they were, so he had a good chance of knowing their true identities. Hiding identities from the Shadows was one thing, but the Elders felt people deserved to know who among them was a Torch or an Eclipse. Perhaps some strange sense of twisted honor prevented him from using their real names, or worse, he didn't care because he thought they'd be dead soon.

"You must be Nelson," Lyssa shouted back. "This is over. The cops will swarm this place and box you in, then we're going to finish kicking your ass. Flame Deva took out your truck, so you're not getting away with the shards."

"Ah, it will be an honor to fight the famous Semi-Automatic Sorceress," the Sorcerer replied with a laugh.

Had Damien been spreading that around? She wasn't sure if she should be impressed or annoyed.

"The police won't come any closer," the Sorcerer continued. "They've received a tip that a dangerous sorcery battle is playing out at the port, and they're waiting for the Society to finish handling it. But for it to be you of all people! Ah, fate."

"You were expecting Torches, just not us?" Lyssa asked.

"I was expecting a confirmation call from Sellers early this morning. When I didn't get it, I wondered what had happened. I thought the FBI had arrested him, but I thought I better prepare, just in case. My planning has helped salvage what could have been a disaster."

"You know who we are, rogue," Aisha spat out, her voice full of bile. "Who are you?"

"A man looking to the future and preparing his position accordingly." The Sorcerer smiled and twisted his wrists. More pieces of metal ripped from the container wall, this time forming a constellation of twirling sharpened metal surrounding him.

Lyssa remained clueless about the regalia, but judging from what she'd seen, the Sorcerer might have a blade essence. It could have been worse, but it could have been a lot better. It'd been years since she'd last seen someone with a blade essence.

"You should finish him off," Jofi said. "There's no reason to leave it to an Eclipse."

"I need to make sure he's the end of this chain," Lyssa whispered. "He can't talk if he's dead, but he's not getting away."

"I've prepared for this eventuality." The Sorcerer raised

his arms. "You can continue to weaken yourself by flinging your bullets and spells against my invisible wall, but you won't survive. Or you can consider another option, a more sensible one. I respect women of intellect and power."

Lyssa rolled her eyes and scoffed. "Skip the part where you offer to cut us in. Neither of us is buying what you're selling."

"Hecate is right," Aisha said. "You can't buy us. You can surrender now, or you can surrender after we beat you into submission. Or you can die. I'm fine with any of those eventualities."

"Surrender," Lyssa added, "and I'll guarantee you'll live until we deliver you to the Society for judgment. Fight us, and there are going to be unnecessary deaths, including yours. I don't want to have to kill a Sorcerer, but I will if I need to."

The Night Goddess schtick wouldn't mean much to most Sorcerers, but she'd make a half-assed try. This wasn't going to come down to psychological warfare. She eyed her Dark Steps. They were growing more transparent.

"You're so much like your brother it hurts." The Sorcerer shook his head. "It's pathetic. The same self-righteousness from someone who is nothing more than a sorcery-powered mercenary."

Lyssa's heart kicked up. "What did you just say?"

It couldn't be. Impossible. He was just messing with her.

"If you let me go, I might have some news for you about him." He laughed. "I've heard you've been looking for him. I've heard you don't believe he's dead."

Lyssa's jaw tightened, along with her grip on her guns.

Fifteen years and nothing. It was too convoluted a plan to leak shards to Phoenix just to get to her.

"He's attempting to undermine your morale," Jofi said. "Your brother was a high-profile Torch. The circumstances of his disappearance are not unknown among your kind."

"How about I offer you another deal?" Lyssa called back. "How about I beat your ass down and force that information out of you? Won't that be fun?"

Aisha cackled. "Well said, Hecate."

"We still have a stalemate, my beautiful Sorceresses," the Sorcerer replied. "No." He shook his head. "I can't let you leave here. Know now that you'll fall before Adrien Allard, bearer of the City Guard."

Lyssa frowned. Giving up his real name to two Sorceresses was one thing, but he'd also revealed it to all the Shadows around him.

She thought it through. Sellers' men were normally the ones who drove the truck, but Adrien had been expecting an ambush. They must have all been his goons.

"Destroy him," Jofi said. "The unknown nature of the remaining shards represents an extreme risk. His full capabilities also remain unknown."

"Flame Deva," Lyssa yelled. "When I give the signal, you focus on his men, and I'll focus on him. Sound fair?"

Aisha let out a snort of disapproval. "You'll have the higher quality opponent, Hecate, but I suppose the numbers make up for it. Very well."

Adrien barked a laugh. "You think you can surprise me while you're openly discussing your plans? You'll never get through this shield. You don't understand how long I've prepared for something like this. Do you think I didn't anticipate Torches or Eclipses showing up? Your arrogance will be your downfall. We can continue to attack you, but you can't get to us. You can't win."

"I think you still don't understand what pure darkness is," Lyssa replied.

"And what's that? Entertain me before you die."

Lyssa didn't respond. She chanted under her breath, her mind filled with a complex series of glyphs and arcane symbols alternated with images of celestial destruction, including a stream of material being ripped off a massive star and heading into a black hole. She shifted her visualizations, mentally drawing the glyphs in strokes in time with her chants. The glyphs were formed in her mind over a field of stars, each star disappearing when she produced an arcane symbol. A swirling void surrounded the front of her left pistol containing the showstopper rounds.

"What are you playing at over there?" Adrien asked, sounding nervous. "I can sense it. Your darkness won't win against my blades. And you never answered my question, Hecate. What's so special about pure darkness?"

"Pure darkness is one important terrifying thing," Lyssa replied. "It's why everyone has a primal fear of it. Pure darkness hides everything from sight, so people inject their fears into what they can't see. In that sense, it's everything, but that's not what it is. What it is, is *nothing*."

She spun around the corner, pointed the gun at Adrien, and pulled the trigger.

CHAPTER THIRTY

Biting cold enveloped Lyssa's body. Deep, impenetrable darkness swallowed the emerging bullet. The blackness flew toward the invisible barrier, dimming the path it flew along but not expanding, as if sucking in the nearby light and leaving a column of shadow.

The bullet struck the barrier. Jagged dark lines shot out from the point of impact, enveloping the barrier in an instant and revealing its shape as a squat dome. Panic covered the faces of the men inside.

The inky dome of nothingness lasted less than a second before dots of light appeared, a few at first, then many, as if it were flaking away into nothingness. Lyssa brought up her other gun, still filled with penetrator rounds, and waited until the dome disappeared.

The man holding the skull shard jerked back as it cracked and crumbled to dust. He yanked out a pistol.

Lyssa smiled, not disappointed with her failure to kill Adrien. She needed to take the bastard alive. Shredding

Adrien's invisible castle had been worth it just for his shocked expression.

"Annihilation," Jofi said, "has a beauty all its own."

Lyssa hadn't heard Jofi say anything like that before, but she didn't have time to worry. She'd know when and if the seals broke. It wouldn't be subtle.

Adrien sprinted from the open container to the container maze, his blades still whirling around him. Aisha unleashed small, fast fire blasts at his men. Her spells exploded on the unfortunate lackeys, burning through their uniforms and sending them to the ground, screaming. The survivors broke away from the container and ran in different directions.

A curtain of flame from Aisha ripped over the ground and cut them off from the container maze. They ran backward as a group, laying down cover fire as they sprinted for smoking ruins of the semi's cab, the only available cover.

The dart man pulled a dart off his bandolier and brought his arm back to throw it. Aisha whipped a fireball at his arm. He released the dart, only for it to meet the Sorceress' attack. The dart exploded in a web of sticky filaments, imprisoning him. He yelled in surprise and toppled forward. Aisha laughed.

She wouldn't be able to keep up that pace after the larger, earlier attacks. Lyssa needed to do her job, too.

Taking her opening, Lyssa jumped for her first conjured step. She'd meant to use the steps to get above potential holes in the shield, but now they would help her track down the fleeing Sorcerer.

She ignored the throbbing from her previous wounds

and the cold and heaviness soaking her body, concentrating on charging up the steps and getting an angle on the fleeing Sorcerer. A bullet flew past her, but the man who'd shot at her went down a half-second later, the victim of a fireball.

Aisha forced the men back, alternating hands as she tossed attacks. Covered by her shield, her bare feet left blackened steps on the road.

The enemy bullets disappeared against the power of her shield, but stray shots to the side exploded on the pavement, staggering her. Aisha had already downed half the men, leaving Lyssa not very worried about her, but she went ahead and added two shots of her own at the shooters from above. Her penetrator rounds blew through the bodies of her targets.

She was out of pity. These men had understood what wielding shards against Torches meant. They'd had their chance to surrender, and they'd insisted on fighting. Like Alvarez and his thugs, they'd learn that shards weren't enough to compete with true sorcery.

Lyssa bounded higher using the disintegrating Dark Steps. She took a side path that helped her spot the fleeing Adrien. She ran forward and leaped off the farther step onto the top of a container, pumping her cold and heavy arms and legs to catch up with him. He ducked behind a container.

Wrenching metal sounded from ahead. Lyssa kept running. Metal ripped from the top of nearby containers, lengthening into sword- and knife-sized blades. They shot out in an arc pointed in her direction.

She jumped down between containers to avoid the

attack. One of the blades sliced into her shoulder, tearing the regalia and the mesh. Blood seeped from the cut.

Lyssa landed with a grunt, stumbling. In her current state, firing another showstopper would drain her too much, and she needed to take Adrien alive anyway. It'd been a risk shooting it directly at him, even behind his shield.

Her shoulder stung, and she glanced at the wound. Thin but shallow. Slicing through her stacked defenses and inflicting even that minor a wound proved both the power of true sorcery and that Adrien's blades couldn't be ignored. Cops or FBI who tried to take him on would be paper dolls.

A quiet whooshing noise sounded from Adrien's direction. She kept close to her current cover, a green shipping container. More hollow wrenching echoed all around her. She needed to get eyes on him.

Dozens of tiny needlelike blades shot up and rained down around the area. They embedded themselves in the containers with a cacophony of pings. Others buried themselves in the ground. None hit her.

"The enemy lacks confidence in his ability to defeat you," Jofi said. "His attacks show desperation. Finish him off."

"Or he's being careful so he can take me out," Lyssa whispered. "I got overly excited, but I need him alive so I can question him. You heard what he said about my brother."

"Taking him prisoner might not be possible," Jofi said. "You have suffered wounds and damage and aren't completely recovered from your encounters with Miss

Khatri and Miss Dale's creation. Your showstopper has sapped your strength and mobility. You can't find your brother if you're dead."

"Then I'll have to make sure I don't die." Lyssa ejected her showstopper magazine and tucked it away. She replaced it with her remaining exploding round magazine, glad Aisha hadn't forced her to use it up in Midland. "I've managed to do that for twelve years. I don't see a reason why I would stop today."

Explosions and gunfire continued to sound behind her, along with a loud, recognizable laugh. At least Aisha was enjoying herself.

The din of nearby battle almost drowned out the whooshing noise, but not enough that Lyssa couldn't track it. She spun around the corner with both guns ready, her eyes narrowed, creeping forward. Adrien was close to her. She could feel his sorcery.

"You've seen what I'm capable of when I get serious," Lyssa shouted, her gaze darting around, seeking the enemy. Knowing he was roughly in front of her wasn't the same as knowing exactly where the next attack would come from, especially with so many potential places for cover among the containers—and that was assuming he hadn't crawled inside one. "This is over, Adrien. I don't know why you thought you could get away with smuggling shards, but this was how it was always going to end. On some level, you must know that."

Lyssa stopped near an intersection of containers. The whooshing was louder but still not close. She spun. Nothing but sharp metal embedded in the ground.

"What you did shouldn't be possible for someone like

you," Adrien called, his voice echoing from ahead of Lyssa. "You're not old enough to hold such power. That shield would defy an Elder."

"That's the thing about having a lot of friends instead of lackeys," Lyssa replied. "When you put your heads together and pool your efforts, you can do a lot. If you're that impressed, why don't you do me a favor and give up?"

She crept along the side of another container. The sorcery sensation intensified. Something glinted ahead. She jumped back and prepared to fire.

No attack came. Thin, shiny blades floated in the air and fanned out at the end of a container. Lyssa wasn't sure what he was up to.

A whistling noise caught Lyssa's attention from above, and she looked up just in time to see the two blades. By reflex, she swiped at one with her guns. It sparked as it slid down her pistols, but she deflected it. The other impaled her abdomen. She bit her tongue to keep from crying out.

Lyssa ran backward as another pair of blades shot up from the opposite side of the container and missed her by inches. Running with a sharp, pointed piece of enchanted metal sticking into her abdomen when she was already wounded and drained wasn't high on Lyssa's list of recommended activities for the day. She stayed in motion, every step jostling the blade and making the pain flare worse.

She continued her defensive dance until she assumed wraith form and ran around the corner. The edged onslaught stopped. Ensconced in wraith form in the long shadow of a container, she was barely visible, but her trail of blood wasn't helping.

"When's the last time you fought another Illuminated?"

Adrien called. "I think you've gotten arrogant, Hecate. You're too used to gunning down weak Shadows and relying on defenses that assume the other side doesn't have true sorcery. Now, because of your miscalculation, you're going to die."

Despite the confidence in Adrien's words, there was a ragged quality to his voice. The man might have had an impressive shard shield, but he'd pushed himself to the limit with his blade sorcery.

"When was the last time I fought an Illuminated?" Lyssa laughed. "I don't know. What time is it?"

"We can make a deal. I'll give you the information about your brother. I know you're hurt. You can just lie and say I escaped. There's nothing to be gained by fighting me and everything to lose."

"In your current state," Jofi began, "victory is not assured."

"Winning never is," Lyssa murmured. "But there's no way he's walking now."

She pulled some more painkiller herbs out of her pocket and munched them. Samuel had better let her rest after it was all over.

There had been no explosions or gunfire for about a minute. The sirens had stayed distant, and flashing red and blue signaled a line of police at the far edges of the port.

Lyssa tried to decide her next move. There was no way Aisha would lose to a bunch of second-stringers using borrowed power. Waiting for the other Sorceress might be a good move, but she also might not be coming. Aisha might have taken Lyssa's declaration as a desire for a beginning-to-end duel with the Sorcerer, or the flame

Sorceress might be exhausted or unconscious and not able to join her.

There was no choice. Lyssa didn't have time to wait for help, Illuminated or Shadow. It was time to end the fight. She stowed her penetrator-loaded pistol and tossed the explosive-loaded pistol into her right hand before conjuring a small cloud of shadow. A quick peek around the opposite corner revealed another fanned set of shiny blades.

She smirked. Mirrors. It was clever of Adrien, but he couldn't hit what he couldn't see.

Lyssa tossed her spell toward the mirrors on one side, swallowing them in darkness before rushing to the opposite side and doing the same thing. She crossed again and charged with her remaining strength, her gun in front of her. The mirror blades flipped onto their sides and shot out in a sweeping arc. She leaned back and they flew over her, one almost slicing her nose.

After snapping back up, Lyssa continued her run. Her form began to solidify in patches. Too many wounds and too many clever tricks had drained her. She didn't care. Adrien wouldn't escape if it killed her.

Her heart thundered. Her soft footsteps turned to heavy boot strikes as the rest of the wraith form failed. There was a shadow from a ring of whirling blades on a container and the outline of a man's body. She knew exactly where he was.

Sometimes Lyssa needed tricks. Sometimes she needed clever psychological ploys. Sometimes she just needed to put a bullet into a man's chest.

Lyssa dropped to the ground right before the corner of

the container, sliding feet first as she cleared it. Adrien stood nearby, his orbiting blades at the ready. They fired in her direction, aimed at what would have been chest height before her slide. They flew over her, leaving her next to the man with a gun loaded with powerful sorcery-enhanced rounds pointed at him.

Adrien stared at her, no blades left. He reached toward the shredded side of the closest container.

Lyssa pulled the trigger. The bright flash blinded her as Adrien jerked back. His regalia was now a tattered mess, his chest mangled and bloody.

He was right; she was too used to fighting Shadows. One penetrator would have ripped through anyone without regalia.

Adrien howled in rage and pain and ripped two new blades from the container. Lyssa fired again. The attack blew off his arm and shoulder. The Sorcerer fell to his knees and coughed up blood.

"Lyssa Corti, bearer of the Night Goddess," Adrien wheezed. "Witness my end."

She hesitated for a moment, almost shooting before holstering her gun. Even a rogue Sorcerer deserved respect as a former Illuminated, and his invocation of the ancient ritual didn't mean he was going to win.

She reached into her pocket for a healing herb and offered it to him. "This doesn't have to be the end."

"Better to die on my terms than suffer the humiliation that would follow." He coughed again. "Bear witness, please."

Lyssa dropped to her knees and downed the herb

instead. She tightened her jaw and yanked the blade out of her abdomen, letting out a strangled yelp.

She took a deep breath and spoke the next words in Lemurian. "I, Lyssa Corti, bearer of the Night Goddess, witness the end of Adrien Allard, bearer of the City Guard. By the blood of Lemuria, may his soul find completion."

Adrien collapsed to his side. "By the blood of Lemuria, may my soul find completion," he replied in the same language. His breathing grew slower, and he switched back to English. "Norman, Oklahoma. Kalander's Storage. Unit 48-B. 06-20-20-15."

"What?" Lyssa clutched her stomach wound.

"You've earned it, but beware of who you tell. I question now why certain shards ended up where they did. Burn away the corruption if you dare, Torch. We live in a world of filth, not illumination, but maybe darkness is the best tool against darkness."

Adrien stopped breathing. His eyes remained open in a death stare.

"What do you think is there?" Jofi asked.

Lyssa scooted over to rest her back against the container. Every part of her alternated between throbbing with fiery pain and numbing coldness. "Something that can wait a few days. For now, I'm going to catch my breath, wait for some of these herbs to give me enough strength to find Aisha, and go from there. We've just created a lot of paperwork for Damien."

Someone's shadow grew on a container to her side. Lyssa groaned and raised her gun.

"Are you dead?" Aisha called. "I thought we had an agreement about that."

"Not dead yet, but if you want to finish me off, this would be a great time."

Aisha walked around the corner, eyeing Adrien's body. She was bloodied and burned, but she didn't look like she'd been stabbed. She leaned over and offered her arm.

"Come on, Corti," she whispered. "You've done enough for the day. You might be a thief from a family of thieves, but no one can doubt you're a demon in battle."

CHAPTER THIRTY-ONE

A week later, Lyssa found herself standing in front of the orange door of unit 48-B in Norman, Oklahoma. She'd sloshed through a flooded parking lot after a surprise storm drenched the area. Ten minutes later, there were almost no clouds above her. Sometimes erratic weather was more impressive than sorcery.

The aftermath of the incident had gone about as well as it could, with Lyssa formally contacting the police and the EAA for assistance over Aisha's objections. She had spent some time resting in a hotel until her regalia and herbs reduced her pain to manageable levels. Even now, she wasn't back to one hundred percent, but she doubted Adrien had set up a long-play trap in a random Oklahoma storage unit.

Elder Samuel hadn't said much when taking her report. He had been brief and to the point, and she wasn't in the mood to be anything but the same.

The Elder had also officially closed out the contract, and the EAA had taken receipt of the surviving shards in Houston and was cataloging them before returning them to the Society. The only thing the Torches had refused to hand over was Adrien's regalia. They had taken it off the body, and Aisha had promised to deliver it to Elder Theodora. It was only a matter of time before it disintegrated and returned to the Vault of Dreams anyway.

Tradition. Lyssa didn't always respect it, but the death of an Illuminated meant something to her. A regalia was more than a costume or a source of power. It was a fundamental reflection of their soul and deserved to be treated as such.

Adrien Allard was blamed as the source of all the shards, and the job was over for both the EAA and the Society, though Samuel mentioned he'd come and chat with Lyssa again after everything settled down.

The rogue Sorcerer's dying words gnawed at Lyssa as she stood in front of the storage unit's door. She hadn't mentioned the storage unit to Aisha, Damien, or Samuel. She didn't know what they meant yet, and her concern about what had gone down lingered. Adrien's mention of her brother could have been nothing but a trick, as Jofi suggested, but it was hard to be a Sorceress and not believe in fate a little.

Did she just *want* to believe? Probably. There was a good chance she'd open the storage unit and find nothing more than some keepsakes.

Part of her hoped that wasn't true, but another part hoped it was. Anything inside that might lead her to her brother would change her entire life. It was easy to say she wanted to find him when she had no real leads. A desire without a plan was nothing more than a dream that would never be fulfilled.

Lyssa took a couple of deep breaths. A building pressure bothered her as she walked down the hallway toward the indoor storage unit, her boots leaving a trail of wet footprints. Whatever was inside, there was some sorcery involved. That confirmed this lead was something more than a humiliating empty trick, but nothing else.

Then and there, she wasn't Hecate in front of the storage unit's door. She didn't bother to disguise her white jacket. The woman checking out the lead was Lyssa Corti, the younger sister of Chris Corti.

She eyed the keypad. Remembering the code, 06-20-20-15, was easy. June 20, 2015. M-Day. She entered it, and the door clicked open.

"Be aware that the man might have been attempting to manipulate you," Jofi said.

"I assumed as much, but that doesn't make him wrong." Lyssa opened the door and stepped inside. Without her regalia, she was forced to resort to turning on a light switch. "And people tend to lie less when they're dying."

Annihilation has a beauty all its own.

She'd been thinking about Jofi's statement over the last week. As unprecedented as it was, he'd not followed it up with anything similar. Telling Lee and having the Sorcerer overreact about an aesthetic preference statement was a bad idea. She'd worry about it if Jofi said anything else odd.

Three large briefcases sat on the floor, aligned side by side. Lyssa knelt and opened the first one. Scattered objects lay inside. An emerald with a fire burning inside. A bone flute. A slingshot inscribed with glyphs. Shards.

Lyssa opened the other briefcases and found more shards, but in the third suitcase, there was something unexpected: a small memory card. She picked it up and placed it in her palm, stepping away from the suitcases.

No sorcery radiated off it. She chuckled.

"What's so amusing?" Jofi asked.

"The Elders in the Society might not want to modernize, but it looks like the rogues have." Lyssa pulled out her phone and inserted the memory card. "Probably has a virus, but what the hell. This is my month for unnecessary risks."

Nothing nefarious happened. The phone didn't explode, and no spells went off. Something extremely conventional was stored on the card: photos identified by the date, most taken three or four years ago.

Lyssa gazed at the first picture. An elegant blonde woman in an elaborate red evening gown was being helped out of a limousine by a handsome older man in a tuxedo.

The second image depicted a slender woman in a billowing gossamer scarlet gown with a tight red and black corset. She stood in the center of a room, a red Venetian mask covering her eyes and a scarf inscribed with glyphs covering her face while semi-translucent birds made of light flew around her. The dagger-like red heels looked painful, and Lyssa was glad she fought in boots.

"Do you recognize that woman?" Jofi asked.

"This is a regalia, the Beautiful Stranger." Lyssa narrowed her eyes. "I met the owner a long time ago, a Sorceress named Helga Strand. She lives in Oslo, I think. She used to, anyway."

"Is she a Torch?" Jofi asked.

Lyssa shook her head. "Nothing like that. Not a Torch or an Eclipse. A performer, an entertainer—high-class, but that's it. She's more the future of coexistence than someone like me."

She flipped to the next picture. She didn't recognize the man but was unsurprised when the next picture contained a regalia for a man of the same build.

Five minutes passed as she continued through the matched picture and regalia pairs, over fifty Illuminated. She didn't recognize all the Sorcerers and Sorceresses on sight, but Lyssa could associate a name with a good chunk of the regalia. Only a small number of Torches and Eclipses she knew about were in the photos, and she couldn't discern a geographical, essence, or regalia pattern.

"What's the point of this?" Lyssa frowned. "Preparing something to send to the internet?"

"To what end?" Jofi asked.

She stared at her phone. "That's the real question. Right now, even the rogues understand that shoving everyone's identities out in public wouldn't work out well for them either. It's kind of like being spies. Even when you know a guy's working for the other side, you don't go screaming it from the rooftops if you don't want attention on you."

"That seems like an unsustainable strategy."

Lyssa snickered. "Yeah, because it is. I'm surprised the Society managed to negotiate our privacy in the Sorcery Control Accords, but I'll take it while it lasts."

"Simple exposure of all Illuminated identities would cause some difficulties, but it wouldn't be a fatal blow to the Society's influence or power."

"True, but these pictures are on this card for a reason, and I don't think it's because some fan collected them."

Lyssa shook her head and continued flipping through the pictures before stopping at a familiar dark-haired man. He looked a few years older than the last time she had seen him, but that was to be expected in more than one way. Slowed Sorcerer aging wasn't the same as not aging.

She double-checked the date. It was three years ago. The photo showed her brother Chris. The next picture, however, was a different Sorcerer and not Chris in regalia.

She fell to her knees. "All these years." She wiped away a tear. "Adrien wasn't lying. Chris is alive."

"We don't know that," Jofi replied. "The dates might not represent when they were taken. This may still be an attempt to manipulate you."

"Maybe. But why would they want pictures…" Lyssa switched back to Chris' picture and pointed to a movie marquee listing showtimes in the corner. "*Rainbow Chicken Screams So Loud* came out the year listed in the filename. I remember seeing it in the theater with Tricia. You've never heard a woman laugh so loud at such a silly movie. I thought she was using sorcery for a while to be so loud." She shook her head. "If somebody faked this, they went out of their way to make it seem like it was only a few years ago. No way. This picture was taken three years ago, long after my brother's alleged death and after M-Day."

"It might not be your brother," Jofi said. "It could be someone using a spell to look like him."

"Then I want to find them and ask them why the hell they'd do that. He's important to me, but it's not like he's important enough for someone to pull that kind of stunt otherwise." Lyssa shook her phone. "This is the first real lead I've ever gotten. I appreciate what Tricia and Samuel said to me, but this proves they were wrong. Chris is still alive."

"Then why hasn't he contacted you?" Jofi asked.

Lyssa's stomach knotted like she'd been punched. She didn't answer because the question had haunted her for years. It would be easier if Chris *had* been killed rather than disappearing in the line of duty. He was the only blood family she had left after their parents died.

"I don't know," Lyssa murmured. "But that doesn't mean I shouldn't find out. I deserve answers, and after all these years, there's no way I'm walking away from this. Why would I? I'd have to be insane to ignore this lead. You heard what Adrien said. Maybe it's not a coincidence that I ended up with this job. Maybe my brother was trying to get my attention."

"That seems a roundabout way to do it versus contacting you directly," Jofi replied.

"What do you want me to do, Jofi?" Lyssa shouted. "Walk away from this? After all this time?"

"In my time with you, I've learned one important thing about human concerns."

"What's that?"

"Closure isn't always satisfying. Please keep that in mind."

Lyssa continued through the pictures, seeking more clues. "No, I'll figure this out. These pictures mean something, and now I know for sure my brother's alive."

"Do you intend to tell anyone?" Jofi asked.

"Not sure. Maybe just Tricia and Fred." Lyssa sighed. "I can't be sure about who I can trust."

She stopped on the penultimate picture. There was no preceding picture of the man out of regalia. A shiver ran through Lyssa. She wished she didn't recognize the regalia.

The outfit wasn't as flashy as some, especially compared to people like Aisha and Helga. The tall, willowy man in the picture wore a pair of loose white pants, a matching belt, and a white shirt, and his face was covered with a white veil held in place with a headband. Long white gloves covered his arms and hands. The only thing visible was the back of his shaved head.

"You seem upset," Jofi said. "Who is this man?"

"This is Tristan St. James. He's an Eclipse, an infamous one. The ultimate assassin. He's taken down some of the worst rogues in the last forty years. Every once in a while, a rumor that he's a rogue himself pops up, but the Elders insist that's not true." Lyssa rolled her tight shoulders. "He sometimes goes by the name Purity. And don't let the look of his regalia, Snow Ghost, fool you; the guy is seriously dangerous. Super-powerful spirit Sorcerer. Sometimes I wonder if the Elders downplay the guy because they're in some sort of Cold War with him that they don't want to admit to, or if he is a rogue but he's taking out other rogues."

Lyssa advanced to the last image. In it, a regal-looking white-haired woman in a dark blue suit was leaving a French restaurant. Somebody looking at the woman might compliment her smooth skin and say she looked great for her age while being fifty years off in their guess. It was Elder Theodora, and she was over a hundred years old.

"You know what I hate most in the world?" Lyssa asked.

"Based on our conversation yesterday, amaretto ice cream."

"Today, the number one on the list changes." Lyssa frowned at the picture. "I hate coincidences. These pictures mean something important. My brother, a grab bag of different Sorcerers, one of the most dangerous Eclipses of the modern era, and an Elder who just happened to send a woman who hates me on the same job as me. That has to mean something."

"I don't think Miss Khatri hates you as much as you think, judging by what she did after the battle and her cooperation during the assignment."

Lyssa still wasn't sure where she stood with Aisha. The flame Sorceress had waited with her while the police and the local EAA agents showed up, and she'd stayed with her the first day to make sure she was healing. It was awkward, and Aisha couldn't go more than five minutes without bragging that her contributions in the final battle were superior because she'd taken down more men, but she hadn't called Lyssa a thieving cat the entire time.

Were they friends now? No. Frenemies who might occasionally help each other take down threats? Probably. Lyssa could live with that.

"That's now, but it wasn't the same then." Lyssa pocketed her phone. "After all, Aisha did try to kill me in Midland when she thought I was working with the Lone Five Stars."

"Are you accusing Elder Theodora of attempting to assassinate you?" Jofi asked. "Why would she do that?"

Lyssa had never been more frustrated by the lack of

emotion in Jofi's voice than at that moment. An outrageous statement like that needed feeling behind it. She wanted someone to be angry on her behalf.

"I don't know what's going on. All I know is I better watch my back, and Chris is alive. I have to be careful about who I trust going forward." Lyssa frowned. "For now, though, I better get these shards taken care of." She pulled her phone back out and dialed. "A little white lie never hurt anyone."

"Agent Riley here," Damien answered.

"I got a little tip for you on more shards. Don't ask where I got it. These things come up when a woman does what I do. You're going to need to call someone and have them collect some toys from a storage unit in Norman, OK."

"Okay. That's good news, I think."

Lyssa chuckled. There was something soothing about Damien's voice. That was what Bill the Boy-Next-Door had lacked: a good, soothing voice.

She could ask him out on a date. Samuel said he was going to direct other Torches toward jobs for a while, but she'd just verified that her brother was alive. It wasn't the right time to worry about dating hot feds.

Sorry, Tricia, she thought. *Looks like my life is on hold for a while.*

"It's good news, Damien," Lyssa replied. "Every shard we keep out of the hands of criminals makes the world a safer place."

CHAPTER THIRTY-TWO

Lyssa paced in her living room, her stomach tight. Samuel had sent her a message via the mirror, letting her know he was going to stop by and an exact time. She'd asked him to come over so they could go over a couple of things concerning the job.

All progress resulting in him becoming more reasonable, however small, was good. The problem was she needed to figure out how to proceed with her brother. There was no way she could follow up on the memory card without help. Even going to Last Remnant to check on things would require an Elder's permission, which meant getting Samuel onboard.

But her suspicions lingered. Adrien might have been trying to mess with her head as one final attack, but it wasn't like he could have set up the shards and pictures in his dying moments hundreds of miles away from Norman, Oklahoma.

She wasn't sure there was a conspiracy. The small number of Torches in the United States meant a given

Torch had a high probability of running into trouble across a multi-state area.

That was why she hated coincidences so much. They could have multiple explanations, which was not a great thing for a paranoid woman whose job involved tracking down dangerous people who didn't want to be found.

Lyssa's perimeter alarm spells sent her to the door before the knock. Samuel wore a different disguise this time, though it was equally nondescript. She opened the door and gestured him inside. Once she closed the door, his form shifted to his normal Gentleman regalia.

She didn't bother to sit this time, instead folding her arms and standing in front of her couch with a defiant look on her face. Depending on how the next few minutes went, the Elder might end up an enemy, and she wanted her enemies to know she would stand up for herself.

Samuel watched her for a moment with an irritated expression. "The Society considers the shard matter officially closed. Some of the shards recovered from the port were originally offered for sale in Japan during those incidents before the relevant parties were captured."

Lyssa nodded. "Then I cleaned up not just for you, but for some other Elders, huh? I think that makes me one badass Sorceress."

"Your success in this matter hasn't gone unnoticed." Samuel stroked his beard. "Nor has your cooperation with Aisha Khatri despite your history of tension with her. You're learning."

"Yeah, about that." Lyssa dropped her arms. "What the hell was Aisha doing investigating this anyway?"

"I thought that was already clear to you." Samuel stared

at Lyssa. "Elder Theodora misunderstood the scope of what I intended for investigation. She apologized for the mistake, but it worked out to everyone's advantage, so there's no point in pressing the issue."

"Really? That simple, huh?" Lyssa chuckled. "She misunderstood the scope, but she never mentioned it to you? Didn't pass you a little message? 'Hey, I've got Flame Deva on this!'"

"No, I wasn't aware of it until after the battle in Houston." Samuel narrowed his eyes. "Which means you also held back from me. Be cautious of what accusations you fling, given your behavior. This situation is considered a positive achievement overall. Don't taint that."

"Held back from you? Aisha and I, as the Torches in the field, had it handled." Lyssa smiled thinly. "And if the Elders can't even communicate with each other ahead of time to keep from messing up on assignments, why should we waste valuable time waiting for orders when we have a hot lead? If we hadn't gone to Houston right away, Adrien Allard would have run off to the next country to sell shards."

"Watch yourself, Miss Corti. Success doesn't mean immunity in all matters. It might not be your intention to impugn an Elder, but your words are coming close to that."

"Tell me that whole situation wasn't total garbage. Convince me, and I'll gladly back off." Lyssa scoffed. "I know you, Samuel, and I know you aren't that sloppy. Even if you were trying to screw me over, you wouldn't do it that way, which points us back to Theodora. I was assigned to the job before Aisha. My involvement with the smuggled artifacts was on the freaking Shadow news and was coordinated with the EAA. This wasn't a super-secret Society-only op."

Samuel watched her silently, his arms folded behind his back as if evaluating her. "The minute three humans gather in a room, politics begin. It doesn't matter if they're Illuminated. Politics can be unpleasant, but they aren't the same thing as a conspiracy."

"That's what this was?" Lyssa asked. "Nothing but nasty politics?"

"Yes." Samuel walked over to the couch and took a seat, a weariness in his posture. "If anything, it's my fault for not foreseeing this. All Elders have a difficult task in the current days, balancing our influence with the Society, Shadow governments, and the Tribunal. Some might become overly enthusiastic about such things but be cautious of reading too much into it. You don't need to find new enemies."

Lyssa shook her head. "Aisha's not the only Torch she could have sent. Sending Aisha was almost asking for an incident. It's like Elder Theodora wanted me to mess up or get hurt."

Samuel's bushy eyebrows lifted. "And was there an incident? According to Miss Khatri, you two encountered each other in Midland and then worked together until you killed Mr. Allard in Houston. Although she has some comments about your family pedigree, her statements suggest you were an effective temporary partner, given the assignment. I was surprised by how positive she was about your involvement, given your history together."

Lyssa narrowed her eyes. Aisha hadn't admitted they'd

had a big fight in the warehouse. She couldn't blame the other Sorceress. It wasn't like Lyssa wanted to either.

It was time for her to make an attempt at politics. She considered her next words carefully. Going to war with one Elder was manageable, but not two.

"I'd say that's an accurate summary." Lyssa shrugged. "But it could have been a disaster. Half the Society knows how much Aisha resents my family over the Night Goddess. She's sticking it in her official reports from what you just told me." She shook her head. "Let me put it another way. Would you have sent me to investigate this if you knew Aisha was involved? Would that strike you as a good plan?"

"I would have selected another Torch." Samuel furrowed his brow. "But in this case, it worked out, so I have little basis to complain about another Elder's decision. Unless you have something else you wish to share with me, there's nothing I wish to say or do."

Lyssa frowned. He might be baiting her, or he might be telling the truth. She wasn't ready to tell him about the memory card, which didn't leave her many options.

"Attempted arson doesn't count if the building doesn't catch fire?" Lyssa lifted her brow. "Come on. That's BS. I'm not saying I want an Eclipse sent after her, but a little more than, 'Hey, it all worked out, so no harm, no foul' would be nice."

Samuel gave her a pitying look. That only enraged her more.

"You're far too young and naïve to play at these sorts of games, Miss Corti," Samuel replied. "I would leave it alone. The dance of Elders may be frustrating and perplexing, but no matter how self-serving it can be at times, the Elders understand that the Society needs all of our Illuminated to be able to survive against the Shadows until we've established—"

"Equilibrium and coexistence." Lyssa waved a hand. "I get it."

"Do you?" Samuel looked doubtful.

"You say the incident is over?" Lyssa asked. "You don't think there's anything left to follow up on?"

"Your part of it is over." Samuel offered the words in a forceful tone.

"Allard's essence was blade." Lyssa patted her stomach where she'd been impaled. "Sure, with time and rituals, he could make some shards, but none of the shards he'd been smuggling centered around that essence."

Samuel nodded. "So? He was a Sorcerer. That meant he had access and knowledge concerning where to acquire them. He'd hardly be the first rogue to collect shards of power from a variety of sources. That proves nothing."

"And you think it's over? Not my part, but the shard-smuggling?"

"Over enough. A thoroughly disrupted supply line and a dead Sorcerer send a powerful message to those who might think about similar endeavors." Samuel gave her a cool look. "If you're implying there are other rogues, of course there are, and there always will be. Perfection is beyond the grasp of even our kind. For now, the American government sees and understands that we can quickly, efficiently, and *brutally* clean up after ourselves. We're quietly offering payments to the people and companies who suffered damaged cargo as well. The lack of Shadow casualties other than the direct servants of the Sorcerer and the middlemen criminals was well appreciated by the American government and law enforcement. They commended your restraint in this matter."

"I did my best not to blow anything up." Lyssa chuckled. "Even Aisha did a good job of restraining herself. It was Allard who made the mess."

"And it has been noticed and noted." Samuel gave a curt nod. "I guarantee you no more assignments for at least two weeks unless they occur within a hundred miles of you. Take your time to rest and reflect." He stood and tugged his jacket to straighten out the wrinkles. "Unless there's something else, I should get going."

"I need permission to go to Last Remnant," Lyssa blurted.

"Why? To go to the Vault of Dreams and check for your brother's regalia again?"

"Something like that." Lyssa licked her lips, wondering if Samuel could tell she was holding back. She wanted to show him the pictures, but he'd dismissed Theodora's interference as nothing more than politics. Overplaying her hand could end with her house disappearing in a mysterious explosion. There was no such thing as being too paranoid in her world.

"No." Samuel shook his head. "The Tribunal wants to reduce traffic to Last Remnant, not increase it, especially in times of tension. You don't have a valid reason to go."

"What?" Lyssa stared at him. "You won't let me go there? It's always tense with our kind. Oh, wait. That's wrong. It's only tense on any day that ends with Y."

"Not right now." Samuel gave her a cool look. "Things

are too chaotic, especially with this incident and others in different countries."

Lyssa frowned. "When, then?"

"Sooner than I'd like, I imagine, but longer than you would." Samuel headed toward the door, readopting his previous disguise in a blur—the advantage of light essence. "You should give up on your brother for your own good." He stopped and didn't turn around. "Unless you have some new information that would suggest this quest isn't meaningless."

"Not yet, just a feeling," she lied.

"Be careful, Miss Corti. These are the most interesting and dangerous times I've lived through since M-Day. You did well working with Miss Khatri to end the smuggling, but I suspect a woman of your predispositions knows that rot seldom occurs in isolation. I know you have your frustrations, and I have them as well, but justice doesn't always come in a timely manner."

"Rot?" Lyssa smiled coldly. "Sounds like I'll be busy."

"Most likely." Samuel stepped outside. "I could convince certain parties to allow you travel to Last Remnant if you had, in their minds, earned it."

"Kick more ass? Take more names?"

"I wouldn't put it that crudely, but yes. Efficient work as a Torch benefits the Society." Samuel headed toward the sidewalk. "Until next time, Miss Corti. Enjoy your time off."

"Do you trust him?" Jofi asked.

"Kind of. Maybe. Probably?" Lyssa shrugged and closed the door. "I don't think he's at the top of the list of people trying to kill me."

"Then what is your plan?"

"To be the best damned Torch I can be until they let me check out Last Remnant."

"And the pictures?"

"Sometimes finesse and stealth are for the best. I need more than pictures before I make my next move." Lyssa headed toward her kitchen. "For now, though, I'm going to have a pint of strawberry ice cream."

The story continues with book two, *Southwest Days,* available at Amazon and through Kindle Unlimited.

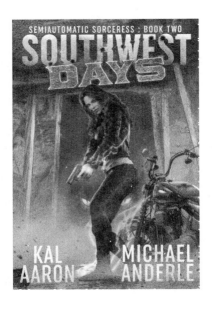

Get your copy today!

AUTHOR NOTES - KAL ARRON
MARCH 2, 2021

Years ago, I had the classic author experience of thinking of a good idea and not writing it down. I thought, "Oh, well, it's no big deal. I'll remember it later." Alas, I couldn't.

Since that fateful day, I've changed my strategy. Whenever I get an idea, I immediately type it into my phone, where the wonders of the cloud back it up to my computer and some mysterious hidden server that probably is sitting in the Vault of Dreams.

When I got the opportunity to pitch a cowrite idea to Michael, I worried I wouldn't be able to come up with something that would work. It's not that I lacked for ideas, but cowriting is a complex dance blending two distinct creative visions to ensure the central ideas and styles of the book are something both authors can get behind. After a lot of thought, I decided to use my lengthy idea list combined with a bit of book reincarnation.

Years ago, I wrote a full draft for an urban fantasy featuring a sassy sorceress fond of motorcycles, mouthing off to her superiors, and taking down demons. At the time, for reasons that escape me now, I decided to set it in Chicago, a city I had only marginal familiarity with.

Not all books deserve a final life, and although there were strong aspects of the story I enjoyed, it wasn't ready for readership and withered away in the virtual trunk. When I was coming up with a cowrite idea, I decided to repurpose that character and shift the focus away from demons while scrapping the demon-hunting plot entirely. I went down my big list of ideas and grabbed several things I'd been dying to add into an urban fantasy book but had never gotten around to. That formed the initial skeleton for the Semiautomatic Sorceress series.

During a lengthy meeting with Michael, we hammered out details and grew excited about the current version of the story. I'd decided to focus on Phoenix, if only because I've lived in Arizona for a while now and I thought it'd be nice for it to get some love.

As a brief aside, I did live in Chicago between the time I thought of the previous book and this one. I'll note between stints Wisconsin and Illinois, I grew to hate snow. You can't slip on sunshine!

Anyway, once we finished setting the general contours of the world for Semiautomatic Sorceress, Michael made an offhand comment that he thought it'd be cool if the main character had sort of a Grim Reaper/Day of the Dead vibe to her outfit. At the time, he just liked the aesthetics of the idea.

That wasn't originally something I'd been considering, imagining a spunkier-looking character with dyed short blue hair. We combined his aesthetic suggestion with the general setting, and that led to the idea of the regalia. It turned into a wonderful way to develop some very distinct and memorable characters both in terms of powers and costumes while also giving an in-story excuse for a sorceress to still have a secret identity in a world where the supernatural is out in the open.

Something intriguing and cool was born out of us bouncing ideas off one another, a long dead novel, and my ideas list. It just goes to show you that you should never throw any ideas away and should always write them down.

I'm excited to see where we can take these characters and setting in the future.

See you soon for book two, *Southwest Days!*

And thanks for reading.

Kal

Please note you can contact me at kalaaron@kalaaron.com. If you want to be added to my new releases mailing list, please go to https://kalaaron.com and fill out the form on the bottom of the page.

P.S.,

If you're wondering about Lyssa's demon-hunting previous life (BTW, she had a different name), that version of the character used an enchanted sword made of blood rather than guns and used it to absorb demons. Magic and monsters were all considered myths and legends.

Other than the attitude and fondness for guns and motor-cycles, not much else survived. Though I will note that, Samuel, Colonel Sanders look and all, is almost a direct port of a character from that series. Mostly, I just wanted to make the herbs and spices joke.

AUTHOR NOTES - MICHAEL ANDERLE
MARCH 5, 2021

Thank you for not only reading this new series but to the back and our author notes as well!

For those who haven't read my work before, I've provided a bit of an introduction below. For those who have read the introduction, just skip to the #GodIAmTired section below.

A Bit About Me

I wrote my first book *Death Becomes Her* (*The Kurtherian Gambit*) in September/October of 2015 and released it November 2, 2015. I wrote and released the next two books that same month and had three released by the end of November 2015.

So, just at five years ago.

Since then, I've written, collaborated, concepted, and/or created hundreds more in all sorts of genres.

My most successful genre is still my first, Paranormal Sci-Fi, followed quickly by Urban Fantasy. I have multiple pen names I produce under.

Some because I can be a bit crude in my humor at times or raw in my cynicism (Michael Todd). I have one I share with Martha Carr (Judith Berens, and another (not disclosed) that we use as a marketing test pen name.

In general, I just love to tell stories, and with success comes the opportunity to mix two things I love in my life.

Business and stories.

I've wanted to be an entrepreneur since I was a teenager. I was a very *unsuccessful* entrepreneur (I tried many times) until my publishing company LMBPN signed one author in 2015.

Me.

I was the president of the company, and I was the first author published. Funny how it worked out that way.

It was late 2016 before we had additional authors join me for publishing. Now we have a few dozen authors, a few hundred audiobooks by LMBPN published, a few hundred more licensed by six audio companies, and about a thousand titles in our company.

It's been a busy five years.

#GodIAmTired

I went to bed late last night after going out to eat early (4:45 reservation at Benihana) and basically played all evening without paying much attention to work. I fell into bed about midnight plus thirty and didn't even bother undressing.

My wife (who stays up later than me) just came in and noticed me on the bed and probably shook her head. I don't know exactly because while I *swear* I was awake and spoke with her…

I don't remember anything.

Fast forward to this morning, where I have one eyeball open and the other closed, trying to sleep while going through my emails.

I had forgotten to set up a call today! I quickly emailed back, and after a few misunderstandings about time (I'm PST, he is Eastern and didn't believe I meant "in 15 minutes," we did an early phone call.

The discussion on the phone was about Indie Publishing. This person was involved in the game industry and is now (thank you, Covid) based out of his home. His love is still writing and creating stories, so I encouraged him to look into what can be done if you self-publish.

You could tell he wasn't buying what I was selling (which was nothing more than "check out indie publishing"), but what did he have to lose? Perhaps some time.

He checked out my suggestion to look on 20Book-sto50k™ and other research before taking me up on my offer to call me and ask questions.

Once I stumbled through getting ready this morning, I got on the phone and was pleased that he both had researched the opportunities and that my suggestion just might be a path forward for him both creatively and financially.

That was all I could hope. Making creatives aware of self-publishing as an option for an author's future is the proverbial leading a horse to water. What they do once they know is up to them. This gentleman called someone HE knew and spoke to them about it.

Both were shocked by what he had learned. I realized at

that moment that the second challenge is now believing what he learned.

It's one thing to believe the mountain exists, even when you can see it. Understanding that you can make it up the mountain is often a leap of faith, as much as a belief in oneself.

So, whatever your passion is, I'd encourage you to learn more about it. If you are a major reader and writing is something you would like to do, know that quite a few people are making a solid living—or at a minimum, a significant addition to the family income—with self-publishing.

I never want to forget to encourage those who wish they could write for a living. I did it, others have done it, and it's still viable.

Have a great weekend (or week...whenever you read this!)

Ad Aeternitatem,

Michael Anderle

CONNECT WITH THE AUTHORS

Connect with Kal Aaron

Website and Mailing List
https://www.kalaaron.com/

Connect with Michael Anderle

Website: http://lmbpn.com

Email List: http://lmbpn.com/email/

Social Media:

https://www.facebook.com/LMBPNPublishing

https://twitter.com/MichaelAnderle

https://www.instagram.com/lmbpn_publishing/

https://www.bookbub.com/authors/michael-anderle

ABOUT KAL AARON

Kal Aaron loves a good challenge, whether it's intelligence analysis, programming, or research science. After years of bouncing around the academic and corporate worlds, he was blessed with a family and the rare opportunity to make a living telling entertaining lies.

When not imagining dangerous fantasy worlds, he spends his time in the deserts of the American Southwest with his feisty wife, children, and pet bird.

Printed in Great Britain
by Amazon

76028870R00200